best buddies

sisters of the heart

soul sister

friends forever

kindred spirits

sister-friends

SISTERCHICKS
in Sombreros!

girlfriends

pals for life

chum

confidante

gal pals

true blue

ally

From one sisterchick to another ...

"I just finished *Sisterchicks Do the Hula!* and had to tell you how wonderful it was! I really can't put into words how this book touched me, deep down in my soul. Like I was thirsty for something and your book was a cool drink of water. As I was reading the last page, I had tears in my eyes, not wanting the story to end and thankful that I could come along on the journey also. Thank you so much!"—LISA

"I am from the UK. Last weekend I bought *Sisterchicks on the Loose!* I can honestly say I never in my life read a book so fast! I laughed out loud, even cried in places, and struggled to put it down. It made me realise I, too, have a Sisterchick who should be treasured."—TRACEY

"A friend gave *Sisterchicks Do the Hula!* to me for my birthday. I couldn't put it down. I'm thirty-five and feeling way too old for my age. Thank you for the breath of fresh air. I felt like God had you write it just for me!—KARA

"I just finished *Sisterchicks on the Loose!* and loved it. In fact, I devoured it. I hated to see it end. It had to be one of the best books on friendship that I have read. Love your sense of humor; I laughed out loud many times reading it. You have such a heart for Jesus and a wonderful spirit."—DEBBIE

"The ladies' book club at our church is discussing *Sisterchicks on the Loose!* next month. I am very excited because I loved the book. I have also read *Sisterchicks Do the Hula!*—it is great. Keep writing! And faster, if you can!"—MARILYN

"Thank you for the return trip to Oahu this morning! *[Sisterchicks Do the Hula!]* It is snowing and sleeting outside, but I was enjoying the beautiful blues that only Hawai'i has. Thank you for giving me a 'garland of hosannas' and for reminding me to do the hula with God's rhythm of grace."—MARBARA

"I just finished *Sisterchicks Do the Hula!* and I loved it! Actually, I found myself sneaking into the bathroom away from my loving husband and ever-present children to read more. You have written marvelous fiction that leaves me feeling closer to God."—MARY

"Look out, Finland! Look out, England! Look out, good ol' U.S. of A.! It's *Sisterchicks on the Loose!*.... Gunn's bouncy, conversational style and steady servings of insight feed the soul and warm the heart. Over forty? The best is yet to come!"—*ROMANTIC TIMES* MAGAZINE

Christie Fisher

a s i s t e r c h i c k™ n o v e l

SISTERCHICKS
in Sombreros!

ROBIN JONES GUNN

Multnomah® Publishers *Sisters, Oregon*

SISTERCHICKS IN SOMBREROS
published by Multnomah Publishers, Inc.

© 2004 by Robin's Ink, LLC
International Standard Book Number: 1-59052-229-X

Sisterchicks is a trademark of Multnomah Publishers, Inc.
Cover image of women by Bill Cannon Photography, Inc.

Unless otherwise indicated, Scripture quotations are from:
The Message by Eugene H. Peterson © 1993, 1994, 1995, 1996, 2000, 2001, 2002
Used by permission of NavPress Publishing Group

Other Scripture quotations are from:
Holy Bible, New Living Translation (NLT)
© 1996. Used by permission of Tyndale House Publishers, Inc.
All rights reserved.
The Holy Bible, New King James Version (NKJV) © 1984 by Thomas Nelson, Inc.

Multnomah is a trademark of Multnomah Publishers, Inc. and is registered in the U.S.
Patent and Trademark Office. The colophon is a trademark of Multnomah Publishers, Inc.

Printed in the United States of America

For information:
MULTNOMAH PUBLISHERS, INC. • P.O. BOX 1720 • SISTERS, OR 97759

Library of Congress Cataloging-in-Publication Data

Gunn, Robin Jones, 1955-
   Sisterchicks in sombreros : a Sisterchicks novel / Robin Jones Gunn.
      p. cm.
   ISBN 1-59052-229-X
   1. Inheritance and succession—Fiction. 2. Canadians—Mexico—Fiction.
3. Women travelers—Fiction. 4. Sisters—Fiction. 5. Mexico—Fiction. I. Title.
   PS3557.U4866S564 2004
   813'.54--dc22

                                         2004015655

04 05 06 07 08 09 10—10 9 8 7 6 5 4 3 2 1 0

OTHER BOOKS BY ROBIN JONES GUNN

SISTERCHICK NOVELS
Sisterchicks on the Loose!
Sisterchicks Do the Hula!
Sisterchicks in Sombreros!
Sisterchicks Down Under! (April 2005)

THE GLENBROOKE SERIES
Secrets
Whispers
Echoes
Sunsets
Clouds
Waterfalls
Woodlands
Wildflowers

GIFT BOOKS
Tea at Glenbrooke
Mothering by Heart
Gentle Passages

www.sisterchicks.com • www.robingunn.com

To Julie, my "almost twin" sister, who planned my
surprise birthday party when I turned sixteen and never
pinched me on the underside of my arm.
Well, maybe once.
I'm so glad we figured out how to be friends early on.
I don't know who I'd be without you.

To Janet, who cruised with me to Mexico,
dined on dancing ladies over tea in Ensenada,
and endured my moaning after the spa treatment that
made her skin well and gave my skin welts.
I'd share sombreros with you any day, dear *hermanachica!*

*"God can do anything, you know—
far more than you could ever imagine or guess
or request in your wildest dreams!
He does it not by pushing us around but by working within us,
his Spirit deeply and gently within us."*

EPHESIANS 3:20

Prologue

Most of my life I secretly admired my sister, Joanne. But until high school, I didn't I like her. And it wasn't until we were in our forties that I treasured her.

We're only sixteen months apart in age. Joanne is the older one. Blond and sweet, with a great laugh. I was known as the bossy baby sister, always ready to make a fuss so I would be noticed.

Our mom used to dress us in matching outfits and tell people, "They're almost twins, you know." Joanne and I hated that. How can you be "almost twins"? Aren't twins supposed to have a lot of similarities? Joanne and I have only two—the same creamy, fair skin and the same funny nose.

By the time I was eight, I had grown a full inch taller than Joanne. That was the year we moved from Saskatoon to British Columbia, and everyone who met us assumed I was the older of the two Clayton girls. I know Joanne shrunk a little every time someone called her Melanie, while I reveled in finally receiving top billing.

When Joanne got her driver's license, our quirky power balance was upset again because I was suddenly at her mercy if I wanted to go anywhere. We argued all the time.

That is, until my sixteenth birthday.

I asked Joanne to drive me across town to a friend's house, but a sassy look crossed Joanne's face, and she said, "I don't know, Melanie. What's it worth to you?"

I snapped back with, "I don't know, Joanne. What's it worth to you not to show up at school Monday with two black eyes?"

Instead of being intimidated, my sister laughed at me. She drove the whole way with a snicker just begging to burst out from her lips. I was so steamed that, when we pulled up in front of my friend's house, I turned to Joanne and said, "When I get my license, I'll never drive you anywhere, even if you have two broken legs and plead with me to take you to the hospital."

Joanne only laughed more.

I slammed the car door and marched up to the house, vowing never to speak to my sister again. Just then the front door swung open, and all my closest friends yelled, "Surprise!" Joanne was standing behind me, grinning like a goose. The surprise birthday party had been her idea down to the last detail.

Stunned, I turned to her, and with an apology that encompassed my entire malicious career as a sister, I whispered, "I'm sorry."

Joanne teared up and said in a sincere but playful voice, "Me, too, Melly Jelly Belly."

I hugged her in front of my waiting friends. "Thanks, Joanna Banana."

And that was it; we became friends.

We always had shared a bedroom, but after that we shared our clothes and makeup as well as our secret crushes and dreams for the future. Joanne wanted to be a nurse. I wanted to be something more glamorous like an interior decorator or a pastry chef and took a variety of classes at the community college, changing my major each semester.

I tried on a variety of careers and was as surprised as anyone when the one that stuck was running the front desk at a dental office, which is what I do even now. That's where I met my husband, Ethan. He came in for a root canal and left with my phone number. That was almost seventeen years ago.

In that same time span my saintly sister graduated with honors from nursing school in Toronto, dedicated herself to long hours healing the infirm, sent generous gifts to my two daughters on their birthdays, and spent five years in India. She worked at a safe house that rescued juvenile girls off the streets who had been sold into prostitution. Now you can see why I admire her.

After Joanne returned to Toronto, I often wondered if she regretted not marrying Russell what's-his-name while she had the chance. It's the sort of question one sister can ask another, but I'd never come right out and asked her.

We fell into a routine with our relationship after we both passed forty. She would call every few weeks and ask about Ethan and the girls and if I had seen Mom and Dad. I'd answer in short sentences, and then I'd ask about her job and her dog, Russell. Yes, she named her schnauzer Russell. After Russell what's-his-name, I presumed.

I kept thinking that during one of those predictable phone conversations I would say, "How's Russell?" And when she started to talk about her schnauzer, I'd say, "No, I mean the *other* Russell." Then I'd find out what really happened and why she took off for India for so long.

But I never quite managed to pull that one off.

That was, until last year, when Joanne and I unexpectedly crossed another bridge between friendship and sistership. Or maybe I should say we set sail on a ship that took us to a new place as sisters because that's literally what happened.

I would never have taken off on such a lark, if the choice truly had been mine. But it wasn't.

I look back now and realize that in the same way we don't choose our relatives, I think it's also true we don't choose the best moments of our lives. God chooses them for us, the same way He chose two sisters like Joanne and me, who are "almost twins," to turn us into the best friend neither of us ever thought we had.

One

*L*ast November, on the last Saturday of the month, I stood in the garage untangling a string of twinkle lights and thought, *Who came up with the term Father Christmas?*

At our house, it's more like Mother Christmas. I'm the one who knows where all the decorations are stored. I organize the festivities, buy the gifts, address the cards, initiate the parties, and single-handedly festoon the house. Without the information stored in my brain and without the loving labor of my two hands, Christmas wouldn't come to our humble abode in Langley, which is a suburb of Vancouver.

I always start with a long list of what needs to be done and tell myself to start earlier than I did the previous year. Untangling the lights on November 29 was a pretty good running start.

That was, until Aunt Winnie called.

"Melanie, dear, you must come over at once. My lawyer is here, and he doesn't speak a word of Spanish."

"Aunt Winnie, what are you talking about?"

"The letter. It has your name on it. You have to be here when the conference call comes through. The call with Joanne. This is most disturbing. Please don't dawdle."

She hung up without saying good-bye, and I growled at the phone. Untangling Aunt Winnie had not been on my list that day.

"What's going on?" my husband asked, as I stomped down the hall.

I repeated the cryptic message and pulled a change of clothes from the closet. Jeans and a sweatshirt weren't appropriate attire to visit Aunt Winnie.

"Sounds strange," Ethan muttered. "Even for your wacky aunt. What do you think she's trying to pull?"

"Who knows? She was completely rattled."

"More than usual?"

"Yes, more than usual."

I slipped into my gray wool skirt and tried to straighten the permanently creased waistband. "And she's not wacky, Ethan. Please don't say that in front of the girls."

"Right. Not wacky. Eccentric. Isn't that what you told the girls?"

"Yes. Is this blouse too wrinkled?" Before Ethan could answer, I pulled it off and grabbed the tried-and-true black turtleneck.

"I thought your aunt was on a cruise to Alaska."

"No, she leaves sometime next week for Mexico, not Alaska. Alaska was last July. Panama Canal was in October."

"That woman goes on more cruises than anyone I've ever met. Why can't you tell her you'll come see her when she comes back from her cruise?"

"Her lawyer is there, Ethan. What am I supposed to do? If you had heard her on the phone, you'd be on your way over there, too."

"Do you want me to go with you?"

"No. I'll call if there's any reason for you to come. Joy has her Girl Guides meeting at two o'clock, and Brianna is babysitting at four, but I should be back by then."

Ethan looked at me skeptically. "If you're not back by five, do you want me to order pizza for dinner?"

"No, I'll be back before then." I brushed past Ethan and reached for my purse. "If you really want to help, you can finish untangling the Christmas lights and pull out all the bins with the decorations."

I backed out of the driveway, chiding myself for being so brusque with Ethan. He was right; Aunt Winnie was wacky. She was demanding. I didn't know why I was defending her instead of siding with my husband. My only comfort was that Winnie would be on her cruise next week, and I could concentrate on what I needed to do at home.

Turning right onto Highway 1, I sped up for the forty-minute stretch into Vancouver and made a mental list of all the possible reasons her lawyer was there.

I wonder if Aunt Winnie is in some sort of financial trouble.

One of the enigmas of my aunt was that no one in the family knew where her money came from or how much she had. Uncle Harlan had passed away three years ago. He and my father were brothers and came from a long line of simple, rural-type Canadians. The money that had funneled into Harlan and Winnie's forty-eight-year marriage came from some undisclosed source on Winnie's side.

Arriving in Vancouver as a mist of chilling rain dotted the windshield, I cut across town on King Edward Avenue and headed for Aunt Winnie's luxurious apartment with its spectacular view of English Bay. As the elevator took me to the tenth floor, I straightened my skirt and checked my posture.

"Is that Melanie?" Aunt Winnie sang out as Mei Lee, her housekeeper, welcomed me inside the permanently rose-scented apartment. Today tinges of burnt toast lingered in the air.

I noticed that the mahogany furniture had been rearranged to make a clear path through the Victorian-style living room for what Aunt Winnie called her "Scoot-About." Several weeks ago she saw the motorized wheelchair advertised on TV and picked up her phone to order one. I wasn't convinced she needed the assistance, but she was enamored with her new device.

"Hello, Aunt Winnie." I went to her side and pressed my cheek against hers. "How are you feeling?"

Her tightly curled silver hair framed her oval face like the crocheted lace on the throw pillows that lined her sofa. She held out a piece of paper to me. "Most disturbing news I've had in a month. No, six months. Most upsetting."

The stationery, I noted, was from El Banco del Sol in Mexico. The only words in English were my sister's and my names, which appeared in the middle of a sentence at the top of the page.

"What does this say?" I asked my aunt.

"I have no idea. Tea?" Aunt Winnie rang a small silver bicycle bell attached to the right handle of her Scoot-About. It was the sort of bell my girls had on their tricycles years ago, the kind that makes a cheerful brring-brring sound with a flick of the thumb. On the front of her Scoot-About hung a woven wicker basket, also of the tricycle variety, complete with pink and lavender plastic streamers.

I was glad Ethan hadn't come with me. No matter what Aunt Winnie had to say, I'm sure my husband wouldn't have been able to see past the basket with the plastic streamers.

"Does your lawyer know what this letter says?" I asked.

"No, I told you: He doesn't speak a word of Spanish. That's why he left. To get it translated. I sent him downstairs to make a copy and insisted he leave the original letter with me. I knew you would be proud of me for thinking of that. He will have the letter decoded by the time he calls us in..." She glanced at her ornate grandfather clock. "Twenty minutes."

"And that's the phone call Joanne will be in on," I surmised.

"The very one." Aunt Winnie triumphantly flicked her thumb against the silver bell.

Mei Lee, ever the efficient housekeeper, appeared with Aunt Winnie's Royal Albert teapot and matching china teacups on a tray. She set the preparations before us with a plate of Nanaimo bars, Aunt Winnie's favorite teatime dainties.

"You don't speak Spanish, do you?" Aunt Winnie asked Mei Lee.

"No." The petite woman shyly dipped her chin.

"But you do speak Chinese." Winnie shook her finger. "If Harlan had bought his summerhouse in Hong Kong, we would have been coming to you for advice. How is the fishing in Hong Kong?"

"Very nice, I'm sure." Mei Lee left the room as I put the pieces together.

"Uncle Harlan owned a summerhouse in Mexico? Is that what the letter is about?"

"Oh, that awful, ugly fish. It was hideous! He insisted on having it mounted. Melanie, will you pour, dear?"

"What fish are you talking about?"

"The one Harlan caught."

"In Mexico?"

"Yes, of course, in Mexico. That's why he wanted the summerhouse."

"And the summerhouse is in Mexico." I held out her cup of tea with a quarter teaspoon of sugar already stirred in, the way she liked it.

"Naturally. Thank you, dear. I only went there once, you know."

"You only went once to Mexico?"

"Harlan's summerhouse."

"And exactly where is Uncle Harlan's summerhouse?" This was the first I'd heard that my uncle had such a place.

"Haven't you been paying attention at all, dear Melanie? His summerhouse is in Mexico."

"Yes, but where in Mexico?"

"Some town with a Mexican name. What about this teapot, Melanie? Would you like this one after I'm gone?"

On a "normal" visit, Aunt Winnie's erratic communication skills drove me nuts. Today I thought I was going to scream. As firmly as I dared, I said, "Aunt Winnie, you said you thought the letter referred to your summerhouse. What—?"

"Oh, it wasn't mine!" she yipped. "It was Harlan's house. I couldn't take the heat. Dreadful! He loved it. But I don't know why we're discussing this. Harlan sold the summerhouse years ago. After his first heart attack. Did I already promise you this teapot?"

"Yes, Aunt Winnie, you did."

She reached for her famous ledger, which I noticed she now kept handy in her little wicker basket. She had started the ledger because every time I came to visit, she gave an inventory of her belongings and offered me first grabs on anything I liked.

I used to say, "Oh, I couldn't ask you for that" or "I'm sure you have many more years left to enjoy it."

My polite approach gave her fits, so about eight months ago I started to say, "Why, yes, thank you very much. I would love to have that someday."

That response prompted her to buy the ledger, and today she wrote down the Royal Albert teapot under my name for the second time.

"You know," she said with a funny little sniff. "It's beach-front property. Gorgeous white sandy beach. Miles and miles of it. I have photos here somewhere."

With her hand on the control switch, Aunt Winnie puttered across the room. She stopped the Scoot-About in front of her antique secretary, stood up, and bent over to pull a box out of the lower drawer. Settling back in the padded seat, she rang her bell and merrily motored the distance of eight feet, back to where I sat on the couch.

"Palm trees." She opened the box and filed through the photos. "Blue water and so many fish. I said I'd never go again, and I never did."

She looked up at me with a blink of surprise behind her glasses. "Harlan and I fought like cats over that fish of his. Do you know that it took twenty years before he finally took the bloated thing off the wall?"

Tilting her head she added wistfully, "Funny, I miss it. Hmm."

The phone rang, and Winnie called out, "Mei Lee!" For emphasis she added a brring-brring of her tricycle bell.

"That will be my lawyer," Winnie said. "You talk to him, Melanie. He said he wanted you to be on the phone with Joanne."

Mei Lee handed me the phone, and what followed was a fifteen-minute conversation that left me speechless. As soon as I hung up, Aunt Winnie squawked, "Well, what did he say?"

"The letter is from a bank in Mexico."

"Yes, yes, I know that. What does it mean?"

"It seems Uncle Harlan listed Joanne and me as the beneficiaries of his summer home."

"Beneficiaries? I told you, Harlan sold the beach house. Eight years ago. After his first heart attack."

"According to your lawyer and the bank in Mexico, Harlan didn't sell the house."

"Are you sure? How preposterous!"

"It's true, Aunt Winnie. Your lawyer has all the documentation."

"Then why did it take those people three years to get around to telling me this?"

"It took a long time to get all the paperwork through the right bank in Mexico. The property still is owned by Uncle Harlan, but since he's gone, it's now deeded to Joanne and me."

"Imagine that," she said with a curious sounding "piffle!" at the end of her sentence. Holding out two black-and-white photos, Aunt Winnie nodded for me to take the square-shaped pictures from her. I guessed them to be from the sixties, due to the white trim around the borders. One photo showed a stretch of white sand and what had to be aqua blue water.

"That's what you see from the front," Winnie said. "White sand, like I said."

The second picture was of Uncle Harlan wearing only a pair of shorts and dark midcalf socks with sandals. He had a floppy straw sombrero on his head and was pouring a bucket of water on a three-foot-high palm tree.

"Harlan had a groundskeeper, you know, but he planted this palm tree himself. Said he needed a place to hang his hammock."

I studied the photos, wishing they showed more of the house and grounds and surrounding area. "By any chance do you remember the name of his groundskeeper?"

"No idea. I think it was a Mexican name. Is it hot in here to you?"

"No, I'm fine."

"Imagine! That Harlan of mine left you the beach house. One last trick up his sleeve. That man! No great surprise that he wanted the two of you to have the place. He knew I would never go there. I suppose it's yours then. Just like that. No papers to sign?"

"Joanne and I have a lot of papers to sign. I asked your lawyer if he could have the bank in Mexico mail everything to us so that Joanne and I wouldn't have to go down there. He's checking into it."

"Mail the papers? I should say not! Such important papers. Why would you want to do that? I for one certainly don't care to wait three more years for another letter written in Mexican. No one around here can read it!"

She rose from her Scoot-About and pointed her finger at me. "You must go! To Mexico. And I have the ticket."

Aunt Winnie had spoken. She reached for her phone and began to make calls.

I didn't arrive home until after five that evening. Ethan had strung the lights and the front of the house looked cheerful. He was in the garage when I pulled in, so we stood on the cold cement floor as I told him the whole story. The concluding shocker was that Aunt Winnie had decided not to go on her scheduled cruise to Mexico next week.

"She had the travel agent transfer the reservation out of her name and put Joanne and me as the passengers."

"Your aunt isn't going on the cruise at all?"

"No, she said it was her Christmas gift so that Joanne and I could go sign the papers at the bank in Mexico and enjoy a little luxury at the same time."

"Wow."

"I know. Wow. It's just beginning to sink in."

"What did her lawyer say about all this?"

"He came back over after the conference call and gave me some additional documents. He said it was a 'smart, proactive expression' for Joanne and me to go because we were bolstering Aunt Winnie's confidence."

"Confidence in what?"

"I think he meant her confidence in naming Joanne and

me as joint managers of her estate once she is gone. He said she is still 'in process' over that decision."

"What was he saying? You're going to be written out of her will if you don't go?"

"I don't know. The whole thing is bizarre. I can't figure out why Uncle Harlan listed me as the primary beneficiary."

"That's easy. He liked you better than Joanne."

"Maybe he thought I was the oldest. Although, it doesn't really matter because the lawyer said Joanne and I both have to sign in front of a notary before the bank will release the rights on the deed. Once the paperwork is clear, we can sell the house and split the profit."

Ethan leaned against the workbench. "What if you want to keep the house and the property?"

For the first time in that crazy, carousel-spinning afternoon, I stopped and let the possibility sink in. "I don't know. What would we do with beachfront property in Mexico? We need the money more than we need a vacation spot we could never afford to go visit."

"You don't have to make that decision right away, do you? You're just going down to Mexico to sign over the ownership, right?"

"Right."

"If it turns out to be some great mansion on the best beach in Mexico, you and Joanne can decide then if you want to keep it."

"Yes, that's my understanding." I kept my voice calm, but

inside I was beginning to grasp some of the thrilling possibilities I could detect in my husband's eyes.

"What are you thinking, Ethan?"

He gave me a charming grin. "This is wild."

"I know. It is." I paused and added, "Is this all too crazy?"

"Too crazy for what? Too crazy for you or too crazy for your wacky aunt?"

"Too crazy for us. For me. For now."

"No, it's not too crazy. Besides, it didn't sound like you had a lot of choice in the situation. Your aunt made the arrangements, right? You need to go. When do you leave?"

I reviewed the rushed schedule: fly to California on Monday, meet Joanne on the cruise ship, cruise to Mexico, go to the bank, sign a few papers, then cruise back to Los Angeles, and fly home on Thursday.

"Sounds like it's a done deal," he said.

I felt little shivers run up my arms. They weren't chilly shivers caused by the cold garage floor. They were thrilly shivers. I was boarding a luxury liner headed to sombrero-land in two days!

"Are you and Joanne going to play shuffleboard and learn to tango or something?" Ethan asked.

"Tango?"

"Isn't that what people do on cruises?"

I laughed. "I have no idea what people do on cruises."

"Looks like you're about to find out."

We headed into the house with our arms around each

other. Ethan added as an afterthought, "Why don't you bring back one of those Mexican blankets? The ones with the stripes."

"Okay. Anything else?"

"Yeah, show me where you keep the pizza coupons. The delivery guy should be here any minute. Maybe I can place a standing order with him for all the days you're going to be gone next week."

Two

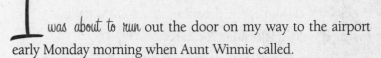

I was about to run out the door on my way to the airport early Monday morning when Aunt Winnie called.

"Melanie, I want the fish back."

I had to think a moment. "Are you talking about the fish you made Uncle Harlan take off the wall?"

"Yes, of course. What other fish is there? I want my Harlan's fish to come home and keep me company."

"Aunt Winnie, listen. When I get back from Mexico, I'll help you figure out what to do about the fish."

She started to cry. "Please, Melanie, promise me you'll get the fish!"

"I have to go now, Aunt Winnie. I'll see you in a few days. Everything will work out. Take it easy, okay?"

"Make sure they give you and Joanne extra towels. I always ask for extra towels."

"I will. Thank you again for setting this up for us." I sensed she was calming down. "Joanne and I really appreciate it."

"It's what my Harlan would have wanted. Oh, I miss him. I should have gone to Mexico with him when I had the chance. A person goes all through life thinking people will always be there, and then they disappear."

"I know. It's okay. I need to go now, Aunt Winnie."

"Yes, yes. Order a dancing lady for me. Good-bye."

I had no idea what her last statement meant, but I wasn't about to pursue it.

"I'll check on her while you're gone," Ethan said, as he backed the car out of the driveway. It was snowing lightly, and I wished we had left earlier for the airport.

"Thanks. I know I'm leaving you with a lot of loose ends."

"Don't worry about it. I can handle it. The girls will be fine. You need to relax. Contrary to whatever it is you're telling yourself, it's not your responsibility to keep the world spinning. You can take a couple of days off from running the universe, you know."

True, I had jumped into pulling everything together for this trip at tornado speed, and in the flurry possibly I'd made too many lists and tried to organize too many fronts. It was also true that Ethan probably thought his comment about taking a break from running the universe was supposed to help me feel at ease about leaving, but it only made me mad. That's how I left him at the airport, with one of those brick-wall kisses that don't fool anyone.

The first thing I did when I landed in Los Angeles was to call Ethan and apologize.

"You know how I meant it," he said. "I was trying to say I hope you enjoy the trip. Relax. Don't worry about anything here. I have it covered."

"Thanks, Ethan. I did sleep some on the plane, and I feel better."

"Good. Now all you have to do is have fun and sign some papers."

"I love you," I said.

"I love you, too."

I grabbed my suitcase at the luggage carousel and ventured outside in my long coat and boots, moving through the crowd with mock confidence, as if this were all an elaborate dream and I was playing the role of a jet-set actress who knew exactly where she was going and what she was supposed to do next.

The sun's glare caused me to squint as I read the names on the sides of all the vans lined up at the center island. A couple in shorts were boarding the van marked "Fiesta Cruise Shuttle." I hurried to get on with them. As soon as the three of us were settled in the last remaining seats, we pulled out of the airport and slowly made our way down the crowded freeway. I kept my head turned toward the window, watching for palm trees. A few popped up here and there, standing proud and solemn despite the congestion and the panorama of asphalt and concrete.

Letting out a deep breath, I began to believe I really was

here. I was going to Mexico. I pulled out the two photos Aunt Winnie had given me of Mexico and studied them some more. If the palm tree Uncle Harlan planted had survived, it would be over forty years old. I wondered how tall it was, and if he ever had used it to secure the end of a hammock.

The shuttle van pulled off the freeway, and I could see our cruise ship docked and waiting. As we drove closer, the ship seemed larger and larger. Stepping out of the van, I stood beside the others while a porter came along and tagged our baggage. In front of me the ship dominated the view. It was huge. Far up on the top deck I could see people leaning on the railing. They were so high up.

An unexpected queasiness came over me, squeezing my stomach and siphoning my breath. My courage had sprung a leak, and I was shocked to realize I was sinkingly terrified.

What am I doing here? I can't do this. I can't go on that ship. I can't go to Mexico. I don't belong here. I need to go home. Right now.

Perspiration poured down my neck. It took every shred of nerve for me not to let out a shriek and run after the airport shuttle as it pulled away. I'd never had a reaction like that before in my life.

Calm down! I commanded my racing heart. *What are you doing? Look, those people are boarding, and nothing terrible is happening to them. Relax!*

"May I see your paperwork, ma'am?" the porter asked.

"I don't have any paperwork." My throat felt tight. The next sentence came out with a cough. "I was told to ask for Sven."

The man stepped away to call Sven, and I tried to breathe in slowly through my nose and release the fear-tainted air through my mouth. What was I frightened of? The ship? That was ridiculous—even though it was a tremendously gigantic vessel.

The porter returned. "Sven will come meet you. He apologizes for not being on hand when you arrived. Is this your only piece of luggage?"

"Yes." I realized that compared to the other travelers on the shuttle, I appeared to be as sparsely packed as a hobo. Stepping to the side, I watched all the other, non-freaked-out passengers with their smiles and eager expressions. They were wearing shorts and T-shirts, and I stood there in my winter coat and boots feeling like a Canadian goose who had flown too far south for the winter.

An older woman in a floppy hat laughed at something her husband said as he handed the porter a five-dollar bill. It struck me that I only had Canadian dollars. That small fact sent my thoughts on a different mental track. I started to plan how I would exchange money when I registered. Knowing that I had a task to fulfill somehow brought my blood pressure back to normal. Charting out my course of action provided a strange sort of comfort. The panic was gone.

"Ms. Holmquist," a deep voice spoke beside me.

I turned and looked up at Sven, my aunt's personal steward. Every time Aunt Winnie went on a cruise, she was assigned a staff person who made sure she was settled in with what she needed. Aunt Winnie made it clear to the travel agent that Joanne and I were to receive the same first-class attention to which she was accustomed.

Sven handed me an envelope and let me know with his engaging accent that he would see to my luggage and walk me through the reservation process.

"Do you know if my sister has arrived yet?" I asked.

"Yes, she is in your stateroom. This way, please."

I was relieved that Joanne was on board. Everything was falling into place. Neither of us missed our flight. Sven would help me with all the details Joanne and I hadn't had time to figure out with our hasty departure. This was going to work out fine. I could do this.

"This card needs to be with you at all times," Sven told me after I exchanged my money and was given my room key. It looked like a plastic credit card. "You will use it to charge expenditures to your room. Also, the time and specified dining room is printed on the card for your dinner reservations."

We passed through another checkpoint where I slid my plastic card into a machine, looked straight ahead, and had my photo taken.

"I think I blinked," I protested.

"Doesn't matter," the woman in the cruise uniform said. "It's only for identification after you disembark in Ensenada."

She sounded like a recording. I wondered how many thousands of digital photos she had taken of passengers during her career and how many had protested like me.

"This way, please." Sven motioned that I should follow him across a secured walkway that led into the ship.

With one foot in front of the other, I held my breath and boarded the ship that had seemed so ominous a few moments earlier. A few short steps, and I entered what looked like the spacious lobby of a luxury hotel. Two dramatic, curved staircases led to the upper level. In the center, between the polished stairways, a pianist in a tuxedo was seated at a shiny black grand piano. His rendition of a classical piece filled the glistening lobby with a touch of elegance. Opulent bouquets of fresh flowers laced the air with sweet fragrance. Dozens of passengers strolled about leisurely in the airy reception area. Many of them held glasses with blended tropical beverages. A waiter meandered from guest to guest, offering appetizers on a silver tray.

Oh, yeah. I could see why cruisin' was Aunt Winnie's cup of tea.

I can do this. Why was I so panicked? Did I watch Titanic *one too many times? My problem is that I don't get out enough. I don't know how to act classy in situations like this. But who cares? Joanne and I are going to have the time of our lives!*

Sven led me to the elevator and then to our suite where a porter delivered my luggage.

"Jo-anne!" I sang out as the door unlocked and Sven, the porter, and I entered.

No reply. Her luggage was open on the bed beside the wall and her coat hung over the back of the chair.

"It's possible that your sister went up to the Port of Call

Café for the welcome aboard buffet. Would you like me to check on her for you or show you to the buffet?"

"No, I think I'll settle in first." I glanced around. The room was larger than I expected. We had two twin beds, a love seat, coffee table, and an easy chair as well as a built-in desk beside the closet. The bathroom was a step up and had a full-size bathtub. A sliding door led out to a small balcony. We definitely had comfortable accommodations. Not quite enough space for Aunt Winnie's Scoot-About to maneuver around this room, but plenty of room for Joanne and me.

"Thank you." I dismissed the porter and Sven with a smile and a nod.

"My pleasure, to be sure." Sven said with a gentlemanly bow. "Please give my regards to your aunt. We hope she is able to sail with us again soon."

"I'll tell her. Thank you." Closing the door, I decided that before I went in search of Joanne on this huge floating hotel, I would take a few minutes to do what I did best: organize.

I had my clothes nearly unpacked when a knock on the door produced another attentive crew member. "Good afternoon. Here are the additional towels you ordered. My name is Raul, and if there's anything I can do for you, please let me know."

"Thank you." I tucked the unnecessary extra towels on the shelf in the bathroom and wondered if Joanne ordered the extra towels, or if Aunt Winnie had phoned and ordered them for us.

Another tap sounded at the door, and a large basket of fruit was delivered, wrapped in yellow-tinted cellophane. The card was from Aunt Winnie's travel agent with a simple message: "Enjoy!"

I barely returned the card to the tiny envelope when another knock produced a gorgeous flower arrangement with a tall, white calla lily in the center. This gift was compliments of the cruise line, congratulating Winnie on her twentieth cruise with them.

My sister is never going to believe all this!

Scooting out the door with the room key and my cruise pass in my pocket, I found my way down the hall and took the crowded elevator to the ninth level. Clusters of chatting travelers milled about. The atmosphere was charged with the hum of anticipation.

I noticed a group of four women who were all wearing the same sort of sassy sunglasses, as if they belonged to a club. The woman in the center of the group was telling a story, and the rest of them were cracking up. I had to stop and watch a moment because the women were my age yet they reminded me of a bunch of high schoolers on the first day of summer camp. I loved the feeling of glee that radiated from them.

Fully motivated to find my sister and let the fiesta begin, I stepped into the large dining area and looked around for Joanne. I didn't find her.

She found me.

With arms outstretched, winding between the closely

positioned tables, my sister called out, "Melly Jelly Belly!"

I would have slugged her, if I hadn't been so happy to see her.

"Joanna Banana!" I echoed, as we wrapped each other in a hug and swayed from side to side, laughing.

"Can you believe this?" Joanne pulled back and grinned at me, her eyes wide.

"Good ole Aunt Winnie," I said.

"And dear ole Uncle Harlan!" Joanne added.

"You look great," I told her. Joanne's hair was much darker than I'd seen it but styled in the same straight, just-below-the-ear cut she had worn last time I saw her. The change I noticed first were the deepened laugh lines around her eyes. She'd gotten older. At the same time, she looked younger. Thinner and more lighthearted than I remembered.

"You look great, too," she said. "Come on! I think we still have time to get our pictures taken up on the top deck by the pool."

She whisked me from the dining room, and we squeezed into another fully packed elevator. Several of the women in the elevator were wearing those same fun sunglasses I'd noticed on the other group of gigglers.

"Do you know where they're holding the chocolate-tasting event?" one of the smiling women asked Joanne.

"No, but it sounds like something we should check out. What do you think, Mel?"

"Before our pictures or after?"

"Oh, are you talking about those sombrero photos?" the woman asked. "I heard they were taking welcome aboard pictures."

"Yes, up by the pool," Joanne answered.

"What do you think?" the woman asked her companions. "Photos first, then chocolate?"

One of the other women made the decision and declared, "Photos before chocolate, everyone!"

"Is that like age before beauty?" Another woman asked as the elevator doors opened.

"If that's the case," the woman who was clearly the oldest of the bunch said, "step aside, girls. Let the aged one pass before you beauties."

We followed the lively, chatty women to where a short line had formed for the photo at the edge of the railing along the top deck. This was the area where I'd noticed people standing when I got off the shuttle and looked up. Now that I was the one standing on deck, it didn't seem so monstrous. Just windy. Near the front of the ship stood a looming climbing wall designed to give adventuresome travelers a place to hook themselves to a few ropes and scale above the deck. Our present altitude was high enough for me.

The other women told Joanne and me to go first since they were still organizing their photo groupings. The photographer handed us two floppy straw sombreros and told us to "let loose" for the camera.

"Sisterchicks on the loose!" one of the women in line called out, and her companions laughed with her.

Joanne flung her arm around me. I reached for her free hand, thinking I could show Ethan the photo and tell him we were learning to do the tango like he'd teased me about. Joanne was letting that hugely gleeful laugh of hers fly about the deck, and I was telling myself, *Don't blink this time! Don't blink!*

With a painless snap, the photographer captured our jubilant moment forever. We handed the sombreros over to the other women, and the older one said, "We found out about the chocolate tasting. It's in the Cove Lounge on the second floor."

"Great," Joanne said. "Sounds like a good way to start off our trip."

A young man in a crisp, white cruise uniform stepped up to us, holding out a tray with tall plastic beverage cups filled with some kind of deep green drink. "Welcome on board," he said. "Would you like to try our signature cocktail, Cruisin' for a Bruisin'?"

"Would it be possible to get some water?" I asked.

"Certainly. Right over there at the bar."

We slid past the lounge chairs where a surprising number of determined sunbathers already were stretched out in the southern California midday. Both of us ordered water and were handed the smallest bottles I'd ever seen. They were so cold that a chunk of ice floated in the center of the bottle like a submerged iceberg. I gave the bartender my cruise pass and asked, "Just out of curiosity, how much is this water?"

"Three dollars," he said. "But let me give you a tip. You'll enjoy the cruise more if you don't keep track of the charges. You're here to relax."

I sipped my icy water and wondered if my husband had been talking to this guy. Why was everyone telling me to relax? Was I the only one who thought it was outrageous to pay three dollars for a bottle of water? Joanne seemed to be taking it all in stride.

We made our way to the Cove Lounge where a woman wearing a fresh flower lei around her neck greeted us. The now-familiar sassy sunglasses were perched on top of her head.

"We were told this is the place to come for the chocolate tasting," Joanne said.

"Yes, welcome. Do you have your Sisterchick passes?"

"Is this it?" Joanne held out her cruise pass.

"No, ours is the yellow one."

Just then the happy quartet stepped up behind us, returned from their photo shoot and still laughing. "Do we need to show our Sisterchick passes?" the leader asked, pulling out a yellow card from her purse. The other three women reached for theirs.

"Go ahead," I motioned to the women.

"Aren't you going in?" the leader asked.

"We only brought our cruise passes," I said, emptying my pocket.

"They're with us," the leader declared. "We were up by the pool having our pictures taken."

"You two are Sisterchicks, right?" the hostess at the door asked Joanne and me.

"Is it that obvious?" Joanne asked. "Our mom used to say we were almost twins."

"I'm here with my sister, too," the older woman behind us said. "She's at the spa right now getting a pedicure. When she saw my toes, that little copycat had to run off and have hers painted, too."

We looked down at the woman's small feet clad in sturdy-looking leather sandals with ten bright pink piglets all lined up in a row, wiggling merrily.

"*Oui, oui, oui!* All the way out to sea!" she chanted with a backup chorus of chuckles from her pals.

"Hey, who's holding up the line?" a tall woman called out from the group that had gathered behind us. "You're keeping us from our chocolate, you know! Are you sure you want to do that?" Over a dozen women were waiting to get into the chocolate fest.

"Go ahead, all six of you," the hostess said, waving Joanne and me through, even though we didn't have the right passes. We joined the lighthearted party already in session, complete with music, balloons, and designated organizers who wore floral leis and name tags. I listened as one of the organizers directed a woman to where she could pick up her name tag and sign up for a free drawing for a gift basket.

I was beginning to think we stumbled into a private party. All these women had the same sunglasses. The napkins were printed with a stylized yellow chick wearing sunglasses, and many of the women seemed to know each other.

"Joanne," I whispered, pulling her out of the line once she filled a plate with white chocolate–covered blueberries, mocha truffles, and macadamia nut brownies. "I think this is a club. We're not supposed to be here."

"But we fit in perfectly," Joanne said. "Look at these women. I'd pick any of them to be my new best friend."

Her comment struck a tender spot in my spirit. I happened to be in the market for a new best friend. Ethan and I had moved four times in the past nine years. The result of so many relocations was that I always lost whatever momentum I'd gained in developing friendships. I'm not the kind of person who goes shopping for a buddy, so if a new friend doesn't come my way, I don't tend to go out looking for one. Did Joanne feel the same way? Was she in a girlfriend slump the way I was?

"I know." I savored a mouth-melting truffle I had plucked from Joanne's plate. "I think this is a great bunch of women, too. But look, they have name tags. If they send us over to that table to get our name tags, we won't be on the list. And if they start singing their sorority song or tell everyone to turn and extend the official handshake, you and I are going to be in big trouble."

Joanne glanced around. "You're probably right. Let me grab one more cocoa-coconut cookie. Did you see that they even have chocolate mint tea?"

With a jerk of my head, I motioned to Joanne that I was heading for the door while she made another daring grab at the chocolates that were meant for these Sisterchicks but not necessarily for us sisters.

"What about getting a pedicure?" Joanne asked once we stepped out of the Cove Lounge.

"What does that have to do with anything?"

"I was thinking of that lady who was showing us her toes and said her sister went for a pedicure. My toes haven't seen the light of day for months. What do you say we find the spa and schedule a little pampering?"

"Sounds fun," I said, thinking how this was a new twist for my sister. I had never known her to pluck her eyebrows, let alone paint her nails. "The spa is on the tenth level."

"How did you know that?" Joanne asked.

"I read the listings when we were in the elevator."

"I'm glad you're here." Joanne linked her arm in mine. "Without you I'd be crashing private parties and wandering around the lobby looking for the spa. Let's face it, Melanie, I'd be lost without you."

The last bit of my chocolate truffle caught in my throat. My sister never said words like that to me before. At home my exasperated husband, who didn't have a talent for details, often told me I "micromanaged" too much or that I was bossy.

I couldn't believe how great it felt to be with the first person who ever called me "bossy," but to have her express appreciation for my skill with details and direction. It was good to be appreciated. Very good. I was ready to celebrate my big sister's approval with a round of pink piggies.

Ah, the power of chocolate to improve a woman's outlook on life!

Three

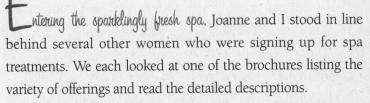

Entering the sparklingly fresh spa, Joanne and I stood in line behind several other women who were signing up for spa treatments. We each looked at one of the brochures listing the variety of offerings and read the detailed descriptions.

"Listen to this," I said. "Guava-mango body wrap and a thirty-minute massage. Doesn't that sound decadent?"

"Or how about this one with the seaweed therapy and a de-stressing scalp treatment?" Joanne suggested.

I made an exaggerated grimace. "Seaweed? Sounds kind of slimy."

"It could be a rejuvenating experience," she said with a grin. "With all these options, I have to say that a plain old pedicure seems pretty dull. I think I'd rather have a facial or one of these body treatments. What do you think, Mel?"

"Anything sounds extravagant to me."

We were at the front of the line before settling on a choice, but making a decision suddenly became a pointless exercise. When we tried to schedule pedicures and body wraps, the receptionist informed us they were booked until the next day, unless we were Crown Members.

I hadn't been convinced I wanted some stranger to rub my back or paint my toenails—that is, until we were told they were booked up. Then I wanted a mango-guava body wrap so bad I could taste it. Or maybe I thought I could taste it because I hadn't had lunch yet, and the chocolate samples had awakened a sleeping giant of an appetite.

"I doubt that we're Crown Members," I said. "But we are staying in a first-class cabin, if that adds any merit."

"If you have your cruise pass, I can run it through the machine to find out your status," the receptionist responded.

I handed over my card, and she fixed her complacent gaze on the computer screen. Suddenly her face brightened. "Oh, I apologize, Ms. Clayton. You're right. You aren't a Crown Member. You're a Platinum Crown Guest."

"Aunt Winnie," Joanne mumbled to me with a knowing nod.

"Our aunt is the Platinum traveler," I explained. "This is my sister's and my first cruise."

"The same benefits apply to you because you're registered under her number," she said. "As a Platinum member, we can take you both right now. Please have a seat, and we'll call you in a moment."

"So, what are we having done?" Joanne asked, as we took our seats.

"Who cares? I'm beginning to see why Aunt Winnie takes these cruises all the time."

"No kidding," Joanne said. "It's worth it for the food alone. The buffet was fabulous."

"Don't tell me about it. I'm starving."

"That's right! I whisked you away to the pool for pictures and then to the chocolate party, where you hardly ate any of the goodies. Do you want to find something to eat and come back?"

"No, I'm okay. Our dinner seating is at six-thirty, so I won't die if I don't get anything until then."

"How did you know it's at six-thirty?"

"It's on the card." I pulled out my cruise pass. "They do two different seatings for dinner: six-thirty and eight-thirty. I'm glad we got the early one."

"Me, too," Joanne said. "The eight-thirty would have been like eating dinner at eleven-thirty for me, with the time change."

"Maybe we can nap during our massages," I said. "Doesn't that sound regal?"

Just then two specialists in white lab coats approached us and asked us to follow them to the private rooms located off the side of the spa lounge.

"See you in an hour," I told Joanne with a broad grin as we were ushered into our side-by-side rooms.

Her wave hinted at nervousness. I thought how good this was going to be for her—for both of us—to start off the cruise relaxed and enjoying the luxury of first-class treatment.

The spa technician assigned to me introduced herself as Shannon and asked a few questions while she made notes on her clipboard. My answers were easy enough: No, I had never been on a cruise before. No, I hadn't experienced a "natural respite" treatment before. No, I had no known allergies. And no, I did not take any prescription medications.

"Lovely," she said with a hint of an Irish accent. "Would you be so kind then as to remove your clothing and put on these spa coverings?"

She held up what looked like a one-size-fits-all bikini made out of a pink paper towel.

"After you've changed, please make yourself comfortable on the massage table. I'll be back in a moment to begin your guava-mango body wrap."

She left, and I followed her directions by donning the paper outfit. I was glad no full-length mirror was in the room. I noticed that even the in-room shower had smoked glass so I couldn't catch my reflection there.

I originally pictured Joanne and me receiving the relaxation treatments on tables beside each other. I imagined us side-by-side, visiting the whole time. Now I could see the wisdom in making this a more private affair. After one look at each other in the paper towel bikinis, we probably would have laughed ourselves silly.

Stretching out on the massage table, I lay on my back and realized I was positioned in the middle of what felt like a giant piece of aluminum foil.

Shannon tapped on the door and entered discreetly. "Ready, then?" In her hand she held a small wooden bowl. With a spatula sort of instrument, she stirred what looked like yogurt the shade of a rotted pumpkin.

"I feel as if I'm about to be turned into a giant tropical fruit burrito."

Shannon's airy laughter filled the small room. "I've not heard that one before. You relax now. I will begin by covering your exposed skin with our special blend of guava paste. It has finely ground mango seeds and might feel a bit chilly at first, but not to worry. You're going to love this."

I closed my eyes and let the beautification begin.

The first area the skin specialist smeared with the fruity concoction was my exposed midriff. I let out a tiny peep, sounding like a bird whose foot had broken through a layer of ice on a birdbath and couldn't pull it out fast enough.

"Everything all right?" Shannon asked.

"Yes, it's just colder than I thought it would be." I felt all my muscles contracting rather than relaxing.

"You'll warm up as soon as we wrap you and let the treatment soak in."

The large sheet of aluminum foil now made sense.

As Shannon's lilting voice explained the benefits of this treatment, I'd like to say that I relaxed and appreciated the natural ingredients and all their healing enzymes. However, I kept getting colder and colder. Every place on my skin where her spatula spread the mixture, I felt a new batch of goose bumps cropping up. My teeth gave an involuntary chatter from the chill. For a Canadian, that's saying something.

I was hopeful, as Shannon covered me with the foil, that I would thaw out.

"Would you like a blanket over you?" she offered.

"Yes, definitely. I feel like I'm covered with goose bumps."

"That's the stimulating effects of the mélange. I'll leave you for a while now. Is the volume of the music too low?"

"No, it's nice." I closed my eyes and told myself to relax. Soft violins and soothing cellos tried their best to lull me, but I still felt prickly all over. I kept glancing at the clock and wondering when Shannon would return.

These overactive enzymes better transform my skin into something wonderful, because they are tickling me to death under this wrap!

Shannon returned with instructions for me to take a warm shower and to use the loofah sponge she handed me. I was to scrub gently all over in the darkened shower stall while she prepared the massage table.

As the water flowed over my arms and shoulders, I warmed up. The potion had dried to a cakelike texture and smelled delicious as it melted off my skin and swirled down the drain.

I noticed after vigorously washing my thighs that they were

red. So was my stomach. Toning down my scrubbing technique, I finished my warm and somewhat-soothing shower and patted dry. Wrapping up in the luxuriously large towel, I returned to the prepared table, eager for a muscle-relaxing massage.

Shannon discretely held up a sheet while I removed the towel and comfortably settled on my stomach. She folded the sheet at my waist so that only my back and arms were exposed. I twitched slightly, still feeling tingly from the shower, and waited for her to begin.

From her lips came a low, "Oh, dear."

"That didn't sound good." I chuckled nervously.

"Melanie, do you have any allergies you didn't mention earlier?"

"No, not that I know of. Why?"

"You seem to be having a reaction."

"Is that why I was so red?"

"Yes. And your skin seems to be developing bumps."

"I thought I had a bad case of the chills."

"No, some of these bumps are growing into welts."

I lay there, helpless, as she continued to describe how the welts were spreading.

"I've never seen anything like this," she said. "I need to bring in my supervisor. Stay right here."

"Where would I go?" I joked, as she left the room.

Now that I knew the bumps were an allergic reaction, I began to itch twice as much as I had when I thought it was a sensation to be expected from the stimulating natural ingredients. A thousand mosquitoes seemed to have used my bare flesh for target practice.

Drawing up my right arm, I watched as new pimple-like dots appeared about every fifteen seconds.

This can't be good! Where did Shannon go?

Desperate times called for desperate measures. Taking matters into my own hands, I slid off the massage table and returned to the shower. If any of the guava-mango mixture remained on my skin, I wanted to wash it off.

"Melanie?" Shannon called, entering the room. "Are you all right? I brought my supervisor with me."

I could faintly make out the shape of another person with her.

"I'm trying to make sure I washed all of the fruity stuff off me."

"Are you allergic to guavas or mangos?" the supervisor asked.

"I don't know. I don't think I've ever eaten a mango or a guava. I know I've never tried smearing either of them on my skin."

"We've called the ship's physician. He'll be here to examine you shortly. I'd recommend that you continue to rinse in the shower until he comes."

"Lovely," I muttered.

"We'll leave some fresh towels here for you, and Shannon will be right outside the door if you need her."

After thoroughly rinsing my inflamed flesh, I wrapped one towel around my now-soaked hair and the other around my body and waited for the doctor to arrive.

His exam was quick. He looked at my arm, top and underside, checked my neck, and then handed me a pill that dissolved under my tongue. He said it was supposed to have an immediate effect on the allergic reaction and gave me a second pill I could take twelve hours later, if the rash persisted.

By the time I had my clothes back on, I felt less itchy but not at all relaxed. Shannon returned with a small bottle of some sort of lotion guaranteed to soothe my skin.

"No charge for the lotion." She handed me some paperwork. "And my supervisor said we'd be pleased to offer you half price for a treatment."

"Half price!" I squawked. "Half price for what? Why are you charging me at all?"

Shannon looked surprised at my outburst. "We thought it might be helpful. You're welcome to speak to my supervisor, if you like."

"I will." I reached for my purse and marched out to the front desk, my wet hair dripping down my neck. Joanne sat in the waiting area, dry and calm, wearing the expression of a woman who had just floated out of a fabulously relaxing experience.

"I already settled our bill." She rose to greet me. "I charged it to our room."

"Well, I'm going to uncharge it," I said with a huff as I approached the reservation desk.

Before I could begin my tirade, a loud announcement came over the ship's intercom system. "In five minutes, our compulsory muster drill will commence. This drill is for the safety of all our guests. When you hear the whistle, you must report to your station wearing your life jacket."

"I need to discuss this with someone," I said to the receptionist, holding up the paper Shannon handed me. "Is your supervisor available?"

"We're not allowed to conduct any business once the drill has been announced," she said. "Sorry. You're welcome to return here afterward."

"What is the drill?" Joanne asked.

"All the passengers must get their life jackets from their rooms and report on deck. The number on your jacket will tell you which station you are to go to."

Joanne looked at me. "What happened to your neck?"

I couldn't pass up the chance to raise my voice, so I stood there and gave her the rundown, concluding with, "The doctor had to give me a pill."

My sister, the nurse, examined my welts carefully. "Must have been Benadryl. Why didn't he give you a shot of epinephrine?"

"I don't know. He gave me a pill. That's all I know. It helped, but I didn't get a massage, and they're still going to charge me. Half price. As if that's going to help."

"No." The receptionist held up her hand. "I heard them discussing you. I told them you both wanted a pedicure. What Shannon was supposed to say was that there was no charge for the wrap, but if you wanted to try one of the other treatments, such as a pedicure, we'd offer it to you for half price."

"Oh."

All the fire went from my belly. My skin continued to smolder.

"You really need to hurry to make it on deck for the drill," the receptionist said. "I'll be happy to schedule you for another treatment, if you come back later."

Joanne turned to go, but I called out to her to wait a moment. I dashed down the hallway and found Shannon with a mound of towels in her arms.

"I'm sorry I snapped at you. I didn't understand what you were saying about the half price being applied to a different treatment."

With professional calm, and I'm sure a pinch of Irish wit, she said, "Well, then. I'll need to be improving my skills with the English language, won't I?"

"And I'll select a different treatment that doesn't involve fruit next time."

She grinned, and I couldn't help but think she probably viewed me as the real "fruit" in this fiasco.

The whistle for the drill sounded before Joanne and I entered the elevator to take us to our deck. We opted for the stairs, moving like two salmon going downstream while swarms of better-prepared salmon were moving upstream. All of them were wearing their bright orange life jackets around their necks.

Joanne fiddled with her room key in the unreceptive door slot while I fished for mine in my purse. More groups of prepared passengers streamed past us in the narrow hallway.

One large man said, "You can't hide in your room. They'll come find you and drag you out for the drill."

We ignored him and tried our best to comply with the ship's regulations.

By the time Joanne and I unlocked our door, donned the jackets, and literally ran to our assigned station, we were tardy.

Breezing out onto the deck, my sister and I had to pass in front of hundreds of standing passengers lined up two deep all the way down the deck. We hurried past them with our heads down, trying to make it to our places at the end of the line, all the while aware of the many eyes that followed us. In the evening air I was aware that my hair was still wet, uncombed, and most certainly sticking out in every direction.

A crewman stepped in front of us just as we sighted the end of the line where we needed to stand. "Madame," he said with a French accent. "Your vest is not right."

He stopped me with a hand on my shoulder and gave a short *tweet* on the silver whistle hung around his neck. Speaking loudly enough to gain the interest of the entire viewing audience, he said, "Attention, please. You will see now how to properly attach your life vest."

He proceeded to remove my life jacket, turn it around, and place it back over my head in the correct position. My sister and the rest of our thoroughly entertained deck mates took note. He then put both his arms around my middle and cinched the straps at the waist.

I let out another peep. This one sounded more like a bird that had fallen head first into an iced-over birdbath. The last thing my skin needed was more agitation.

"Too tight?" He worked with the straps in the back, loosening them.

I caught my sister's eye where she stood with obnoxiously straight posture at the end of the line. Her lips were pressed together, and she looked like the perpetually good student who snuck past the truant officer unnoticed. I knew she was dying to let that huge laugh of hers come rolling down the deck and knock me over like a bowling pin.

The ship's captain came on the loudspeaker and gave a few instructions before sounding the all clear. I stood to the side while the other passengers broke ranks.

"Teacher's pet," Joanne muttered, coming alongside and tugging mischievously on the strap of my life vest.

I responded with a low growl.

Not intimidated in the slightest, my sister confidently linked her arm in mine, and with our orange life vests bumping together as we walked, we returned to our room.

"Did you bring something nice to wear to dinner?" Joanne asked, as she unfastened her vest and tossed it on the love seat.

"I brought a dress, but I want to wear the loosest, most free-flowing clothes I have so this rash doesn't get more irritated."

"Good idea. Do you remember when I told you on the phone the other night about my friend Sandy?"

"Was she the one who went on the cruise to the Bahamas a couple of years ago?"

"Yes. She said we have to be on time or else they close the doors, and they won't seat us for dinner."

"I'm not going to miss dinner, if I can help it!" I said. "What do they do with the people who don't make it in time? Seat them at the eight-thirty dinner?"

"I guess. Or else they go to one of the other restaurants on the ship. Have you noticed how food is an important part of this cruise?"

"Actually, no. I'm still looking forward to experiencing some food on this cruise." I glanced in the mirror above the built-in dresser drawers and squawked, "Joanne, why didn't you tell me my hair was this hilarious? I stood out there on deck with my wet hair flipping around in the breeze, and look how it dried! How come you didn't say something?"

"Because I thought you'd get upset."

"Upset?"

"You used to always get upset if I made any comment about your hair or clothes needing adjustment."

"I did not."

"Yes, you did. You can't tell me you don't remember the fights we used to have over your hair."

"My hair? What fights?"

Joanne looked incredulous. "You seriously don't remember?"

I shook my mangled mane. "Name one time I got upset about my hair."

"Okay," Joanne said. "How about the morning before school pictures in sixth grade, when I told you to put your hair behind your ears when they took your picture? You decked me with a pillow and broke my turquoise necklace."

"No, no, no. You told me *not* to put my hair behind my ears because of the funny way my ears stick out. You said I had deformed ears, and I should get an operation."

"I never said that."

"Yes you did!"

"You don't have deformed ears," Joanne said with a wry grin. "At least you better not because you and I have the same ears."

"No, it's our noses that are the same." I knew our dispute was at an impasse. I scrunched up my nose, and we both looked in the mirror together, Joanne mimicking my scrunch.

"They are the same, aren't they?" Joanne said. "I always wanted your eyes. Mine are too wide. So is my mouth. You got Mom's mouth. I got Dad's big cavern." She opened wide, and I laughed because it made me feel as if I were back at the dentist's office and some patient was trying to tell me, the front desk receptionist, which tooth was bothering her.

"But you inherited the personality," I told her. "Not to mention the perfect skin that doesn't break out all the time." I stretched up my chin to examine the receding bumps on my neck.

Joanne pulled back and looked at me. "Miss Personality. Thanks a lot. That's like being the runner-up, I guess. Miss Big Mouth with the nice skin and the great personality."

If I'd realized I was going to touch such a sensitive area in Joanne's psyche, I never would have said anything about my hair or our noses or anything. We hadn't been together for two hours yet, and here we were, back in our old habit of tearing ourselves down in front of the other in high hopes that the other sister would build us back up. Joanne had tossed out the invitation for me to boost her, and I had given her nothing more uplifting than "you have a great personality." Bad choice.

I didn't know what to say to elevate the down-turned mood.

Joanne was the one who buoyed up the conversation. "We better scoot along, or they'll lock the dining room doors on us, like Sandy said."

"I need to take another shower." I glanced at my watch. "A quick shower. Then will you rub this lotion on my back?"

I realized the beauty of being sisters meant that we could walk away from a potential pity party with all the telltale streamers suspended in midair and return any time we wanted. It also meant I could ask her to touch my afflicted skin without wondering if she was really grossed out by the thought but willing to do it to be nice.

That's the beauty of sisterhood. Our relationship didn't require extra maintenance to ensure that we always would be connected with each other, the way a friendship did. Joanne and I were bonded for life.

So, if that's true, why haven't I ever asked her about Russell?

I stepped into the steaming shower and decided tonight would be the ultimate slumber party after dinner. At long last Joanne would tell all.

Or I'd pulverize her with all the extra bath towels.

Four

Twenty-five minutes later, we trotted down the hall to the elevator with Joanne wearing a semiformal, sequined-bodice gown she had borrowed from Sandy, her friend who had cruised the Bahamas and had invested in a proper wardrobe for such a journey.

I tagged behind Joanne looking much less elegant. My white button-up shirt was freshly ironed but untucked, hanging casually over my nicest pair of black pants. The rash had been arrested, but the itch factor was still at large, and I was trying to keep my clothes loose and breezy. I gave up on wearing any jewelry because even the silver necklace I brought felt itchy on the back of my neck.

Entering the large dining room, we were shown to a table in the center area that was set for six people. Four others already were seated. Most of the people in the dining room were dressed casually, I noticed. No one was as dressed up as Joanne.

Joanne turned to me and muttered, "Apparently this short cruise has a different dress code than Sandy's Bahamian cruise."

"You look lovely this evening," the wine steward said diplomatically, as he filled Joanne's glass with water. "Most of our guests save their formal wear for our dinner on the final evening."

"Oh, I see." To her credit, Joanne seemed to shake off the discomfort of being ahead of the rest of the ship on the evening dress code. Instead, she entered into the introductions around the table as warmly as if she were wearing jeans and a T-shirt like the woman on her right. That was the strength of Joanne's personality. She could flex much better than I could.

The couple on our right was from Montana and celebrating their fifteenth anniversary. The couple across from us was from Newport Beach, California, and said this was their second trip to Mexico on this cruise line.

"We had such a great time, we decided to come again. The food is exceptional." The friendly man from California was in his late fifties or early sixties with what looked like a burn scar running up the side of his neck and ear. His eyes twinkled as he said, "I can personally recommend every one of their desserts. Especially the ones they serve at the midnight buffet."

"One meal at a time, Robert!" his demure wife, Marti, said, as she received the menu being handed to her.

"My sister and I have never been on a cruise before," Joanne said, nodding to me. "Any advice you have will be greatly appreciated."

"The evening shows are entertaining," Marti said, laying aside her menu. "However, the shopping tomorrow in Ensenada isn't much to speak of, unless you're in the market for clay pots. I personally enjoy the ice sculptures at the midnight buffets. They are beautifully done."

The ship seemed to let out a long groan, a sort of wide-mouthed yawn. The floor gave off a low vibration.

"Ahoy!" Robert called out. "We're on our way out to sea."

So it wasn't my imagination; we were moving. The movement was a strangely subtle sensation. I had pictured our departure from the harbor to be something from the movies, complete with streamers and confetti and people on the shore waving to us as we glided out to sea.

Instead, we were seated in a fancy dining room listening to Natalia, our waitress, as she ran through the details of the feast we were about to enjoy. She was darling and sparkly and spoke with a heavy accent.

When she stepped away from the table with the order for our appetizers, Joanne said, "Now I can see why Sandy gained ten pounds on her cruise! They make all the food sound so good you want to try everything."

"I made sure I tried every dessert offered on our last cruise," Robert said.

"I have a solution for the weight gain," Marti interjected.

"Don't take the elevators the entire cruise. Always take the stairs."

Just then a young man dressed as a pirate came over to our table with a stuffed parrot. A photographer joined him, and before we could pose, the pirate positioned himself between Joanne and me and placed his parrot puppet on my shoulder.

"Arrrgh, maties!" the pirate growled as the camera flashed. "Ye can pick up your photos at the lower level of the lobby after dinner. Arrrgh."

We laughed as the pirate made his way around the table, and our appetizers were delivered with a flourish. My daring sister had ordered escargot, which was served in rounded pewter dishes with small, sunken pockets for each of the garlic- and butter-saturated curlycues.

"You're going to share this with me aren't you?" Joanne asked.

Robert also ordered the escargot, and he dove in with great verbal admiration for the tenderness and quality of the delicacy.

I was having a hard time moving past the thought that these people were putting snails in their mouths, biting into them, and swallowing. Joanne forked one of the tidbits and gave me a sly eyebrows-up glance before putting the bite in her mouth. I watched her carefully.

"Superb," she said with calm sophistication.

Superb! Ha! I doubted she had ever tried escargot before or had anything to compare it with. I also didn't particularly enjoy watching her enter into a new experience before me.

Not to be outclassed, I reached for a small fork, knowing that if I didn't take the challenge, this crazy power balance between us would forever be tipped in Joanne's favor. I had to eat the snail. I mean, escargot.

Drawing the fork to my mouth, I placed the rubbery morsel on top of my molars instead of on my tongue to avoid contact with my taste buds. With two quick, sufficient chews I swallowed. The garlic taste overpowered my senses. With a polite nod to the observing dinner guests, I borrowed Joanne's word. "Superb."

Joanne laughed at me. It was a soft, tender, sisterly laugh and not meant to embarrass or demean.

Two minutes later I excused myself from the table. Trying to walk slowly and appear calm, I made my way to the little girl's room. Apparently snails don't enjoy being the only visitor in a stomach that, aside from some pulverized airline peanuts, a smuggled chocolate truffle, and antihive medication, had been vacant since breakfast.

I took the long way back to our table, making sure my stomach was settled. The salad I'd ordered was waiting for me. Poached pear with caramelized walnuts. Thankfully Joanne didn't begin a medical interrogation. She was in the middle of a conversation with Robert, and as I listened in, I ascertained he was in real estate and knew a few things about land ownership in Mexico.

"The bank in Mexico still holds the trust for our property," Joanne said.

That's when I knew that in my absence she had disclosed to our dinner guests that we were owners of beachfront property in Mexico. I wondered how her announcement had gone over.

Robert nodded. "Mexican banks hold 100 percent of the control of all coastal and border lands purchased by foreign investors. Make sure you check your dates on your documents. Most trusts only run for fifty years, but the government is obligated to issue a new permit for another fifty years no matter how much time remains on the original trust."

"That's good to know," Joanne said.

"I shouldn't have gotten him started on real estate." Marti leaned over and gave the appearance she was confiding in Joanne and me. "I should know by now to avoid the topics of real estate and golf if I want to stay in the conversation."

The couple across from us talked about water skiing, and Marti clicked out of the conversation altogether. I felt equally disconnected. What amazed me was how my sister came across so warmly responsive to these people she just met. She appeared comfortable with any topic and any combination of table companions.

I felt ready to have Joanne all to myself after dinner. The first thing she asked, once we were away from everyone else, was if I felt okay. I filled her in on the details.

"Do you think the ship's movement set you off? We could see about getting you a seasickness patch to put behind your ear."

"No, it was the snail. I didn't have lunch, remember? But

let's not talk about the appetizers. The rest of dinner was great. I'm fine now."

"This hasn't been a very enjoyable trip for you so far, has it? First the hives and then the nausea."

"I hope that means everything can only get better."

"It will," Joanne said confidently.

"You know what's strange?" I asked. "All this pampering and fancy food is supposed to be a luxury. We're supposed to experience a taste of how the other half lives, but to be honest, I'm not impressed yet."

"This isn't exactly how the other half lives. Do you know how many millions of people live with barely enough clothing and food to make it through each day?"

I regretted starting my sister on this topic. She was passionate about how clueless people were regarding the conditions the rest of the world lived in. "If even a fraction of the comfortable people in the western world would share just the smallest percentage of their wealth with the rest of the world, so much could be changed," Joanne said. "I told Sandy I didn't think I'd be able to relax and enjoy all this lavishness, but she scolded me and said I needed to be thankful that this cruise had been given to me and to learn to receive graciously."

"It is a gift," I agreed. "I haven't been very grateful yet, either. I think it's hard to receive sometimes when you're used to being the one who does the giving."

Joanne nodded.

We strolled side by side in silence through the lobby area

and decided to check out the photo gallery on the lower level. The pirate photos weren't posted yet, but the picture of the two of us in sombreros was adorable—not because we looked so great in goofy, oversize straw hats, but because we looked like us. And we looked young and happy even with our silly pose. Without hesitating, we each ordered a copy. The picture seemed to represent for both of us how to enter into this gift with delight.

Deciding that a stroll on deck would enable us to enter into the joy of the journey, we headed out on the side of the ship where we had gone earlier for the lifeboat drill.

Pausing at the rail, Joanne and I stood close together, peering down many stories below. Subtle glimmers of white-laced waves let us know we were truly at sea, moving south through the calm Pacific waters. I lifted my chin to the bracing wind, drawing in a deep breath. The night air carried with it a mysterious hint of the vast ocean that surrounded us, hidden in the dark cloak of night. Moist droplets of salty air clung to our eyelashes.

Laughter floated our way from the pool area behind us. We turned to see that several people were soaking in the elevated hot tub under a wide canopy. The steam rising from the elaborately designed area made me think of a cartoon scenario where unsuspecting victims were roasting in a cannibal's stew pot. Only these roasting people looked happy about their predicament.

Below the hot tub the large and brightly lit swimming pool

was void of night swimmers for good reason. The water wildly sloshed from side to side, creating a confined tidal wave.

"I think I'm the one who's about to feel seasick now," Joanne said with a laugh. "We'd better keep walking."

Rounding the side of the ship, we spotted Robert walking toward us. He waved and greeted us by name. On a ship filled with nearly two thousand people, it was nice to be recognized.

"Beautiful night, isn't it?" Robert called out. "I'm supposed to walk off my desserts before meeting Marti for the Broadway Hits Review at nine o'clock. If you two don't have plans, you're welcome to join us."

"Thanks," Joanne and I said in unison.

"You know, I didn't mention this at dinner because I knew my wife would kick me under the table if I dominated the conversation with real estate talk, but I have an associate who is developing some property here in Baja. He bought his acreage in the late seventies and just now is turning it into a golf resort. It's coming along nicely. About eighty acres. If it would help you to have his name and number, I'd be glad to give it to you."

"I don't know if we'd have anything specific to ask him," I said. "I'm sure our property is nowhere near that size."

"I thought he might help to clarify some of the details on the deed or help you to find a notary you can trust. Do you know if your property is north or south of Ensenada?"

"I'm not sure. It's in a town called San Felipe." I realized as I said the name that one of the many tasks on my to-do list had been to locate San Felipe on a map. I couldn't believe that detail had slipped past me.

"San Felipe?" Robert repeated. "Are you sure?"

"Yes, San Felipe."

"Is that near where your friend is building his resort?" Joanne asked.

"No. Actually, San Felipe is on the east coast of Baja. On the Sea of Cortez."

"Are you saying San Felipe isn't close to Ensenada?" My stomach rumbled deeply, and I felt sick all over again.

"It's on the other side of the Baja Peninsula. My guess is San Felipe is about 150 miles east of where we dock tomorrow." He tilted his head. "If you don't mind my asking, how do you ladies plan to get there?"

I was lost. I felt as if I'd just failed a geography pop quiz. I had assumed far too much knowledge from my neurotic aunt and her less-than-competent lawyer. This stunning news flattened me.

"We'll rent a car," Joanne said optimistically.

"It's too far," I sputtered. "Even if we rent a car, the ship only docks in Ensenada for the day. We would have to drive to San Felipe and be back to the ship by five o'clock. We can't do that."

"Sounds like you'll have to adjust your plans," Robert said.

"We need a map," I said.

"We need Sven," Joanne said. "Let's go to the lobby and see if he can sort this out for us."

"You know, renting a car isn't a bad idea." Robert followed us to the elevators, where I kept pushing the Down button as if my anxiety would hurry up the mechanical contraption.

"You could rent a car in Ensenada tomorrow, drive over to San Felipe, stay a few days at your uncle's place, sign the papers at the bank, and then drive back to Ensenada."

"We'd miss the boat," Joanne said.

I felt like saying we'd already missed the boat in more ways than one, but I kept my lips sealed. I was trying to think.

"You'll miss the return trip on *this* cruise," Robert said. "But these cruise liners come down here twice a week. Instead of sailing home on Wednesday, you could catch the next big bucket home on Saturday."

His suggestion had merit. However, the last thing I wanted to do was step into an even more unplanned and unregulated situation.

"You know, Joanne." I tried to sound as if I'd thought this through. "Maybe we should finish the cruise, go home, and start all over with the San Felipe part. We need to put more time and organization into our plans instead of running head-long into chaos."

"This isn't chaos, Melanie. We're on a free luxury cruise that's taking us within…what?" She turned to Robert for backup.

"One hundred and fifty miles, roughly."

"Within one hundred and fifty miles of Uncle Harlan's beach house. How can we turn around and go home when we're so close? What would our options be? Wait for the bank to send the documents?"

"You don't want to do that," Robert said. "Not after what I saw my friend go through with his paperwork for the golf resort. It takes months. Years sometimes."

"We know," Joanne said. "It took the bank in San Felipe three years to notify us that we were the beneficiaries."

Robert let out a low whistle.

Joanne was on a roll now, and I knew she wasn't about to let up. "It doesn't make sense for us to go home and then turn around a month later to fly back to Mexico. Do we even know if San Felipe has an airport? You and I could end up flying back to Ensenada and driving the 150 miles anyhow. We might as well do it now."

I didn't want to do it now. I didn't want to take off in some rental car and drive across Mexico to a fishing village where it was unlikely anyone spoke English. The lure of beachfront property held little appeal to me at the moment. I didn't want to be away from home for an additional three days. Luxury cruise or not, I didn't want to be here at all. I was losing the tug-of-war I'd been having all day with the anxiety monster, and my unhappy gut was telling me fear was about to take me down.

"We need to think this through," I said as calmly as I could.

Everything felt out of balance. I was supposed to be the bossy one, not Joanne. I was supposed to have all the facts about the distance from Ensenada to San Felipe, not Robert, the dessert connoisseur.

The light above the elevator door flashed, notifying us that our ride would be here in a moment. Robert pulled a business card from his pocket and wrote on the back. "Here's our suite number, and this is my cell phone number. If Marti and I can help in any way, please let us know. And you know what? I'll say a little prayer for the two of you."

"Thank you." Joanne reached for the card. "We appreciate your help. I think God must have some sort of surprise in mind for us. He seems to be directing us to something we certainly didn't dream up."

Robert grinned. "God is like that, isn't He? Always dreaming up adventures we could never imagine."

Joanne flashed a warm smile at Robert as the elevator door opened. The two of them seemed to be members of some special God club. I had the same feeling around them that I'd had around the Sisterchicks. I didn't belong.

Robert gave us a wave as the elevator door closed, and Joanne and I rode it to the lobby level. The crew member at the front desk paged Sven, and within a few minutes our personal steward appeared. With calmness and steadiness, Sven listened to our plight and made several recommendations. The one that made the most sense was the one I liked the least.

"This is unusual," he said twenty minutes later, when he handed me a printout of our rental car reservation. "But we are always pleased to make accommodations for our Platinum Crown members. As a reminder, when we dock in Ensenada around nine o'clock tomorrow morning, you need to have your luggage ready. Anything you don't wish to take with you to San Felipe, I will store for you, and it will be waiting for you on your return trip at the end of the week."

I took all the papers from Sven, thanked him again, and numbly made my way toward the stairs.

"Wow," Joanne said.

"Yeah, wow. This isn't at all what I had in mind for this trip."

"I meant 'wow' about the music. Just listen to that." Joanne leaned on the railing that circled the sunken center stage area of the lobby. A classical guitarist was positioned next to the grand piano where the musician had been playing when we first entered the ship. The guitarist's head was bent forward in concentration as he strummed what sounded like flamenco music to my untrained ear.

"Isn't that incredible?" Joanne asked, as if none of the upset in our plans in the past half hour bothered her and all she had to do was leisurely listen to the guitarist. Tears glistened in her eyes. "It's so beautiful," she whispered, smiling at me.

I smiled back even though I didn't understand what she was reacting to so emotionally. She talked about the symmetry and deliberate passion of the music. I nodded, but the only sounds floating in my head were a scattered cacophony.

Five

"Do you know if the midnight buffet is tonight?" Joanne asked me.

"No, it's tomorrow night. Why, are you hungry?"

"Not at all. I was interested in seeing the ice sculptures." With a grin Joanne added, "And trying out some of those famous desserts. I guess that will have to wait until our return trip."

For the past hour Joanne and I had been sequestered in our spacious room with the flowers and fruit basket adding the only cheer to the quarters. Well, actually the most cheer came from the elegant terry cloth swan that greeted us when we returned. Apparently our room attendant had been busy while we were at dinner. One of our abundant white bath towels had been twisted and bent into the shape of a long-necked swan and sat perched at the foot of Joanne's bed like a stuffed animal.

Joanne leaned against the headboard, reading a Baja tour book Sven had dropped off for us. He said it was "his contribution to our courageous endeavor." I'm not sure what he meant, but I told Joanne that if I was listed as the beneficiary on her life insurance policy, she still had time to change that, in case we both expired somewhere in the Baja desert. She only laughed.

I directed all my efforts to frantically organizing for our departure to San Felipe in the morning. The extra length of our trip wasn't going to be a problem for me at work because I had unused time off and had scheduled to be gone all week.

What bothered me the most was the way my husband had readily agreed that driving across Baja was the best choice for Joanne and me "since we were so close." I half hoped that, when I called to tell him the upsetting change of plans, he would say something like, "I don't think that's a good idea" or "You better come home and plan to go back to Mexico later."

Instead he said, "I think God is doing the organizing for you and Joanne on this trip."

It infuriated me the way everyone was spiritualizing this problem. I secretly wanted to blame God for the mix-up while Joanne, Ethan, and even Robert were giving God extra credit for His creativity.

"It says here—" Joanne rose from her bed and walked toward me with the tour book in her hand—"that outside San Felipe is a place called the Valley of the Giants. It has a cardón cactus that's estimated to be eight hundred years old."

"An eight-hundred-year-old cactus?"

"Look at this thing. It's the largest cactus in the world."

The small photo showed a tourist in shorts dwarfed by a massive cluster of spiny green fingers reaching into the clear blue sky. The tallest spear rose at least forty feet into the air.

"This is getting pretty exciting, Mel. We've never seen these kinds of natural wonders in our quarter of the hemisphere. Look at these rock formations."

She held up another picture of a narrow road that wound over a desolate-looking hill covered with desert shrubs and lots of dry, pale yellow dirt. In the distance rose boulders that looked like the cartoon town of Bedrock, where Fred and Wilma Flintstone lived. A customized VW bug was the only vehicle in the picture. From the roof jutted a tall antenna, and a cloud of dust rumbled out the back.

"Did you read this?" I asked. "'Off-road racers from around the world flock to Valle de Trinidad where their adventure begins on Highway 3.'"

"Highway 3? Isn't that the road we're taking to San Felipe?" Joanne asked.

"Yes, and did you take a close look at this picture? The road is not paved, Joanne."

"I'm sure that's only the off-road portion. I can't imagine Highway 3 would be marked so prominently on this map if it wasn't paved."

"How do you know? It could be that in Mexico, a road is a road. Paved or unpaved."

"You worry too much." Joanne took the book back from me.

"One of us needs to."

"Not necessarily. Worry doesn't get us anywhere. What did Mom used to say? Worry is like a rocking chair. It keeps you busy, but you never go anywhere."

"I don't think our mother ever said that."

"Well, maybe it was Aunt Winnie who said it."

I looked at her skeptically. "How can you be so nonchalant about all this?"

She shrugged.

"You didn't used to be this easygoing."

"I think my time in India changed me. Nothing was certain there. Sometimes we had electricity; sometimes we didn't. Sometimes the medical supplies arrived; sometimes they didn't. We all learned to flex because none of us could control the daily situation. I see this detour to San Felipe as another chance to learn to be flexible."

As much as I detested hearing Joanne say that, I knew she was right. Flopping on my bed, I let out a long sigh and told my headache to go away.

"Joanne," I said flatly, "I have control issues."

"Oh, really?" Joanne smiled broadly. I'm sure she was trying very hard not to bust up laughing at the obvious.

"Maybe I should have gone to India for a few years before I got married and had kids."

"You would have hated it," Joanne said.

"Thanks a lot!"

"You would have. Hardly anything ever went the way we

planned. It was like trying to paint a mural with a toothpick." She paused and for added emphasis included, "In the middle of a circus with juggling clowns balancing on your shoulders and your pants on fire."

"Okay. I get the idea." I held up my hand to stop Joanne from going on one of her exuberance jags.

"Those five years changed me. Every day brought enough insanity to send any one of us over the edge."

"But you didn't flip out. You even stayed longer than you first agreed."

"That's because it was the best place for me to be at that time in my life."

I tilted my head and studied my sister's serene expression. "I'm sure you know this, but you seem younger and more lighthearted than you used to be."

Joanne grinned. "That's because I'm in love."

I froze only a moment before throwing my arms around her. First I hugged her, and then I grabbed her shoulders and gave her a friendly shake. "Why didn't you tell me? Who? When? Where?"

"You know him," Joanne said with a coy expression.

"I do?" My eyes opened wide. "Is it Russell?"

"Russell? My dog?"

"No, Russell what's-his-name. The guy you brought home for Christmas when you were in college."

Joanne laughed. "Russell Wyzanowski? I can't believe you remember his name."

"I didn't remember his name. Only the *Russell* part. He's the only guy you ever brought home; of course I'm going to remember his name. I thought that's why you named your dog Russell—after your old boyfriend."

Joanne laughed again. "No! I never thought of that connection! My pooch was named Russell when I got him from a lady at work. I told you, didn't I? She was moving to an apartment and couldn't have pets."

"Quit stalling. Who's Mr. Wonderful?"

Joanne grinned. "It's God."

I waited for an explanation to what seemed like a miserly joke.

"I'm serious, Mel. I started to pursue a deeper relationship with Christ, or maybe I should say He pursued me, and I responded. I don't know exactly how it happened, but if I seem more content it's because I'm genuinely in love with God."

Joanne and I had grown up in a strict, traditional church, and we both were baptized when we entered junior high. She never had talked about devoting her life to God before.

"Did you take a vow or something?" I asked cautiously. "When you were in India?"

"Not exactly."

"Then what do you mean? It sounds as if you're planning to stay single and offer God a lifetime of service."

"No, it's not like that. I'm not trying to become a nun or anything. I would love to get married. Of course, I'd have to meet the right man first, which, as you know, has been the problem for quite some time now. That brings me to another topic I wanted to discuss with you on this trip. What would you think if I moved back to Vancouver?"

"To meet men?"

"Possibly. But that's not my main motivation. I've been thinking about this for a while. Do you remember Darren and Hope?"

I shook my head.

"You know, our cousin Darren in Connecticut. He and his wife, Hope, have three boys."

"Is she the one who opened the tea shop a couple of years ago?"

"Yes. Have you ever ordered any of her ladybug tea? It's wonderful. So is the hula hips tea."

"Joanne, what does this have to do with anything?"

"I received a Christmas card from them last week, and Darren and Hope had a baby last spring. A girl, after three boys. They always wanted a girl."

I still wasn't tracking with her and used my aggravated expression to let her know.

"My point is, Darren is our age. Hope has to be at least forty. They just had a baby. In their forties. It's not too late for me to start something new in my life or to make a change. I've been floating through life ever since I got back from India, and now my life is about to take some turns."

"And moving back to Vancouver is one of those turns."

"I think it is. You've been the one who's had to make all the extra effort to look after Aunt Winnie and Mom and Dad. I can find a job there easily enough, and I have more free time than you. I thought if I moved to Vancouver, I'd at least have family nearby, and that's becoming more important to me the older I get."

"I love the idea of your being close enough to help out," I said. "Especially with Aunt Winnie. You're not thinking of moving in with her, are you?"

"No! I'm not trying to become her self-imposed caregiver. I'd get my own place. So, what do you think?"

"I'm all for it. But why now? What's prompting you to make this decision after all these years?"

"Let's just say there's a man who is no longer at the top of my list of people I want to be around, and so, to be perfectly honest, I'd have to admit that 40 percent of my decision is based on the opportunity to move far away from him."

"Joanne!"

"What?"

"This is all fairly significant information you're handing to me all of a sudden."

"We didn't have a chance to talk like this earlier today," she said. "I was going to tell you about the potential move while we were walking around the deck after dinner, but then we ran into Robert."

"I'm just surprised you didn't say anything about all this

when we've talked over the phone the last few months."

"I don't like talking about intensely personal information over the phone. You know that."

I looked at my sister carefully and realized that, no, I didn't know that. What else didn't I know about her? For instance, who was this man she wanted to get away from?

"Joanne." I reached over and gave her hand a squeeze. "I want you to feel free to tell me all the significant details of your life."

"Okay, what do you want to know?"

"Everything. Whatever you want to tell me. I'm trying to say that I want to be in your life more. You know how you said the older you get, the more you realize how important it is to be close to family?"

"Yes."

"Well, the older I get, the more I've come to realize I only have one sister, and I don't think I fully appreciated you when I had the chance."

Joanne teared up. "Better late than never."

We hugged, and she pulled away with a bright expression. "I came to love you late! That's been the message God keeps bringing to me."

I wasn't tracking with her again.

"You have to hear this." Joanne hopped up and pulled a journal from the outside pouch of her suitcase. "Listen."

She stood in the center of the room and read to me from her journal.

"I came to love you late, O Beauty so ancient and new; I came to love you late. You were within me and I was outside where I rushed about wildly searching for you like some monster loose in your beautiful world. You were with me, but I was not with you. You called me, you shouted to me. You broke past my deafness. You bathed me in your light, you wrapped me in your splendor, you sent my blindness reeling. You gave out such a delightful fragrance, and I drew it in and came breathing hard after you. I tasted, and it made me hunger and thirst; you touched me, and I burned to know your peace."

She looked up at me, her face glowing, and I thought, *My sister has turned into a fascinating woman. I didn't know she had such deep and passionate thoughts locked up inside her.*

"That's powerful," I said. "Did you write that for anyone in particular?"

"Oh, no, I didn't write it. Augustine did."

I probably should have known who Augustine was, but I didn't. My ignorance wasn't something I wanted my sister to know so I merely remarked, "Oh."

"It's astounding to me," Joanne went on, closing her journal and putting it back in her suitcase. "That a monk in the fifth century could articulate so clearly the same things I felt when I came into this fresh relationship with Christ."

"Oh," I said again. "Yes, he's very articulate."

"Of course, he wrote that in Latin, but I bought this modern English translation, and I think I've read through the little book five times."

"Oh," I said for the third time. I couldn't figure out what was going on with my sister. At least, I thought she was my sister. She looked like Joanne, but she kept surprising me with traits I'd never seen in the Joanne of my childhood.

"I should probably finish packing." I rose to my feet and tried to find a task. Being busy with my hands was usually the best way for me to clear my mind, and at the moment, my previously overloaded brain was about to spin out of control.

Joanne fell asleep before I did. I felt a heaviness pressing against my chest. Her last words before she snuggled under the covers, with the strangely adorable twisted swan towel still at her feet, were, "Don't worry about anything, Melanie. God is going to work out everything in ways that will make our hearts swell and our mouths drop open. I love you, Melly Jelly Belly."

I told her I loved her, too, but I didn't call her Joanna Banana because I still wasn't sure who she was. Or maybe I should say I didn't recognize who she had become. I also wasn't sure I liked the idea of my heart swelling or my mouth dropping open.

In the engine-humming, slightly rolling silence of the cruise ship, I lay in the darkness and reviewed the clues to the mysterious woman in the bed next to mine. She was in love, but the romance was reportedly with God and not a new boyfriend. She was not planning to be a nun, yet she was reading and quoting a monk's ancient confessions. She was hoping to move from Toronto to get away from some unnamed man, and to top it off, I had found out after all these years that she didn't name her dog after Russell what's-his-name.

I closed my eyes and felt the subtle sway of the ship. It hadn't seemed very noticeable while we were moving around our cabin, but now that I was lying still, I felt like a baby being rocked to sleep in a cradle.

Releasing a long, low sigh, I thought maybe I should pray. I'd been too frantically active the past few days to even think about praying. Now that I was lying still in the comfort of this cocoon, being lulled by the gentle sway, my mind played with some of the lines Joanne had read to me. I remembered something about "rushing around like some monster loose in God's beautiful world" and how "you shouted past my deafness."

Have You been shouting to me? I asked in an inaudible prayer.

The answer was apparently "no," because only silence prevailed in our stateroom. For a long time I lay still, barely breathing, only thinking.

At last my heart whispered, *I won't run around like a monster anymore. I'll control my temper and stop being so full of anxiety about everything, okay?*

I knew it wasn't a confession comparable to Augustine's, but it was all I had at the moment. At least it was a start. Apparently that was enough to calm my mind, for I fell asleep.

Joanne was up early. I know she was trying to tiptoe

around, but it's hard to open a sliding glass door quietly.

"What time is it?" I muttered without opening my eyes.

"Seven o'clock here. Ten o'clock by my head."

"Are we docked yet?" The motion of the boat seemed to have stopped, or else I'd become used to it.

"Yes, we're in Mexico. You should come see this." Joanne had wrapped up in one of the long terry cloth robes that were hanging in the closet when we arrived. She stood out on our small balcony, and the cool air from the new day filled our room. The faint scent of burning trash came in along with the air.

I grabbed the other thick robe and joined my early bird sis on the balcony. Variegated panels separated our balcony from the ones on either side, but we could hear our neighbors on the right side. It sounded as if they were moving their patio chairs around.

On the deck underneath us, the covered lifeboats were lined up and secured in place. Far below the lifeboats was the dark gray water of the Port of Ensenada. The day had not been roused for very long from its early December snooze, and though fully risen, the sun seemed to shine on us with the same grogginess I felt.

A faint haze floated in the air as Joanne and I leaned against the railing and studied the panorama before us. Low hills rose behind the sprawling city of Ensenada. Houses dotted the hills, their adobe-colored tile roofs blending with the dusty browns of the landscape. Directly below us was a modern-looking dock area complete with an outdoor restaurant, paved walkways, and a duty-free store. Just beyond the newly developed tourist stop sprawled a soccer field void of a single blade of grass. It was more like a dirt lot that was set up to one day become a soccer field. However, from the general appearance of the town's worn-looking structures, it seemed we were looking at a soccer field that was used regularly.

I couldn't relate to any of this—the touristy area in the foreground, the dirt lot that served as a soccer field in the middle of my view, or the sprawling, foreign-looking jumble of buildings that made up Ensenada. But my stomach didn't tighten at the thought of disembarking and heading out into the city on our own.

"You ready for the morning buffet?" Joanne asked, stirring me from my reverie.

"It's so early. I was considering another half hour of sleep. We won't be able to pick up our rental car until ten o'clock, so there's no rush to disembark."

"But we're up," Joanne said. "We might as well go to breakfast, then dress and have a little time to look around town before we pick up the rental car."

"Don't you mean dress and then go to breakfast?"

"No, we can go in these robes. Sandy said on the cruise she went on everyone walked around in their bathing suits and pajamas, as if they were at a big, floating slumber party."

I had to admit the thought of sliding my feet into a pair of slippers and shuffling off to a bountiful buffet sounded decadent. "Okay, let me wash the sleepies out of my eyes first."

"Do you think our family is the only one that says *sleepies*?" Joanne called after me.

"Possibly."

"Hey, did you bring any sunscreen?"

"No."

"It doesn't seem that hot right now, but it might be a good idea to buy some before we take off on our trek across Baja."

I plunged my hands under the running water in the bathroom sink and realized my stomach hadn't lurched when Joanne brought up that we were going to drive across the desert today. That was a good sign. I wasn't completely ready for the journey ahead, but at least I no longer was knocked sideways by the thought.

Tucking our room keys and cruise passes in our bathrobe pockets, Joanne and I trotted down the hall toward the elevators. An elderly couple, who looked as if they were dressed for a day of touring Ensenada, complete with fanny packs and bottles of water, joined us in the elevator. They wore matching dark red pants and tropical print camp shirts, and both of them had on bright yellow sun visors. I noticed they glanced sideways at Joanne and me, as if we were dressed funny in our slippers and robes.

The Port of Call Café was filled with morning people. Instead of sleeping in, half the vacationers appeared to have opted for the early buffet. Joanne and I headed for the end of the long line, and I realized people were turning around in line and looking at us.

"Joanne," I whispered, "it looks like you and I are the only slumber party girls on board."

"What do you mean?"

"Do you see anyone else walking around in a bathrobe?"

Joanne scanned the room. "No, but that's their loss as far as I'm concerned. We're comfy, and they're not. Here, have a plate. Don't you love these big, oval-shaped plates? These jumbo platters make it easier for us to load up on food without looking like a couple of crazed foodies."

"Crazed foodies? Why not? We already look like hospital escapees."

"No we don't." Joanne reached for a slice of pineapple. "We look like two relaxed chicks on vacation. Trust me, I've seen hospital escapees, and we don't come close. Can you believe all this fruit? Look at the watermelon! In the middle of winter, no less."

For a moment Joanne reminded me of Aunt Winnie the way she skipped around topics. Her lightheartedness was catching, though, and I decided if I stayed close to her, I wouldn't look so strange strolling around in my robe.

"What do you think this is?" Joanne reached for a slice of plump, deep orange fruit. "Papaya, maybe? Star fruit is yellow, isn't it? This is probably a mango or maybe guava. Do you want some?"

"I'll pass." I held up my hand as Joanne tried to add a slice to my plate. "One tropical fruit disaster is enough for me on this cruise, thank you very much."

"That's right!" Joanne chuckled. "Maybe I shouldn't get too adventuresome in trying new fruit, either. We share the same DNA, but no offense, I'm not eager to share the same maladies."

Like a couple of discerning gourmets dressed in fluffy lab coats, we gathered samples of only the breakfast items whose ingredients we could identify with a reasonable amount of certainty. Joanne was enthusiastic about the huevos rancheros and eggs Benedict. I was more interested in the chocolate-filled croissants.

Finding an open table proved to be a challenge. We wandered around with our filled plates, watching people eat and gauging how close they were to being finished.

"People are still staring at us," I muttered to Joanne.

"It's not the robes," she said. "It's the way we're circling like vultures."

"Come on, let's see if we can find any places open on the other side." I led Joanne to several large tables by the windows where two seats were open across from each other at the end. The rest of the table was filled with vacationers.

As soon as we asked if the end seats were available, the woman nearest the open seats said, "You two were smart." She nodded at our attire. "I wanted to wear my robe, but I thought I'd be the only one."

As soon as she said it, she pressed her lips together, as if she realized she just pointed out the obvious.

Joanne laughed. "Well, now you know you wouldn't have been alone!"

The woman laughed and pulled out a chair for me. "Are you two going to spend the day shopping, or are you going on one of the tours?"

"Actually," Joanne said brightly, "we've rented a car, and I guess you could say we're going on our own sort of tour."

We suddenly had the attention of all the other diners at the table. It was as if Joanne whet their appetites for something oh so much more thrilling than rifling through stacks of woven Mexican blankets from a street vendor.

"Where are you going?" another woman asked.

I wondered why Joanne had been so open with our private information, but then I felt a cool breeze on my legs under the table and realized that a woman who walks around in public wearing a bathrobe has very little power to conceal any of her secrets.

Six

After Joanne told the people at our breakfast table that we were driving to San Felipe, one of them said, "I wish we had planned something like that. Your overland trek across Baja sounds much more interesting than the tour we signed up for."

"What tour are you going on?" I asked.

"We're taking a bus to see La Bufadora."

"What's that?"

"A blowhole. According to the brochure, it's a hollow rock formation at the coast where the incoming tides send a spray of water shooting into the air like a geyser."

"Sounds interesting," Joanne said.

"I'm more interested in the vendor carts that sell *churros* in the parking lot."

"Those are the long donuts, right?" Joanne asked. "The ones with the cinnamon and sugar?"

"Do they dip those in chocolate?" another woman at our table asked.

"I don't think so, but if you're interested in a little chocolate this morning, you should go to the cake-decorating event in the main lobby," the woman next to me volunteered.

"My sister used to want to be a pastry chef," Joanne announced.

I gave her a pained expression. "That was a long time ago, Joanne."

"I know, but don't you think a cake-decorating contest sounds like fun? We need to start this day with a little zip. Our cruise didn't exactly get off to the best start yesterday."

But Joanne was right. Our spa treatment wasn't stellar. Showing up for breakfast in our robes didn't exactly enhance my sense of relaxation. We already were packed but couldn't pick up our rental car for several hours. A cake-decorating contest might be fun.

"We could even show up at the contest in our robes," Joanne said.

I wasn't the only one at the breakfast table who strongly suggested we change. As soon as I swallowed my last bite of cantaloupe, Joanne and I trotted back to our room to dress for the day and join the lively bunch in the center of the downstairs lobby.

The event was set up in the same area where we had watched the guitarist last night, but the space was transformed. The plants and baby grand piano had been pushed aside to make room for three rectangular tables that formed a U shape, open to spectators who now lined the steps and railing of the sunken center arena.

Joanne and I were given poncho-style aprons along with floppy chef's hats and instructed to take our place at number eight behind the table. We were the last two to get into position. Two round cakes awaited us on individual cake stands. The double-layer cakes already were covered with a light chocolate glaze. I formulated a plan. A nice basket-weave border around the cake's sides would be elaborate and impressive. If time was short, perhaps I could just make an inverted scallop trim around the top.

As I was planning, a slender, lively blonde stepped up to the microphone. "Welcome, everybody. I'm Lillie, your cruise director. Is this a great way to start the day? Chocolate cake for everyone! As you can see, our teams are ready to go. Each team will have four minutes to decorate his or her cake."

"Four minutes!" I squawked along with some of the others.

"To give the teams a little help, we've asked our fabulous onboard pastry chefs to serve as pastry coaches."

Spontaneous applause burst from the gathering crowd as a row of eight official cruise chefs marched over to the tables and faced each of us with their hands behind their white chef's coats. Their hats looked more impressive than ours, and their serious expressions made me think either this would be a lot of fun but they were trying to play along as stoics, or they were repressing their aggravation over being taken from their kitchens.

One of the female spectators burst out, "We love your éclairs!" Her friends all laughed and clapped. I noticed a bemused expression on our chef's face, whose embroidered name on his jacket was Francois.

"First, each team must select a captain."

Joanne turned to me. "I think that's you, Captain Melanie."

The cruise director didn't allow time for discussion. She jumped right in. "Okay, captains, stand behind your first mates. First mates, hands behind your backs. Captains, slip your arms through the opening in your first mate's arms and reach for the tube of frosting, which, by the way, is chocolate. Chocolate frosting and chocolate cake. Does that sound good to anyone?"

An approving cheer rose around us.

Clearly we were going to be part of a humorous production, as I provided the hands to do the decorating but was dependent on Joanne's eyes and her directions to know where to apply the frosting.

"Your personal chefs will demonstrate how to decorate your cakes on the cakes in front of them. First mates, with only your words, you are to direct your captains. Captains? Ready? Begin!"

With no preparation time, I took the frosting tube in my hand and tried to see around Joanne's floppy hat. It was pointless.

"Mel, he's starting on the top and making the frosting kind of go back and forth in little zigzags all around the edge."

Okay, I know how to do that.

I fumbled to find the base of the cake stand and to connect with a point of reference. My thumb mashed into the cake's side.

"That's okay," Joanne coached. "Keep going. Put the tube on the edge. That's good. Now start making those zigzags."

I went nice and slow, but Joanne spewed commands. "He's done with his trim. Don't worry about finishing ours. You can come back and do the trim at the end, if there's time. Now, with your left hand, pick up the plastic gizmo on the table and hold it steady. He's using his to make a rose."

I'd done roses before with the same sort of tool and thought I might be able to do this part with some ease. It was getting hard to hear Joanne's directions over the yelling from the other teams and the cheering from the enthusiastic audience.

"Okay, that's good enough," Joanne said with a lot of laughing. "It almost looks like a rose. He's going on, so put the rose in the center. No, more to the right. I mean the left. Right, the left. No over."

"Right or left?" I yelled in her ear.

"Doesn't matter. Just put it on the cake. He's doing the base now. Make a long line with a space followed by a circle and then a space and another line."

"I don't understand. What kind of line and what kind of circle?"

"It looks like about an inch for the line. Start with a dot and then break and do a dash, then a dot and another dash. Got it?"

"One more minute to go," cruise director Lillie announced.

"And it looks like one of our chefs is calling out for help here in the final sixty seconds. Francois at station eight is decorating the base of his cake with the Morse code for SOS."

Everyone laughed, and I realized what Joanne had been trying to describe as a dot-dash sequence. I gripped the cake stand with my left hand, turning it toward Joanne while quickly applying the pattern with my right.

"Thirty seconds," Lillie called out.

"He's writing a word on top of the cake," Joanne said. "Move your hand away from me. That's it. Start right there. Now write something."

"Write what?"

"Ten, nine, eight..."

"Anything! Hurry!"

With a loop of my hand, I made a capital *J*.

"Three, two..."

I followed the *J* with an *O,* and completed it just as the cruise director called out "One! Time's up! Frosting tubes down. Let's see what kind of confectionary delights our teams have created here. Captains, you may join your first mates by coming out from behind them."

Stepping next to Joanne, I got a good look at our joint creation.

"That's pathetic!" I moaned.

"No, it's not," Joanne protested. "Well, except maybe for the rose. And you didn't finish the top border. But you spelled my name right."

Energetic Lillie held up the cake created by team one. The design on the chef's cake was several perfectly straight lines across the top. The contestant's duplicate looked like a mutilated tic-tac-toe game board.

The laughter continued around the tables. Team five's cake was dubbed the "moon cake" because of all the places the captain had inserted the tip of the frosting tube while trying to find a place to start.

"Look at all those craters!" Lillie said.

The team next to us had spent most of the time cracking up and yelling at each other and laughing some more. Their fun was reflected in their cake, which turned out to be a squiggly-giggly mess, and nothing at all like their chef's elegantly decorated cake.

"Oh, my!" Lillie exclaimed when she stepped over to us with the microphone. "Look at this work of art! It actually resembles the chef's cake. I think we may have a winning team here. What are your names?"

She held the microphone in front of me. "Melanie," I said. My voice seemed to explode in a booming echo.

"Joanne," my sister said as the mike was held up to her. "That's my name on the cake. Jo."

"Look at that!" Lillie held up our cake and made a smooth half-turn so all the spectators could see the *Jo.* "What do you say? Do we have a winner here?"

The applause that rose around us was embarrassing but great fun. I couldn't remember the last time anyone had clapped for me for any reason. Tight little tear bubbles filled my eyes.

"Your prize—" Lillie turned to all the other contestants before adding—"is that each of you gets to try the first bite of the cake you decorated."

An approving murmur arose, but then Lillie added, "However, we have one stipulation. The captains now must stand to the front, and the first mates are to step behind. That's right. You first mates now become the hands that cut the first slice and feed it to your captains. And captains, may I remind you, it's not a good idea to bite the hand that feeds you."

The spectators seemed to be especially tickled by this turn-about and cheered on their favorite teams. With my hands behind my back, I felt Joanne literally breathing down my neck as she inserted her arms through my open arm loops and asked, "Which side is the knife on? I didn't see it."

"It's on the left. It's a butter knife, and it's sitting close to the edge of the table with the blade facing the cake."

She immediately made contact with the butter knife. As I continued to direct, Joanne inserted the knife just under the mushed-up rose. A wave of laughter came rushing over us. I stretched to see across to the second table where one of the first mates had foregone the knife and was feeding her beloved cap-tain a fistful of cake.

"Don't get any ideas," I told Joanne, turning and speaking loudly over my shoulder.

"What are they doing? Having a food fight?"

"Just about. You have the first incision just right, Nurse Joanne. Move the knife over just a squinch, make another cut, and you'll have it."

"Actually, I won't have it," Joanne teased. "You'll have it! But not all over your face, I promise. I'll be nice."

I thought of how many truces my sister and I had agreed upon using that simple phrase, "I'll be nice." The good thing was that whenever we said it, we meant it, and we managed to be kind to each other, even if the sweet spell only lasted for an hour.

Taking her time, Joanne offered her precisely cut slice of cake, which I bent forward to nibble. The cake was delicious, and I suddenly thought I wouldn't mind having this cake and frosting all over my mouth and chin.

Someone in the crowd called out, "Go ahead! Dive in, team eight! You're the last one."

I didn't need to dive in. My sister brought the cake up to my face, and with a playful smash, she plastered me.

The crowd was pleased, Joanne laughed, and I felt unexpectedly young and cheery.

"You're not mad?" Joanne looked me in the eye as the chef handed me a towel.

"No, the cake is scrumptious. Here, try some."

Before Joanne saw it coming, I pinched a handful and delivered a sizable chunk to her face. She cracked up, and I remembered, for the first time in a long time, the mischievous glee of being "almost twins."

"Thank you, ladies," Lillie the cruise director called out in a singsong voice. "You've all been great sports. I think all of them are winners, don't you?"

The spectators showed their agreement with Lillie by applauding.

"As our special gift for each of you, we'd like you to take your cake with you. Your chef will provide a pastry box for your creation—or what's left of it, as in the case of team number five."

"*Pour vous.*" Francois handed us a square, pink box. "Congratulations."

"Thank you," I said. "Your cake is beautiful."

"*Merci.*"

"What are we going to do with a whole cake?" I asked Joanne as we headed up the stairs to our room to collect our luggage.

"Almost a whole cake," she corrected me. "This is just a really wild suggestion, but why don't we eat it?"

"Now?"

"No, on the road. It will be a treat."

"It'll be a puddle of melted cocoa by noon," I protested.

"We can't give it to anyone," Joanne said. "Not after *some* of us stuck our fingers in it."

I grinned. "I couldn't resist."

Joanne stopped midway up the wide flight of stairs and impulsively wrapped her arms around me. With a big, smacky kiss on the side of my head, she said, "You know what? I can't resist you. I love you, Mel. Did I ever tell you that? You are the coolest sister ever."

Startled by her outburst, I jokingly said, "I think you were around those Sisterchicks a little too long. Their crazy antics are wearing off on you."

"Crazy or not, I've decided there's nothing wrong with loving somebody and telling them so," Joanne said stubbornly. "I've lived too long without openly expressing what's in my heart."

She grinned at me.

I smiled back. "I love you, too, Joanne."

My declaration was no less true than hers, but it certainly didn't carry the zing her announcement had.

As we cleared our final paperwork with Sven and disembarked, I thought about the contrast in Joanne's vibrant declaration and my sincere echo. She had changed. With her freshness and openness, she was the one who was irresistible.

As Joanne and I stepped down the gangway that led to the dock and tourist area we had seen from our suite that morning, I noticed a crew member dressed up with a wide sombrero and wearing a serape. He was waving to each of the travelers as they disembarked and inviting them to have their photos taken by the ship's photographer.

I took several steps toward him in the wide cemented area, thinking Joanne and I should at least pose, even if we weren't going to be around that evening to pick up the print.

A pregnant woman in zebra-print capris and impractical

spike-heel sandals hurried past me, trying to catch up with her runaway toddler. She was yelling at him in a language I didn't recognize. Her voice suddenly elevated into a shriek, and I turned just in time to see the willful child run to the edge of the concrete dock and topple into the water far below.

My startled cry was drowned by the mother's terrified scream. She ran toward the narrow channel of water that separated the huge ship from the dock, wailing like I had never heard before. The heel on her shoe broke in her dash, and she stumbled. An older woman standing a few inches away caught the pregnant woman before she could fall. It was clear she intended to leap into the water to save her child.

Before anyone could fully comprehend what was happening, a second splash let us know a rescuer had gone into the water only seconds after the toddler fell in.

My heart pounded, and I turned to grab Joanne and to say I couldn't believe all this was happening.

But all I saw was my sister's abandoned luggage.

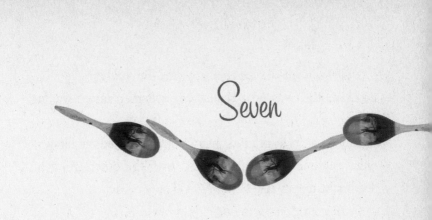

Seven

Joanne!" I screamed, and the toddler's mother wailed at the top of her voice. The older woman restrained the distressed mother from leaping into the water. I ran to the edge and screamed again when I saw nothing but oily, dark water.

Just then Joanne's head surfaced, followed immediately by her hands, lifting up the child.

"Joanne!" I shrieked. "Help! Someone help her!"

Beside me flashed the frame of a male passenger jumping into the water. A crewman rushed up beside me and tossed down a life preserver tied to a long rope.

The child choked and coughed and let out a tremendous screech so that Joanne couldn't hear the man, who was now in the water, giving her instructions. She held firm to the little boy, who was panicked and trying to climb on her neck, forcing her head back under the water.

"No!" I screamed. "Get the baby! Get him off her!"

The mother was now beside me, collapsed into a wailing heap.

Joanne's head resurfaced, and the man grabbed the life preserver with one arm and the child with the other. Then he yelled for Joanne to take hold of the life preserver.

"Grab it, Joanne! Hold on!"

A number of people had gathered by now, and many of the men stepped forward to toss a second life preserver to Joanne, whom they proceeded to pull up to the dock. She rose coughing, soaked, and battered against the side of the dock. Someone wrapped a Mexican blanket around her shoulders.

"Joanne!" I threw my arms around her. "Are you okay?"

She coughed and nodded. I could feel her shivering and held her close.

"The baby," she sputtered. "Get the baby."

"They have him," I said. "He's okay."

We stood holding each other, watching as the gathering group of assistants gave up on pulling the man and the toddler to safety with the life preserver. Instead they lowered a long ladder over the side for the man to climb up with the screeching child secure under his arm.

The moment the mother reached for her child, I burst into tears. The boy instantly stopped crying and was wrapped in a blanket. His wet hair dripped over his unblinking eyes as he shivered and whimpered in his mother's embrace.

"Is he okay?" Joanne touched the mother on her shoulder.

"Thank you, thank you, thank you," the trembling woman repeated over and over with a thick accent. "Thank you." She kissed Joanne on both cheeks and thanked her again.

All the color drained from Joanne's face. She was leaning into me, relying on my strength, as if her knees might buckle at any moment.

"Let's find some dry clothes for you." I drew Joanna closer.

She nodded. The use of her voice seemed to have evaporated along with the use of her leg muscles.

"You okay?" I bolstered her up.

She didn't reply. I thought she might faint.

"Take a deep breath," I said. "We'll stand here a moment. Is that better?"

She nodded. Someone handed us another blanket. I wrapped it around my wet shoulders and steadied Joanne as we took a few steps back to our luggage.

"Let me take that for you," the ship's photographer said. He handed his camera to the young crewman wearing the sombrero and reached for our luggage.

Joanne gazed over her shoulder as we headed up the gangway. The mother and her son were being assisted to the inside of the ship as well. The passenger who had jumped in after Joanne was standing still, dripping wet and holding on to the life preserver. No one seemed to know what to do or say. The shock remained in the air like electricity as the crowd silently dispersed.

I couldn't believe what had just happened. The incident

couldn't have lasted more than three or four minutes, but my heart felt as if I had held my breath that entire time. I gasped for air so sharply it hurt.

"Where can we go?" Joanne's teeth chattered.

I quickly explained to the photographer that we were on our way off the ship and had checked out of our room. He led us back into the lobby and placed our luggage on the floor. We stood close, Joanne still dripping, me wet from holding her up, and both of us wearing the brightly colored Mexican blankets around our shoulders.

"Ladies, what has happened?" Sven appeared and stood with his mouth open as the photographer pieced together his account.

"Come." Sven motioned for another crewman to pick up our luggage. "We will take you to the spa for warm showers, and then I will obtain new keys for your room."

Numbly trotting after him, Joanne and I were shown into the private shower and sauna area of the spa. Everyone was in a flutter to assist us, but this time it wasn't because we were Platinum Crown members. We showered and changed while our clothes were taken away to be cleaned and returned to us on our trip home. As we emerged, still stunned but feeling fresher, the receptionist asked if we would like to have a massage, compliments of the captain.

I can't explain why that didn't seem like a good idea. Yes, we were both tense, and it would have helped us to relax—as long as I wasn't allergic to the massage oil. But a luxurious body treatment felt out of place after being so close to a life-and-death situation. We asked if we could have the massages on our way home, and the receptionist said the captain's offer was for that day only. We still declined.

"This has been a memorable trip for you two, hasn't it?" the receptionist said.

Joanne and I looked at each other. Neither of us had any words to respond.

Sven offered us new keys to our suite and asked if we would like to return to the room to rest.

"I think we should get on the road," Joanne said in a tranquil voice. "We need to pick up our rental car and start for San Felipe."

"Joanne, are you sure you're ready to travel?" I asked.

"I'm okay."

Her calm was unnerving. My mind kept reviewing the near catastrophe. All it would have taken was one significant swell of the ocean while Joanne was in the water, and the mammoth force of steel would have pushed my sister into the unyielding dock and crushed her to pieces. Or the toddler could have forced her underwater and drowned her. What if she had jumped in and been unable to find the toddler under the water? What if...?

"Mel?" Joanne touched my shoulder lightly. "Is it okay with you if we get our rental car now?"

"It's fine with me. Are you sure you're ready to move on?"

She nodded and reached for the handle of her wheeled

suitcase. I followed Joanne off the ship, well aware of the looks the informed crew members gave her. My sister was a hero. A saint. And I was treading in her footprints.

We boarded a small shuttle that would take us the mile or so into the main tourist area of town where we would pick up our rental car. The radio blasted a lively song in Spanish, and the driver chattered in Spanish on his cell phone. The language change made it feel as if we had left all that was familiar behind.

Part of me wanted to wail at the top of my lungs, "Stop the shuttle! Take me back! I can't do this!" The panicky sensation was the same I'd felt before I had boarded the ship. Only this time the feeling was smaller and deeper, like something dropped into the nuclei of my otherwise balanced brain atoms.

As the yellow light turned to red, the shuttle drove through a main intersection. Three more cars followed the shuttle, as if the red light were merely a suggestion. Cars coming from the opposite direction didn't hesitate to move forward, horns blaring, drivers swerving to invent new traffic patterns.

"This is not a good sign." I said.

"I don't mind driving." Joanne glanced at me.

"Shouldn't you rest a little?"

"For the tenth time, Mel, I'm fine."

It was as if we were teenagers again, arguing over who would be the one to drive the family car to an event we both were attending. In the past I usually won these squabbles because Joanne would acquiesce to save time. I didn't know how my new "superwoman" sister would respond, but I continued my role as the determined underling.

"I know you're fine, but I can drive, Jo." My tone was bossy enough to will away my terror of the unknown.

Joanne gave me an exasperated look. "We'll take turns. Come on." She rose from her seat and carried her wheeled suitcase down the shuttle's steps. I followed her on the uneven sidewalk crowded with cruise ship tourists. Both sides of the street were lined with small shops that boasted the "best prices" with signs hand-printed in English but listing the "best prices" in pesos.

A leather handbag in the window of one of the newer-looking shops caught my eye. I knew we didn't have time to shop now, but I told myself to remember this shop so we could stop when we returned from San Felipe.

"*Hola,*" a young man greeted us at the doorway of the shop next door. His small, narrow space was loaded from floor to ceiling with Mexican blankets, guitars, leather coats, embroidered blouses, and leather sandals that hung on a rope.

We both smiled politely and continued down the street without stopping to haggle with him over a souvenir or two. Three blocks down we came to the car rental place. It appeared more up-to-date than many of the shops we passed, and that gave me hope the car we had rented would be modern.

"Hello," I greeted the young man behind the counter. He was wearing a cotton short-sleeved shirt with the car company logo above the pocket. "We have a reservation." I pulled out the papers Sven had prepared for us and handed them to the young man.

He looked at the papers and spoke Spanish over his shoulder to someone in the back office. An older man stepped out and greeted us with a wide smile that showed off his gold-capped tooth. "You want a car?"

"Yes," I said. "We have a reservation."

"You were not here when this time came." He pointed to the printed pickup time on the papers. "We don't have this car anymore."

"Certainly you have other cars," Joanne said.

"Yes, but not for this same price. We have better cars. I can get you a good price on a better car."

"No thank you," I said firmly. "We'd like the same price we were quoted when we made the reservation."

"We have no more cars for that price."

It didn't take a lot of insight to see the setup. Did we stand here and try to fight with this guy or take what we could get and pay the higher price with the hope that we would be given a reliable vehicle?

Joanne stepped closer to the front desk. "What cars *do* you have for the price we were quoted?"

"No cars. Not for that price." The man with the golden grin looked at the younger man.

With a straight face, the younger man said, "My brother has a burro he can rent to you for a low price."

This was obviously not the time to take names and try to

report these two to the Ensenada Better Business Bureau, if such an organization existed. They saw us coming—two women with luggage in hand and no other options available in town. We were being taken, and we had to take what we were given. The mental image of Joanne and me plodding through the desert on the back of a burro for 150 miles did not bring a smile to my countenance. It only made me mad.

"Okay," I said firmly. "What do you have?"

We were shown a laminated sheet of paper with pictures of a Mustang convertible, a seven-passenger minivan, and an all-terrain Jeep.

"The convertible looks nice," Joanne said right away.

"No more today," the man said.

"We'll take the minivan then," I said.

"The van is rented until tomorrow. Do you want to come back tomorrow?"

"No, we don't want to come back tomorrow. We want you to give us a fair deal on a rental car today. What do you have available?"

"This." He pointed to the picture of a Jeep. "I will give you a good price." The man seemed to enjoy this game far more than any compassionate human being should.

"I guess that means we take the Jeep," Joanne said.

With a gleam he said, "*¡Excellente!*" and sent his young associate to bring the vehicle.

The paperwork was reprinted, and the rate was listed in pesos. I tried to calculate the price in my head, converting the pesos to Canadian dollars. By my sketchy estimate we were going to be paying close to sixty dollars a day for the Jeep.

"We don't have much choice," Joanne said in an effort to calm me down. "Let's just go with it and take out all the extra insurance we can."

By the time we finished the paperwork, my tolerance was stretched to its limits, and I knew we were paying far too much to drive across the Baja Peninsula in what turned out to be a canary yellow Jeep that had no roof.

"It's not so bad." Joanne loaded our luggage into the back. We still had the two Mexican blankets we had been handed when she rescued the toddler. Earlier we tried to return them to Sven, but he insisted we keep them. It was a good thing because the blankets provided covering for our two small suitcases in the back of the open Jeep.

"As long as it doesn't rain," I said, heading around the front of the vehicle.

"Melanie." Joanne stepped between the driver's seat and me. "Let me drive. You're much better at navigating than I am. You can tell me how to get out of town, and then we'll switch, and you can drive. I'm not good at reading maps."

"You just want to have control of the car, like in high school." I tossed the accusation at her with a hint of surrender. If she was going to be so stubborn about this, I'd let her have her way.

Joanne laughed, and it sounded good to me. "Are you

going to make any threats about what might happen if both my legs get broken?"

"Not yet," I teased back.

"Good," Joanne said, her snappiness rising. "Then get in the car and pull out the map."

We edged our way into the two-lane street just as loud music blared around the corner. Joanne stopped at the first *alto* sign, and an old convertible with fins turned in front of us. Speakers were fixed to the front and back of the long vehicle. On the top of the backseat perched a humorous-looking costumed character with a huge head. He waved at us with white-gloved hands.

"What do you suppose he's saying?" I shouted to Joanne as the driver picked up a microphone and blasted out his advertisement over the loud music.

"Who knows, but you better start waving. We're part of the parade!"

The convertible slowed to a sputtering ten miles per hour, and we were in the wake of his exhaust and noise as the waving character attracted the attention of all the tourists and store owners along the main shopping street in Ensenada. We couldn't pass the one-car parade because the traffic on the opposite side of the street had slowed to watch the spectacle.

From the street corner, next to a cart that was stacked with woven backpacks and strung-up marionettes, a cluster of women stood waving at the big-headed goofball in front of us. One of the women from our cruise ship recognized Joanne and me and called out something we couldn't hear over the blare of music from the convertible.

"Hey, look!" Joanne called to me. "Wave! It's some of the Sisterchicks from the elevator!"

Joanne honked the horn in time to the obnoxious music as we laughed and waved. Cars facing the opposite direction joined in the honking, and we made our exit from the shopping district with all the commotion of a couple of rock stars trying to get out of town after an amped-up event.

"Turn right, Joanne."

"Aww, can't we keep going straight and stay in the parade?"

"If you really want," I shouted over the voice of the announcer, who was giving his rousing speech once again, complete with exaggerated rolls of his *r*'s. "But the road to San Felipe is to the right."

"*¡Adios! ¡Adios!*" Joanne called out, laughing and waving with one hand as she made the right turn onto a four-lane road.

We quickly noticed that, even though the thoroughfare was marked as four lanes, that didn't hinder the Mexican drivers from creating five, and in some places six, lanes of traffic.

"Don't forget about the stoplights," I said, as we approached a green light. "If it turns yellow, you better keep going, or you'll be rear-ended by the locals, who seem to take yellow as an invitation to speed up."

"Got it." Joanne clearly was enjoying the thrill of being behind the wheel in the midst of this chaos. "This reminds me of Calcutta. Except I never drove there. I only rode in cabs and rickshaws. Hold on, I'm changing lanes."

"Joanne, stay in this lane! We have to make a left at the next intersection."

It was too late. Joanne was in the far right lane and forced to turn right. We ended up making a big circle that took us back to the front of the car rental place.

"If you want me to navigate, then you have to listen to me," I scolded.

"I know, I know. Don't get so riled up, Melanie. I know where we are now. Hey, look at those sombreros. We should buy some for the trip."

"We can buy souvenirs when we come back to Ensenada in a few days. Get ready to turn up here at the intersection."

"We need the hats now," Joanne said. "They'll be our roof."

At first I thought she said, "They'll be our goof," and I was going to say I felt conspicuous enough in the Jeep. Then I realized she said *roof,* and I agreed that it wouldn't hurt to have some covering for our heads against whatever elements waited ahead for us.

Making a quick turn into an open space in front of a street vendor, Joanne leaned over and called out, "Two sombreros, please! *Dos.*" She held up two fingers to the surprised cart owner and asked me, "Isn't that Spanish for two? *Dos sombreros, s'il vous plaît.* Wait, that's French. How do you say *please* in Spanish?"

The vendor, wearing blue jeans and a long-sleeved tan

shirt, approached the Jeep and handed me two of the floppy straw sombreros like the ones we wore in our cruise photo. "Two?" he asked.

"Yes. *Sí.*" Joanne left the Jeep running and reached for her purse.

"I have some money." I pulled out my U.S. dollars and held them out to the vendor. "Is American money okay?"

"Yes. Ten dollars."

"Each?"

"Yes, ten dollars each. You need anything more? A purse? I have nice wallets."

"No, just the hats. Thanks."

"Excuse me." Joanne leaned over in front of me. "Would you consider selling us the hats for nine dollars each?"

I couldn't believe she was bargaining with him. Drive-up souvenir shopping, and my sister was trying to strike a deal.

He put up his hand and shook his head. "No. Ten dollars for the sombreros. I have some key chains. Three for five dollars."

"No," I answered for both of us. "We don't need any key chains. Thanks. *Gracias.*"

"*De nada,*" the man said with a friendly wave. A smile graced his expression as we drove off with our sombreros on our heads and the cords secured under our chins.

"I wonder if we paid the going rate," Joanne said. "Or do you think he saw us coming and ripped us off like the car dealer? It's hard to know what a fair price is for souvenirs."

"He definitely saw us coming the way you pulled up." I laughed. "Everyone on this side of town saw us coming in this Jeep, and now they're all going to see us go with these goofy hats. Or should I say our *roofy* hats?"

Joanne ignored my pun. "Is this where I turn?"

"No, the next intersection. *Ruiz* is the name of the street we're looking for. You turn right on Ruiz and then left on Benito Juarez."

"Got it."

Joanne followed my directions this time around, and with only two near collisions, we managed to reach Highway 3, the route that would lead us straight across the Baja Peninsula to San Felipe.

I know I should have been clutching the seat or clenching my teeth at this point. We were driving away from civilization and heading into terrain that wasn't exactly hospitable to a couple of Canadian sisters who didn't know enough Spanish between us to form a complete sentence. I should have been right in the middle of a serious panic attack while concealed under the floppy sombrero. However, I was overcome with a strange and unfamiliar sensation. I wanted to see what would happen next.

Eight

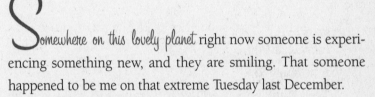

Somewhere on this lovely planet right now someone is experiencing something new, and they are smiling. That someone happened to be me on that extreme Tuesday last December.

As the tires of our Jeep rolled over the paved road leading away from Ensenada and our overland trek was officially underway, I realized I wasn't panicked.

"This has been quite a day." I tried to fold the map so it wouldn't flap around so much in the air.

"And it's not even noon yet." Joanne calmly grinned under her sombrero shade.

"Does any of this seem strange to you?"

"Strange? In what way?"

"A week ago I was doing all the normal things I do every day: going to work, making dinner, helping the girls with their homework. But today I started the day dining on a cruise ship

wearing a bathrobe in public, winning a cake-decorating contest, then watching you leap into the ocean to rescue a
drowning baby."

"Toddler," Joanne corrected me.

"Okay, toddler. Then we rented a Jeep for far too much
money, were caught in a parade behind an overgrown
Muppet, and now we're driving across the Baja desert with
chocolate cake as our only provision and these ridiculous
sombreros as our only shade." I leaned back and examined
Joanne's serene expression. "Does any of this strike you as out
of control?"

Joanne grinned and shook her head. She was at peace.

"That's what I thought."

Joanne laughed.

"I keep thinking I need to pinch myself to make sure all
this really is happening."

"I'll pinch you." Joanne's fingers headed my direction,
overly eager to do what she had become professional at by the
age of five.

"Keep your pinchers to yourself. I still have the bruises you
gave me years ago."

"I never gave you bruises."

"Uh, what about the time you pinched me when Dad was
going to take us to ice cream after piano lessons, but I started
to tell him we already had a snack at Mrs. Morton's house?"

"I didn't pinch you *that* hard."

"Yes, you did."

"Well, you didn't have to ruin our chances for ice cream by being so upright and honest."

I scowled a moment and then confessed, "Ethan tells me I have an 'enlarged sense of justice.'"

"He's right." Joanne settled in the driver's seat. She looked like she drove lemon yellow Jeeps for a living.

"Joanne?" I asked a few moments later when a singular, lingering question wouldn't leave me. "Do you still think I'm bossy?"

"Yes."

"You didn't have to answer so fast."

"Well, you asked."

"Don't you think I've gotten better?" I decided against filling her in on my recent anxiety attacks.

"You're better than what?"

"I'm doing better than I thought I would be with this whole trip. That's improvement, isn't it?"

Joanne nodded, and her sombrero flopped back and forth. "Relinquishment is a beautiful thing."

"Relinquishment? I don't think *relinquishment* is a word."

"If we were playing Scrabble, I'd let you use it."

"We're not playing Scrabble," I protested.

"Okay, how about *surrender*? Surrender is a beautiful thing. I think the more we surrender of ourselves to God, the more He takes over and leads us the way He wants us to go."

For a moment I regretted bringing up my victory in the control department. I didn't want Joanne to overly spiritualize my breakthrough. In my mind I hadn't relinquished or surrendered anything. I simply managed to harness the fear.

What had my prayer been the night before? Didn't I tell God that I'd stop running around like a monster and stop being so anxious? From my perspective, I was calmly accepting the situation because I was doing what I said I'd do. That's how things happened with me. If I said I was going to do something, I did it.

"Have you ever read the devotional *My Utmost for His Highest*?" Joanne asked.

"No."

"Oswald Chambers wrote it, and for the month of January, there's an entry that says, 'Get into the habit of saying, "Speak, Lord," and life will become a romance.' That's what this past year has been for me, a fresh, adventurous romance."

"Does this have anything to do with the guy at work whom you now want to get away from?" I asked.

Joanne looked at me with her mouth twisted to the side. "What are you talking about?"

"Last night you said you wanted to move to Vancouver because you didn't want to be around someone at work."

"Oh! No, no. I definitely wasn't having a romance with him! I'm talking about this new romance I'm having with God. He's putting all the steps of my life in place like never before."

"So there's no man in your life who's contributing to this romance."

"No. And you know what? For probably the first time in my life, it feels deep-down okay. God has plans for me. Good plans."

In our quietly conservative Christian family, we didn't talk openly about God. Joanne was beginning to make me more than a little uncomfortable. I changed the topic. "Do you want me to drive yet?"

"No, not yet. The road is in much better condition than I thought it would be. Do you think we stay on this road all the way?"

I studied the map. "Yes, almost the whole way."

"Off we go, then." Joanne picked up speed as we roared through the hilly terrain. The landscape was dry and scruffy-looking, with clumps of sagebrush and lots of trash along the side of the road. As ridiculous as the two of us probably looked in our sombreros, I was glad we had them. As long as the tie was secure under my chin, the hat served as a shelter from the wind and the sun.

I noticed that the sunlight was different from the sunlight we had at home. Being so much farther south made the sun shine down on us instead of at a lower angle. It wasn't too hot, but the air was definitely warm.

We rode in silence for a while. I shot glances at Joanne every now and then and noticed how calm she seemed. Her profile reminded me of when we both had the chicken pox at the same time. I was nine, so that made her ten. Our mom turned our bedroom into a mini–hospital ward and put us on a strict routine.

Every morning we took turns in the bathtub. While Joanne was soaking in whatever oily concoction Mom added to the bath, Mom changed the sheets on the vacant bed, fluffed up the pillows, and brought in a pitcher of water with two clean glasses. Joanne would come back to bed in freshly washed pajamas, snuggle under the crisp sheets, and fold them back neatly just under her chin. That's when she would close her eyes and that same calm expression would appear on her face.

I would take my bath next while Mom changed my sheets and aired out our room. Slipping into clean pajamas, I would fall back into bed and wait for Mom to place her cool hand on my spot-covered forehead.

During those ten days of our confinement, I remember looking over at Joanne every morning and thinking she looked so serene, lying there on her back with her funny nose defining her profile like a distinct range of mountains. Her lips were together, and the corners of her mouth turned down, as if she were in mourning. I thought strange, mysterious thoughts like, *Is that what Joanne would look like if she were dead?*

Now, as I glanced at her under her shade of woven straw, I thought she looked like a different sister. Healed, certainly, of the cruel chicken pox but healed of something else as well.

Joanne turned and looked at me. "What are you thinking?"

I hesitated before saying, "I was thinking about when we both had chicken pox."

"Chicken pox? What made you think of that?"

"I was thinking of how Mom played nurse and washed our sheets and pajamas every day."

"All I remember was how she would take our temperature

three times a day and write it down. I looked forward to that because that's when she would put her hand on my forehead. I thought the sweetest sensation on earth was her cool hand on my burning-up skin."

"I remember that, too," I said.

Our mother was a reserved, traditional homebody who wasn't overly expressive. We knew she loved us. I'm sure Joanne felt the same way I did about that, but we rarely were pampered. That's why the surprise birthday party Joanne arranged when I turned sixteen was so important. Our birthdays were generally small family affairs with cake after dinner and a simple gift that was wrapped and waiting on the coffee table in the living room. We grew up with sufficient affirmation but not an excess of celebration. All in all, I had very little to complain about when it came to my childhood.

"Do you think we had a healthy childhood?" I asked Joanne.

"We weren't sick too often," Joanne said. "Is that what you mean?"

"No, I mean do you think either of us grew up with a lot of scars from our parents?"

"I don't think so. Why?"

"I was just wondering. So many people I know say they had damaging childhoods. I think ours was pretty good."

"It was. Why are you reviewing our childhood?"

"I don't know. Being out of my comfort zone causes me to think about things I wouldn't normally have time to think about. It's as if my brain has room to turn over and look at things I never pay attention to in the routine at home."

"Oh, no!" Joanne tapped the display behind the steering wheel. "I don't believe this!"

"What? What's wrong?"

"We're almost out of gas."

"How can that be? We've only been on the road for half an hour."

"I didn't pay attention to the gas gauge when we picked up the car, did you?" Joanne asked.

"No. Do you think they sent us out with less than a full tank?"

"Sure looks like it."

I pulled out the map and tried to estimate the number of kilometers between us and the next village down the road. "We should turn around and go back. The next stop looks pretty small on this map, and who knows if they have a gas station."

"Are you sure we have to go back?"

"To be safe, yes. We need to go back. Turn the car around." My sense of supreme justice kicked in, and I hollered, "What a rip-off! Those guys are going to pay! We're going back there, and we're going to make sure they fill it right this time, and we're going to get them to adjust our bill for time lost. This isn't right. They shouldn't be allowed to stay in business with such unethical practices."

Two minutes earlier I was applauding my ability to stay focused and composed in the midst of uncertainty, but now I was ready to bite someone's head off. When I get cranked up like this at home, Ethan usually takes on my grievance and makes sure that whatever wrong has come our way is righted.

My sister, however, laughed, as if she found my tirade entertaining.

"Why are you laughing? This is completely unfair!"

"Yes, it is." She slowed to make a U-turn. "Much in life is unfair."

Her flippant attitude bugged me.

"It's okay." Joanne raised her voice, as we were now heading west and facing a stronger headwind. "We discovered we need gas now rather than finding out in the middle of nowhere. Everything will work out okay, Mel. Relax. This is supposed to be a vacation for us, remember?"

"This isn't my idea of a vacation. None of this has been relaxing since the very beginning. I wish we hadn't come. I don't care about the beachfront property or any of it."

"Melanie, listen to yourself!"

"What?"

"Snap out of it!"

I couldn't remember the last time anyone had talked to me like that. I also couldn't think of anyone else from whom I would take such a rebuke. Even though I accepted her chiding, I still snapped back with a defensive, "I don't like being taken advantage of, that's all."

"I don't either," Joanne said quickly. "But this is what it is. We can't change the situation. We can only go from here. It's not worth it to turn into a couple of crybabies. The world is full of injustice."

"Okay. Fine." I folded my arms and looked away from Joanne.

Our twenty-five-minute drive back into Ensenada was silent. I was struggling with the urge to pout or shout or maybe even get out to demonstrate to my sister how exasperated I was with all of this. But I stayed in my seat and kept silent. Joanne drove the speed limit, carefully made her way through the now-familiar intersections, and found the car rental place without any assistance from me.

"We need gas," Joanne called out to the gold-toothed employee, who was standing in the driveway when we pulled in. "You sent us on our way without any gas."

"No petrol?" the man asked.

"No," I stated with a frown. "You gave us a car without any petrol. Where do we go to fill up the tank?"

He pointed to a filling station across the street. "Petrol."

"Are you saying the gas isn't included in the rental?"

He shook his head and shrugged his shoulders.

"Come on," Joanne said, backing up. "Let's fill the tank and get out of here."

It was so hard to hold my tongue and not to scream about how unfair this was, but I didn't want to invite another scolding from my sister.

We filled the tank but wondered if the price was comparable to what we paid at home. I was too mentally exhausted to do calculations. Joanne already had steered the Jeep back onto the main street, pointing us out of town; this time without a blaring parade to lead us.

Not until we were nearly to the same place on Highway 3 where we had made the U-turn did we speak to each other again. Joanne was the one who ended the standoff.

"I'm sorry I wasn't more sensitive to you earlier."

"That's okay," I mumbled. "I'm sure I overreacted."

"Regardless, I don't think I was sensitive to what you were feeling. I'd really like to hear what you're going through with all this."

"I don't even know anymore. At first, I admit I was intrigued with the news of our inheritance. I mean, who wouldn't want to inherit beachfront property? Then it seemed too much. Now we're here, and I'm trying to keep it all balanced in my mind. I'm not brave like you, Joanne. I'm not an adventurer. This isn't my idea of a dream vacation."

Joanne nodded but didn't add her usual cheery commentary.

"Why? What are you thinking?" I asked. "How does all this make you feel? You run toward dangerous experiences. This must be your idea of a dream come true."

"I wouldn't say it's my dream."

"At least we agree there," I said.

"But I'm thinking this might be God's dream for me."

"Why do you keep saying stuff like that? What does that mean?"

Joanne glanced at me, her expression brimming with delight. "I don't know if you'll want to hear this, but I started praying something in January, after I read that line I told you about earlier how life is a romance when you say, 'Speak, Lord.'"

"Was it one of those prayers for serenity or prosperity like Aunt Winnie has on cards around her home?"

"I don't know. What kind of cards does Aunt Winnie have?"

"She sends money in to television programs, and they send her prayers on cards."

"No, I've never seen the prayer I started to pray on a card," Joanne said. "It's not a formula or anything. It's just something that happened in my heart. I thought about how I've spent so many years of my life setting goals and trying to be strategic about my plans."

"That's how we were raised," I said. "I don't see anything wrong with that approach to life. Look where you are now because of all your planning."

"Yes, but I thought about how I'm forty-two years old, and all these years I've pursued *my* dreams, *my* goals. While I was praying one night, I wondered if maybe God had a few dreams for my life that hadn't come true yet. So I prayed, 'Father, may all *Your* dreams come true. I don't want to get in the way or hinder You from fulfilling any of the plans You had for me when You dreamed me into being.'"

"You're right," I said. "I've never seen a prayer like that on one of Aunt Winnie's laminated cards."

"It's not so unusual, really," Joanne said. "It's sort of a variation on the Lord's Prayer. You know, 'May Your kingdom come and Your will be done on earth as it is in heaven.' For me it was a significant turning point, though. It was a big step to surrender to God all my ideas of how I thought my life should be going."

"Is that why you said earlier that surrender was a beautiful thing?"

Joanne nodded. "Letting go was the most freeing thing I've ever done. Ever since I began to pray that way, I can see more clearly how all the pieces fit together. Everything happens for a reason."

"I agree with that," I said.

We had been driving uphill for a number of miles, but now the road leveled out. The air was cooler than I expected. Joanne and I both had on light jackets, which we zipped up.

"I think everything happens for a reason, including our having to turn around and go back for gas."

"And what do you think the reason is?"

"I've no idea." Joanne shrugged contentedly.

She was beginning to remind me more and more of Aunt Winnie, and I wasn't sure that was a good thing.

"I think that with any great romance, timing is everything. Living life in this great big romance with God has messed up my timing terribly, but I keep seeing how His timing is perfect. All kinds of amazing stuff keeps happening."

Pointing to a herd of cattle grazing in an open field, I tried to redirect the conversation. "I thought from the picture in the tour book that we'd be driving through desert the whole time. This is pretty."

"It is nice. Do you have the map handy? Isn't there a small town up ahead?"

Checking the map, I told Joanne we were coming into a town called Ojos Negros. "Are you thinking of stopping?"

"If they have bottled water, I thought it might be a good idea for us to buy some."

We drove on, the wind flapping our silly sombreros. I was relieved that Joanne didn't return to the topic of how God was making all this "amazing stuff" happen in her life. Part of me was feeling a little edgy about her ethereal romance. Was it a big cover-up for her not having an earthly romance? Another part of me was curious to hear about the guy at work she was trying to get away from. If she didn't have a romance with him, why was she eager to move away from him?

Approaching the question cautiously, I asked, "Joanne, what's the story on the guy from work?"

She paused, as if thinking about where to start. I knew a polite friend would say, "You don't have to tell me about it, if you don't want to." But I wasn't her polite friend; I was her sister. I wanted to hear everything. Besides, I hadn't exactly accumulated any polite points during the previous two hours; why should I start now?

"It's just a work situation that's become a little complicated," Joanne began. "The man is one of the administrators at the clinic where I teach. About six months ago, one of the students came to me and said he was making advances toward her. I had to file reports and work through a whole counseling process for the student."

"Is it settled yet?"

"Not exactly. After three months of my working with her and going through the tangle of paperwork and meetings, the student said she had made up the incident and dropped all the charges."

"Did she make it up?"

"Who knows? She withdrew from the course, and I was left with an administrator who still won't speak to me because he says I should have had more discernment. He said my skills are in question, if I'm not able to accurately evaluate a student's accusations."

"That's ridiculous!"

"I know. I personally have doubts about the administrator's character, but I don't have proof about anything. Now you can see why I'm considering other job options. Moving to Vancouver is certainly at the top of the list."

"I'm sorry you had to go through all that, but as I said last night, I'd love it if you moved to BC."

"The job situation has been fairly aggravating," Joanne said. "But through it all I feel as if I'm protected under an umbrella of God's grace." She tapped the edge of her broad hat. "Or maybe I should say I'm under a sombrero of God's grace. He's protecting me from the elements, so to speak."

I was fed up with Joanne's turning every topic into a spiritual lesson. Unfortunately, I couldn't shake from my thoughts the concept she just conveyed about God's protecting her from the elements.

In my mind, God had always been the major "element" of life to watch out for, not to hide under. I thought that as long as I didn't do anything really wrong, God would be happy with me. I grew up making sure I didn't bother Him unless I needed something important.

Just like I felt toward Dad when we were growing up.

Rolling down the road, in the middle of Baja California, I realized for the first time in my life that I viewed God, my heavenly Father, the same way I viewed my earthly father. The relationship was adequate; I had no complaints. At the same time, I couldn't say I had a deep and special love for God the way Joanne did. I didn't have any desire to ask God if He had unfulfilled dreams for me. The risk was too great. What if His answer was yes, and those dreams weren't my idea of a good dream?

Nine

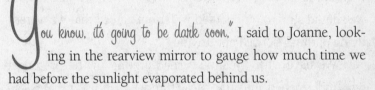

Y ou know, it's going to be dark soon," I said to Joanne, looking in the rearview mirror to gauge how much time we had before the sunlight evaporated behind us.

"Are you tired of driving?" Joanne yawned and looked around.

I'd only been behind the wheel for a little over an hour and wasn't tired yet. Joanne drove the first hour and a half of our trek. Our sombreros had come off when I started to drive and the sun moved behind us instead of over us.

The road had been fairly easy to navigate, but every so often we would hit a portion that was in need of repair, and I'd have to slow down and carefully swerve around potholes big enough for a pig to fall into them.

I told Joanne I didn't mind driving. "I just wish we had more daylight left. I'm not looking forward to the unknown road conditions ahead. Who knows what it will be like to drive in the dark?"

"How far do you think we are?" Joanne asked.

"More than halfway, I'm sure. Maybe three-fourths. It sure has taken longer than I thought it would."

"I know. It's getting chilly. Are you hungry?"

"Yes. Are you? We should have stocked up on supplies before hitting the road," I said.

When we had approached the town of Ojos Negros earlier, we passed a small store that advertised on the outside of the building it carried beer and cigarettes. We briefly discussed if we should stop to buy bottled water but agreed that we weren't dying of thirst, so we kept driving.

"We have cake." Joanne turned around in the passenger seat and reached into the back, fumbling under the Mexican blanket to pull out the pastry box with the remains of our decorated cake.

"Wow!" she suddenly called out. "What a gorgeous sunset. Can you pull off the road, Mel? We can eat our cake and watch the sun go down."

I put on my turn signal, even though we hadn't seen another car for the past ten minutes. The side of the road was narrow and sandy, so I stopped mostly in the middle of a level stretch of highway and put on the emergency flashers. I hoped no one would come roaring out of nowhere and run into us.

A moment after I had that thought, a Volkswagen beetle with a tall antenna sticking out the back sputtered past us going in the opposite direction. I guessed we must be close to the area where the tour book mentioned the popular off-road races because that was the second car we had seen that looked like it could do some serious hill climbing and desert driving.

Joanne pulled the smashed cake box out of the back and opened it to view the less-than-stellar-looking prize cake. "I'm sure it will still taste good."

"It's food." I got out of the car and stretched my legs. I loved the dry, fresh air and drew in a deep breath. A hint of sage and something that reminded me of eucalyptus floated in the air. I was so used to moist, chilled air that this contrasting atmosphere was invigorating.

Handing me the open cake box, Joanne said, "After you."

I took a pinch of cake and dropped it into my mouth. "Still tastes good."

"Just look at the peach colors in those clouds against the pale blue sky." Joanne leaned against the back of the Jeep. "It's so gorgeous! What's that old saying? 'Red sky at night, sailors' delight'?"

"Only we're not sailing with the rest of the ship," I reminded her. "They're probably pulling up anchor right about now. I hope we're doing the right thing, driving to San Felipe like this." I broke off another wedge of the gooey cake and let it melt on my tongue.

"I wish I'd brought a camera with me," Joanne said. "This would be a moment to remember. Chocolate cake at sunset in the middle of nowhere. Fabulous. Absolutely fabulous. If we were on the ship right now, we wouldn't have had this experience."

"True." I reached into the backseat for my coat. "It's going to get cold fast. I'm glad we have the Mexican blankets and our winter coats."

"We'll be okay," Joanne said. "Look at those colors, will you? Incredible."

While I noticed that the peach and blue had deepened to orange and periwinkle, in the distance we heard a faint howling.

"Did that sound like a coyote to you?" I moved closer to Joanne.

"It sure did. We probably shouldn't be standing around like this with food," she said. "Are you ready to go?"

I was about to say yes when I heard another sound coming toward us. It was the sound of a sputtering car, not a wild animal. I guessed this would be another off-road vehicle coming from the opposite direction of the one that had passed us a few moments earlier.

"We should get in," I told Joanne. "Just in case they don't see us in the twilight and run into the back of our Jeep."

Joanne squinted into the sunset to see the car. "They have their lights on. They should be able to see us. No, wait. Their lights just went out. No, they're back on. Do you think they're trying to signal us? Are they blinking at us?"

"I don't know." I jumped into the driver's seat. "But let's not stand here waiting to find out. Come on!"

As soon as Joanne closed her door, I said, "I'll wait until they pass us, and then I'll pull back on the road."

The gray Volkswagen beetle with a long antenna continued to blink its headlights at us. As we waited, it sputtered to a halt only a hundred yards or so behind us. The driver turned off the engine, and the only sound Joanne and I heard was a rattling of metal upon metal, as if pieces of silverware were being tossed at a spinning fan.

"We should see if they need help," Joanne said. "It sounds as if their engine isn't cooperating."

"That's not a good idea, Joanne. You are far too trusting of strangers. We can drive to the next village and try to alert someone of the problem, but we shouldn't stay here and wait for trouble to overtake us."

"What trouble? They're the ones with the car that won't start. They're probably tourists like us," Joanne said. "How would you feel if we were the ones sitting in a car that wouldn't start out here in Nowhere Land?"

"How do you know they're tourists?" I turned on the engine, released the emergency brake, and put on my turn signal, prepared to bolt out of there.

"They're in a Baja bug. Isn't that what those cars are called? They probably rented it to go off-road racing around here like the tour book said, and now they have engine trouble. We can't leave them, Melanie."

"Yes we can. It's not safe to try to assist strangers on deserted roads in the middle of Mexico! Didn't the tour book say anything about that? Come on, Joanne, don't make this a big deal. We need to be safe; we're leaving."

"Just wait!" she yelled at me. "Stop being so paranoid and pushy and wait one stinking minute! If someone gets out of the car and comes toward us, and we don't feel safe, we can bolt. But what if it's two women stranded out here in the dark?"

"What would two women be doing out here?" I snapped.

Joanne lowered her chin and gave me that all-knowing big-sister look. "Maybe they've inherited beachfront property and are trying to drive to San Felipe. Maybe they went to a car rental place that didn't fill their tank with gas or maybe—"

"Okay, okay," I muttered. "I got your point."

The driver's door and the passenger's door opened at the same time. "If you see that they have guns," I crouched to get a good view in the side mirror, "you holler, and I'll punch the gas pedal, and we'll scream out of here."

"It's a little boy," Joanne said.

"A child is driving the car?" I turned to look over my shoulder just as a tall man approached. The boy had popped out of the passenger's side and was waving his hands over his head, trying to get our attention. In the darkening light around us, it was difficult to make out any of the man's or the boy's features. Clearly, though, they had nothing in their hands. Specifically, no weapons.

"Hello!" the man called out, waving at us as he approached. "¡Hola!"

"I'm still going to bolt, if I think for one second that we're not safe," I told Joanne.

"Fine! But just give the guy a second. We can't leave him stranded here with a little boy."

Something inside me wanted to say, "Haven't you filled your quota for saving lives for one day, Mother Joanna?" But I could see now in the glow of our taillights that this guy wasn't a local. Joanne probably was right; they were stranded tourists. We should help them.

"Hello," the man said breathlessly as he jogged up to my side of the car. "I was hoping to catch you. We passed you earlier, but when the car started to go out on us, I turned around hoping you hadn't gone too far."

As soon as he said the word *out,* Joanne and I knew he was Canadian.

"I have to get to one of the ranches about five kilometers from here, but my car isn't going to make it. We received a call that one of the workers broke his leg."

"Oh!" Joanne responded like the trained medical professional she was by jumping out of the passenger's side, pushing back our luggage, and motioning for this stranger and the boy to hop right in.

"I need a few things out of our car," the man said.

"Melanie, turn us around."

I complied but shot Joanne a stern look. I did not like this predicament. She appeared as confident and in control as if this twilight rendezvous were planned.

Grabbing a small duffel bag and with the car keys in his hand, the man directed me to continue west, back toward Ensenada.

We are never going to make it to San Felipe the way we keep going forward then turning around and going backward!

"Watch for a dirt road that intersects with this main road on the right side. It should be about a kilometer or less up here."

"I'm Joanne," my cruise director sister said. "This is my sister, Melanie. What part of Canada are you from?"

"Vancouver. Is it that obvious?"

"To another Canadian, yes. I'm from Toronto. Melanie lives in Langley."

"No kidding. We're neighbors then. I'm Matthew Henderson. This is Cal. I apologize for putting you out."

"It's no problem." Joanne spoke freely for herself but not for me. I wanted to pinch her. If she started to share private information with this man the way she had when I left the dinner table the night before, I definitely would pinch her.

"How did you find out about the rancher with the broken leg?" Joanne turned toward our hitchhikers and seemed to study them intently.

"I come down a couple of times a year to volunteer at the clinic in San Felipe. One of the ranchers called in on the radio. I was the only one available to come. The details were sketchy, but it seemed they weren't able to transport the guy to the clinic."

"I'm a nurse-practitioner," Joanne said. "So please, if I can be of any assistance, let me know."

"You're serious? You're a nurse-practitioner?"

"Yes."

"Slow down, slow down." Matthew grabbed the back of my seat. "I think the turnoff is right up here. It comes fast. There it is. Turn right."

The Jeep took the bump onto the uneven dirt road like a champ, but I had my mouth open and bit my tongue when we took the dip. The taste of blood mingled with the last bits of chocolate cake, and tears welled up in my eyes.

Don't cry, you big baby! Keep your eyes on the road.

We rambled over what felt like ten miles of rough dirt road with only the headlights to guide the way. Matthew directed me, encouraging me for doing such a great driving job. All I could think of was how Joanne and I would have to drive back over this in the dark alone and then make the rest of the trek to San Felipe in the deep darkness. At the core of my being I was more frightened than I'd ever been in my life.

Matthew directed me to slow down, and we inched along, using the headlights as feelers until we came to a gravel road that led about half a mile to a ranch house. Two lanterns hung from wooden beams that jutted out from under the adobe roof. Matthew said he had been here two years ago and was grateful he remembered the approximate location, because otherwise it would have been easy to pass it by.

The sound of our wheels on the gravel roused the occupants,

and a man and woman rushed out to greet us, speaking rapid Spanish.

Matthew answered them in Spanish and then instructed Cal to go into the house with Señora Valdepariso while he went out to the ranch hand's quarters with Señor Valdepariso.

"I could use your help," Matthew said to Joanne.

"Sure." Joanne turned to me. "Are you going to be okay?"

I nodded, trying to hide my fear. "I'll wait with Cal in the house."

Joanne fell in step with Matthew and Mr. Valdepariso, who took one of the lanterns. The señora motioned graciously for Cal and me to follow her into the humble dwelling. She wore a dress covered by a full apron. Her graying hair was wrapped in a thick coil on the back of her head. Reaching for the other lantern, the gracious woman spoke to Cal and me in Spanish.

"I'm sorry; I don't understand," I said.

"I think she asked if we're hungry," Cal said. "*Hambre* means 'hungry.' *Hombre* is 'man.' I learned that yesterday. I think she said *hambre.*"

"*Sí?* Hambre?" She said a few more words.

"*¡Yo!*" the boy answered. I thought that was a rather disrespectful way to respond to someone who had just offered him food, but then I realized *yo* was Spanish for "me," and he was indicating he was hungry.

By the lantern light, I could see the young boy's distinctive features. I guessed him to be about eight or nine. He had sandy red hair that stuck straight up in front.

"Cal, did you see that white box on the Jeep's backseat?"

"The one with the cake in it?"

He obviously had looked while we bumped down the road.

"Yes, could you bring it in?" I was thinking we could share the cake, but I also was thinking of wild animals that might be attracted to the food, if we left it in the open car.

Cal jetted back to the Jeep, retrieved the box, and handed the mangled gift to our slender hostess. I guessed her to be in her early fifties. Maybe older. It was hard to tell. Her face was weathered with as many wrinkles as the peach-tinted streaks we had watched in the western sky only an hour or so earlier. But her skin wasn't peach toned. It was a rich reddish brown hue that looked warm in the glow of the lantern. She was smiling at us as if we were old friends who had stopped by for a scheduled visit.

Her acceptance of the situation, such as it was, spread calm over me, and I found my heart returning to a steady beat and my tears of fright evaporating.

I realized when we entered the house that she was still holding the lantern because they had no electricity. Simple furniture filled the open space. A wooden table with four straight-back chairs. A small wood-fed stove, a single basin sink, a wooden cupboard, and a narrow folding table that held plates and metal bins in which I guessed she stored her perishables.

She motioned for us to sit at the table, and we obliged

quietly. Part of the floor was covered with carefully placed, reddish-colored Tecate tiles. The tiles went only so far. Then it looked as if they had run out of tiles, and the floor turned to smooth dirt.

I pasted a polite smile on my face and tried not to appear to be staring in shock as I gazed around the room. I knew people in the world lived like this, but I'd never imagined I would be in such a hovel.

A faded green floral curtain gathered on a shower rod separated the main area from what I guessed to be the bedroom or at least another room. The walls were uneven blocks of adobe bricks the size of shoeboxes. Bits of straw stuck out of the mud bricks that were wedged tightly together and sealed with more of the brown dirt.

Despite our sitting on dilapidated chairs, which I would have thrown out long ago, inside a house made of mud bricks with our feet on a dirt floor, everything around us was tidy and orderly. I felt the strangest sense of being safe and protected.

Under a sombrero of grace, I thought. Then I stopped myself before I started sounding like my romantically religious sister.

Señora Valdepariso lit a fire in her woodstove, and the room filled with the scent I'd smelled at a Mexican restaurant we ate at once in Vancouver that cooked all its food over mesquite wood. She was speaking to us cordially, as if we could understand her. I nodded occasionally and kept a goofy grin on my face. Cal sat politely at the table, swinging his legs and looking around.

As I watched, the señora poured water from a plastic water bottle into a ceramic bowl, and with her weathered hands, she worked with some sort of dough.

"It's okay." I motioned that she could stop. It seemed she had so little to give. "You don't have to feed us. We're fine."

She smiled and kept working, taking a lump of dough in her worn palms and rapidly flapping it back and forth until she had formed a flat tortilla.

"Cool!" Cal rose from his chair and stepped closer to watch her. "How do you do that?"

She reached for another lump of dough and with amazing speed flattened another tortilla.

"Can I try?" Cal made hand motions, indicating he wanted to make a tortilla.

Like any mother in any corner of the world, the señora reached over, examined the young man's hands, and pointed at a painted ceramic water pitcher and bowl on a small stand by the wall. Her directions to him were in Spanish, but I understood the universal "go wash your hands first" command.

Rising, I directed Cal to the basin and told him to place his hands over the round bowl while I poured the water from the pitcher. He rubbed his hands thoroughly. I spotted a small wedge of soap and told Cal to use some soap. I thought of all the times at home that I had thrown away pieces of soap twice that size just because it was annoying to try to pick up such a small piece.

He shook his hands dry, the droplets flinging across the

tiled area of the floor. I washed my hands, lathering with soap and then pouring the water over each hand.

"Should I toss this water outside?" I pointed to the bowl and then pointed to the door.

The señora said, "No." Wiping her hands on her apron, she picked up a knife, reached for the lantern, and motioned for Cal and me to follow her out the front door. I carried the basin of dirty water as we followed her several yards away from the house. Her lantern lit up a row of cactus. She indicated I should pour the water at the base of the cactus. Then with her knife she carefully sliced off one of the round, flat "ears" of the cactus. I couldn't imagine how she managed to grasp the big, green elephant-ear piece without all the spiny needles going into her hand. Obviously she had done this a time or two.

The three of us returned to the house with Cal asking, "What are you going to do with that hunk of cactus?"

She answered, but neither of us knew what she said.

Returning to the bowl on her narrow worktable, the señora motioned for both of us to reach for a ball of the tortilla dough. She proceeded to demonstrate how to flatten it. Cal and I both laughed at the same time. We definitely didn't have the knack for this. Cal's hands were still damp, and the dough stuck to his palms. I got the motion down, not as swiftly as our expert cook, but I managed to make the dough resemble a tortilla. Sort of. The señora had two perfect tortillas done by the time my first one was serviceable.

With a scoop of her knife into a metal tin, she melted a

wad of lard on the top of her cast-iron stove and lay the tortillas on top as gently as if she were placing a baby bird back in
its nest. Her nimble fingers turned the tortillas by grasping the
edges, and the room filled with a wonderful fragrance.

In any other context I don't think I would have considered
the combination of lard and tortillas to be a wonderful fragrance, but here, at this moment, the scent represented home
and hospitality and nourishment for weary travelers. All my
normal pickiness set aside, I knew I would gratefully eat anything this woman offered me in her modest home.

The scent seemed to arouse more than just my appetite.
We heard a strange shuffling sound from behind the green
sheet door. The fabric fluttered slightly, and a small pig trotted
out of the bedroom, snout to the ground, looking for leftovers.

I wanted to burst out laughing. Cal said, "Cool!" and went
over to take a closer look at the curious fellow.

The señora wasn't happy the scrounger showed up unin-
vited. With lots of Spanish words and a flapping of her apron,
she corralled the critter to the front door and used her foot to
make him scoot outside. The wooden door didn't close well or
latch entirely shut, so I could see how various animals easily
could wander in whenever the door was left open, which I
imagined would be often since that was the only way to air out
the house or vent the stove.

Reaching to flip the last tortilla, our cook placed a cast-iron
skillet on the stove and went to work extracting the stickers
and slicing up the piece of cactus. Clearly we were going to be

served this delicacy. I reminded myself that I had thought only a moment earlier that I would eat whatever was offered to me. When I considered how few of these flat appendages were left on the row of cactus we saw, I realized she was giving to us extravagantly out of the little she had to offer.

I stared at this kind and generous woman, feeling as if I'd never been shown such hospitality in my life. I certainly never had expressed this sort of hospitality to anyone who came to *my* home.

Years ago at a church luncheon I heard a speaker talk about hospitality and how the literal meaning of the word was "the love of strangers." It stuck with me then because I didn't think that could be right. I never looked it up but always intended to because I thought it couldn't be true hospitality—or at least not safe, secure hospitality—if you were showing love to a stranger. Such an act would be risky and foolish, not God-honoring and lovely.

However, this night, I saw how wrong I was. What the woman was offering us was extravagantly beautiful. From the hand-flapped tortillas to the cut-up slices of her paltry supply of cactus, she was saying she loved us.

And she didn't even know our names.

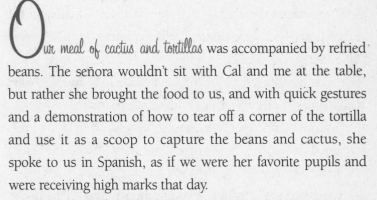

Ten

Our meal of cactus and tortillas was accompanied by refried beans. The señora wouldn't sit with Cal and me at the table, but rather she brought the food to us, and with quick gestures and a demonstration of how to tear off a corner of the tortilla and use it as a scoop to capture the beans and cactus, she spoke to us in Spanish, as if we were her favorite pupils and were receiving high marks that day.

"This is delicious," I told her, holding up my fourth wedge of tortilla. "Thank you."

"*¿Delicioso?*" she repeated as a question.

Young Cal was quick to respond. "Sí. Muy delicioso. Gracias."

"Yes," I added. "Gracias. Muchas gracias."

"De nada." Touching her heart, she continued to say something that I'm sure was very tender.

She urged us to eat more, as if all the food on the platter was for the two of us. It seemed we should save some for the others.

"Did you eat yet?" I pointed to the food and then to our hostess.

"Sí, sí."

She tidied up the kitchen area, chattering to us the whole time. I took one more bite and patted my tummy to indicate I was satisfied. She was surprised and motioned for me to eat more.

"No, gracias. I'm full. It was very delicioso. I thought the cactus tasted like green beans. What do you think?" I asked Cal.

"Exactly like green beans," he said. "My mom always makes green beans out of a can. I like this better."

"What's your name?" I asked our hostess.

She didn't understand. I patted my chest. "Mel-a-nie. That's my name. Melanie."

I touched the arm of my young dinner date. "This is Cal. Cal."

"Cal," the señora repeated. "Cal."

"Yes, that's Cal, and I'm Melanie."

"Mel..." She hesitated.

"Mel is good. That's what my sister calls me. You can call me Mel." I patted my upper chest again. "Mel."

"Mel," she repeated, pleased with the ease of *Cal* and *Mel*.

I pointed to her. "What's your name?"

She touched her chest, and with a gentle smile, she rolled off her name like a well-rehearsed line of a beloved poem: "Rosarita Guadalupe Yolanda Rosario Valdepariso." Then after a pause she shortened it to "Rosa Lupe."

"Rosa," I said.

"Rosa *Lupe,*" she corrected me.

"Rosa Lupe."

"We have cake." Cal pointed to the pathetically smashed cake box. "Do you want some cake?"

Rosa Lupe opened the box and let out a delighted cluck of her tongue.

"It doesn't look like much." I shook my head. "But it tastes good. Please, have some."

I made the same sort of gestures she had made when trying to get us to eat more.

With a childish grin, Rosa Lupe wiped off her knife and cut a modest sliver.

"Go ahead." I motioned some more. "Please, eat it."

Her eyes opened wide as the cake went into her mouth. She made all kinds of yummy sounds as she swallowed the chocolate, and with a womanly smack of her lips, she declared, "¡Delicioso!"

I grinned and nodded.

What was that we heard on the cruise? No true Sisterchick can turn down really good chocolate. I believe it now! Sisterchicks are everywhere!

The front door opened, and Rosa Lupe's husband entered

without a lantern. He nodded to us humbly, as if he were inter-rupting something instead of Cal and me being the interrupters of his evening. We were eating his dinner.

Standing with his back to us, Mr. Valdepariso discussed something in hushed tones with his wife. It didn't matter what he was trying to say so privately. Cal and I couldn't understand him anyway.

"I bet they're talking about where we're all going to sleep," Cal said to me in a low voice, leaning closer.

"We're not spending the night here," I said.

"You're not? Where are you going?"

"San Felipe. How long did it take you guys to get here from San Felipe?"

"A long time. Like an hour."

"An hour? I didn't think it was that far."

"You can't go very fast on the road," Cal said. "Especially if your car keeps breaking down like ours."

"Were you planning to spend the night here?"

Cal nodded. "Out in the straw in the barn. That's where I said I want to sleep."

"You may get your wish." My eyebrows caved in with the worry weight of the world now sitting on top of my head. It was one thing to offer a ride a few miles out of our way and to accept a meager meal prepared by Rosa Lupe. But expecting these kind people to find lodging for all of us in their hacienda was far too much to ask.

Cal apparently was right, though, because soon after Mr.

Valdepariso went back outside, and Rosa Lupe took me over to the hanging green sheet. She pulled back the curtain, and with an all-encompassing sweep, she indicated that their bedroom was at our disposal.

I touched her shoulder and smiled as sincerely as I could. "We can't take your bed. This is your home. You and your husband need to sleep here."

She didn't understand me, so I reverted to the one word I knew was the same in both languages, "No." I pointed to the small bed with the torn blue-and-white bedspread covering it and neatly smoothed out to the corners. "No, we can't sleep in your bed. We'll sleep somewhere else."

"In the barn," Cal added.

I don't know what Cal had pictured in his mind for a barn-sleeping experience, but I was pretty sure the Valdeparisos didn't exactly have the fresh-straw-filled sort of barn that kids in the movies run around and jump in.

Rosa Lupe kept talking and motioned for us to follow her outside. We walked several yards in the light of the lantern. I looked up to the inky dark canopy above us and involuntarily gasped. The heavens were alive with thousands of brilliant stars bursting through the night sky. It was wondrous, providing a quiet luminescence of its own.

"*Estrellas.*" Rosa Lupe looked up with me.

"Es-tray-yaws," I repeated. "Stars. Es-tray-yaws."

"Sí. Estrellas. ¿*Bonitas*, no?"

"Yes, they're beautiful," I said. "It's a beautiful night." Even though it was much cooler than it had been during the day, the air didn't feel at all like the winter air did on a clear night at home. I filled my lungs with the chilled oxygen and knew that my sister would really like this—the stars, the air, the beauty of this unfamiliar place.

Rosa Lupe stopped in front of a smelly area where I envisioned the little piggy's family enjoying a merry wallow in a swamp of mud and mess. Cal was given the task of carrying the lantern, and he was swinging it every which way so I couldn't see how frightening the animal area really was.

Rosa Lupe said something and then kept walking, leading us past the animal area to another adobe structure. This dwelling had a central area inside with a table, a long bench, and a small area that looked as if it had been used for cooking.

An uncovered doorway led us to the second room where we found Joanne and Matthew working together. They were making the final loop of a long bandage that was wrapped around the patient's leg. A primitive splint ran under his leg all the way up his thigh. His torn pant leg was stained with blood. I could only imagine what this man must have gone through in the hours between when he broke his leg and when we arrived.

He looked up at us from a bed covered by only a crumpled blanket stained with blood. On the floor I noticed two empty tequila bottles. His eyes rolled back, and I thought, *That man is stinking drunk!*

The mother in me wanted to shield young Cal from this startling sight. I wanted to take him back outside to look at the beautiful stars. But in the severe honesty of this remote place, it seemed fitting to let the boy see life as it was.

I offered the patient a sympathetic nod and what I hoped was a comforting smile. In the depths of my heart I knew that if I'd broken my leg so severely that the bone had punctured the skin and if no immediate medical assistance or pain relievers were available, I might have been tempted to get thoroughly drunk as well.

"Mel, do you have any aspirin with you?" Joanne asked.

"I might. In my purse. I left it in the Jeep." Stating aloud that I had willingly left my purse in an open vehicle shocked me. At home I won't even leave my purse in a shopping cart at the grocery store. I have to have it over my shoulder at all times. What had happened inside my head to allow me to leave my purse unsecured and to walk away from it without a second thought?

The startling truth was that I trusted these people and this situation and maybe even trusted God that this was His idea for us to be here.

"He won't need the aspirin until morning," Matthew said. "But if you have any you can spare, I'm sure he'd greatly appreciate it."

"Sure. Of course."

After a fair amount of discussion that flowed through Matthew, since he was the interpreter for both sides, it became clear the only sensible option was for all of us to stay here for the night.

"Hombres *aqui*," Rosa Lupe said.

"This is where the guys sleep," Matthew interpreted. "The three of you women will have the main house. The señora says we are welcome to come and eat."

"It's delicious." I smiled at Rosa Lupe. "¡Delicioso!"

She grinned back at me.

"I'll clean up here and see you in the morning," Matthew said.

"Aren't you going to eat?" Joanne asked him.

"No, I'm fine. Cal and I will bed down for the night. You ready to get some sleep, Cal?"

The adventuresome young man had lifted one of the tequila bottles and was sniffing it. "Okay."

I looked around. The only bed was the one occupied by the now-snoring patient. The table and bench in the other room might work as beds, but I saw no extra blankets. The floor was dirt.

"Do you two have sleeping bags or air mattresses or anything?" I asked Matthew.

He seemed amused by my question, and I realized how ridiculous it was. I knew he only had the small duffel bag with him. He and Cal were wearing sweatshirts but had no coats or extra blankets. If the Valdeparisos had extra bedding, I was certain they would have offered it by now.

"You can use our blankets," my generous sister said before

I could inform her that the other house had only one bed and no extra bedding waiting for us in some hidden linen closet.

"Are you sure?" Matthew asked.

"Yes. Is that okay with you, Melanie?"

Everyone but the drunken man stared at me. All I could say was, "Of course."

At least we still have our coats.

I pictured myself wrapped in my winter coat, lying on the edge of the tiles that partially covered the floor while my feet were being inspected by the roving piglet in the middle of the night.

This can't be happening. Not really. Any minute now I'll wake up, and Ethan will tell me I was talking in my sleep, and I'll tell him about this crazy dream. We'll laugh together and...

It struck me that according to my sister's view of life, this very well could be a dream. God's dream. Not necessarily my dream.

Rosa Lupe and her husband left one of the lanterns with Matthew and Cal and used the other to lead Joanne and me back to the house. I watched the couple grasp hands as we walked. Tapping Joanne's shoulder I pointed up at the grand recital of the celestial cast of stars overhead.

"Ohhh!" Joanne sighed at the beauty, just like I knew she would. "Look at that!"

"*Entranas* bonitas," I said, eager to show off my new Spanish words to my sister.

Rosa Lupe stopped walking and turned around. They both

looked at me as I tried out my new words one more time.

"¿Entranas bonitas?" I said.

Rosa Lupe released a tender chuckle. Her husband grinned widely and told me something in Spanish. I'd obviously not said "beautiful stars." In the morning I'd ask Matthew to interpret for me and find out how badly I had slaughtered what was meant to be a sincere expression of praise.

"No matter how you say it, the stars are beautiful," Joanne murmured.

"Yes," I said, sticking with English. "It's an incredibly beautiful night."

Our host couple helped us lift our undisturbed luggage and purses from the open Jeep and insisted on carrying them for us. We entered the house, and the first thing I noticed was a dark bug at least an inch long scuttling on creepy, short, skinny legs across the table. As soon as the light shone in its direction, the hideous insect skittered away from the covered food so quickly it seemed to disappear. I watched the floor to see where it went, but in the glow of the lantern, I caught sight of no unwanted creature.

"*La cucaracha,*" Rosa Lupe said with great distain.

I recognized that word. As a child I'd heard a song with that word: *La cucaracha, la cucaracha...*

"Cockroach," Joanne said quietly.

"A la cucaracha is a cockroach?"

She nodded.

"I always thought the song was about a little bird."

"I guess it was about a cockroach," Joanne said mournfully. "How horrid to sing about a cockroach."

"I know. That couldn't have been a cockroach on the table, though. It was too big." Our cockroaches at home were the size of a thumbnail. I'd only run into a few in my career as a house-keeper, and they were polite enough to check into the Roach Motel traps I set for them on the very first night the motels opened for business. I didn't imagine Rosa Lupe had any Roach Motels set up in the corners.

"It was a cockroach, all right," Joanne said. "They grow big in the tropics. Trust me."

I scanned the floor a second time. Suddenly I wanted the little pig to come back in and busily snoot about.

"I'm not sure I can do this." I lowered my voice as if Rosa Lupe could understand me.

She was busy motioning for Joanne to sit down and to eat. I wondered what the cactus tasted like cold. At least the ceramic bowl that covered the plate of food had kept the unwanted dinner guests away.

"What are you saying?" Joanne asked. "What can't you do? Eat this food?"

"No, I already ate a lot. It's very good. I don't know if I can sleep with the cockroaches and the pigs."

"Melanie." Joanne gave me a withering look. "No pigs are in here."

"There was one!"

Joanne shook her head, as if she didn't believe me. I

wanted to see her world rocked just the tiniest bit. Just once. I needed to be reminded that she was human after all. Obviously blood and broken bones didn't turn her stomach. The cockroach hadn't fazed her. As she sat down at the table, I said, "See the green stuff? It's cactus."

"Right." She shook her head.

"It is. Just ask Rosa Lupe. We went outside and picked it for supper, and then I watered the cactus."

Joanne looked as me, as if I were thoroughly entertaining. "Cacti don't need water."

"This one did."

Mr. and Mrs. Valdepariso ceased their conversation and observed our sisterly banter while exchanging a knowing look.

"*¿Hermanas?*" Rosa Lupe pointed to the two of us with her finger wagging back and forth.

"Yes, we're sisters," Joanne said, as if she understood what Rosa Lupe was asking. "Is it that obvious? Our mother used to say we were 'almost twins.' Of course, Mel and I never agreed with her. But then I don't know that we grew up agreeing about a lot of things."

Rosa Lupe nodded politely, as if she understood every word and then launched into her own story in Spanish. I had no idea what she was saying, but Joanne listened as if she might catch a word or two she understood.

Mr. Valdepariso joined Joanne at the table, and the two of them finished off the rest of the tortillas and cactus-bean dip.

"It's green beans," Joanne said.

"No, it's cactus," I pressed. "It just tastes like green beans."

Rosa Lupe presented the dilapidated remains of the cake to her husband, as if it were a great prize. He made some sort of appreciative-sounding comment while she served him a large piece with what appeared to be the only fork in the house.

I leaned back in the wobbly chair and thought of how much Mr. Valdepariso reminded me of Robert, who had ordered three desserts at the dinner table on the ship the night before.

Was that really only last night? I can't believe it.

Twenty-four hours earlier my sister and I had dined on escargot, prime rib, and crème brûlée. Tonight it was hand-flattened tortillas with beans and cactus and chocolate cake. I didn't think my imagination could handle what dinner might consist of tomorrow night or where we might dine.

The contrast between the cruise ship and the country *casa* became even more acute when Joanne and I finally understood the intended sleeping arrangements. Mr. Valdepariso left after he ate to join the other hombres. Joanne and I were to share the prized bed with Rosa Lupe. All three of us in a double bed. Hopefully, without cockroaches.

Before we bedded down, Rosa Lupe led Joanne and me to the outhouse located a hundred yards behind their home. We took turns holding the lantern outside, and let's just say it was a wise choice not to have too much light illuminating the situation inside the outhouse. I never knew I could hold my breath so long.

Washing up inside the house with the ceramic pitcher and basin, I told Joanne I wished we had brought the cruise ship robes with us.

Her reply was, "True. They would have made a nice gift for Rosa Lupe and her husband, but I don't think they would have understood the principle behind the luxury of a French terry cloth robe."

I was thinking the robes would have been nice for us, but I didn't say that.

We both opted for our sweatpants and T-shirts, layered under sweaters. The color combinations were not at all stylish, but we were warm. We were also blessed. I realized when I opened my suitcase and had a half-dozen articles of clothing available to me that, even though what I brought with me represented only a fraction of my wardrobe, it was still twice what Rosa Lupe probably had.

She slept in a long flannel nightgown that was rubbed through in some spots. Her long hair came down for a quick combing and then went back up in a twist on the back of her head.

Pulling back the worn comforter and the top sheet, Rosa Lupe made a welcoming motion, indicating that Joanne and I should have first choice of positions. The bed didn't have pillows and there was no bottom sheet covering the mattress. Joanne and I had brought our coats with us to drape over our feet, but in the close quarters, with three in the small bed, it soon became apparent we wouldn't need the coats.

"I don't mind sleeping in the middle," my saintly sister said. "Last night I slept with a swan. Tonight I'll sleep with two swans."

"Sweet," I said, remembering the folded-up swan towel from the cruise ship.

Rosa Lupe doused the lantern just as I was crawling into bed next to Joanne. The bed bounced up and down as Rosa Lupe got comfortable on the other side. Joanne and I were both on our backs, shoulder to shoulder, thigh to thigh. Her foot wandered over and gave my bare foot a friendly hello tickle.

"Don't start something you can't finish," I teased her.

Joanne giggled.

Rosa Lupe let out a long, contented breath and began to recite in the darkness. A poem? No, the reverence with which she spoke made me think it was a prayer. Her rounded Spanish syllables rolled over us sweet and tender as a mother's cool hand on a feverish forehead. I felt calmed and no longer giggly. The day was done. The time for sleep had come.

"Amen," Rosa Lupe whispered.

"Amen," Joanne echoed.

"Amen."

It was the last word I remembered hearing from my own dry throat until some time in the middle of the deep, dark night when Joanne yelled in my ear, "No, don't let him drown!"

"Joanne." I halfway sat up, reaching in the darkness to grasp her shoulders and wake her from the all-too-understandable nightmare. "Joanne, it's okay. Wake up."

"The baby," she whimpered. "He fell in the water."

"Yes, I know, Joanne. It's okay. Shhh. It's okay. You're both safe now." I slid my arm around her back and held her, as if she were the terrified toddler wrapped in the blanket and not blinking.

I could hear her breathing slowing and returning to a steady, light rhythm. If the outburst woke Rosa Lupe, she didn't indicate it by moving or by entering into our squished comfort session.

Lying back on the lumpy mattress, I kept my arms around Joanne in a loose circle.

"Melly," Joanne whispered, "don't let go."

"I won't," I promised.

Eleven

Morning came as luminous as a searchlight, wearing unveiled sunlight and slipping in through a large crevice in the adobe wall. I watched the brightness of the new day reveal the startling surroundings without making any apologies. The beauty was in the light. Simple splendor rode on those sunbeams.

I was surprised to find that I was the only one in the bed. Joanne's soft voice floated from the other room. I could smell the wood burning in the stove. A moment later I heard the sizzle of the melting lard followed by the rhythmic pat-pat of Rosa Lupe's skilled hands shaping the morning tortillas.

At home I'm always the first one up. I make the day come. I am the rooster, awakening everyone else. Ethan says I'm a regular "Miss Merry Sunshine." He's sarcastic, of course, because usually there's nothing "merry" or "sunshiny" about me in the morning. I'm all business. The list of daily tasks always is long, and daylight always is short.

Here, on the flipside of the great western hemisphere, I woke with a stiff neck, a flattened arm, a cramp in my calf, and a smile in the sunlight. The contentment made no sense. I should have lain awake all night fretting that if I fell asleep and opened my mouth, a cockroach the size of a baby dill pickle would fall in, and I'd choke to death.

Instead of moaning and dreading the untold adventures that awaited us in the new day, I lay quietly in the solitude of that uneven bed. I thought about Joanne, my only sister. I thought about her sterling heart, a heart that had through the night beat right beside me for the first time in many years. I knew that it had been in the rapturous celebration of sister-hood and the gracious hospitality of these humble people that I had slept well.

"Good morning." I stepped into the other room and smiled at Joanne and Rosa Lupe.

"*Buenas dias,*" Rosa Lupe greeted me. "*¿Tienes hambre?*"

"That means, *hungry,* right? Yes, I would love one of your fabulous tortillas."

"Did you see how fast she makes these?" Joanne asked.

"I know. She's amazing."

"How are you doing?" Joanne asked.

"Good, actually."

"Did you get any sleep?"

"Yes, I did. How about you?"

"Off and on."

"You had a nightmare. Do you remember that?"

Joanne nodded with her lips solemnly pressed together. She lowered her eyes to the journal in front of her, and I told myself this was a topic I definitely should bring up later.

"I was just reading the señora some verses I copied several months ago. After we saw the stars last night, I was trying to remember where I'd read about God's making the stars, and here it is in my journal."

"Does Rosa Lupe even understand what you're reading?"

"I told her it was from the Bible."

"*La Biblia,* sí." Rosa Lupe nodded and indicated that Joanne should keep reading as Rosa Lupe flap-flapped her hands, creating an abundance of tortillas.

"Here it is," Joanne said.

"The LORD merely spoke, and the heavens were created.

He breathed the word, and all the stars were born....

Let everyone in the world fear the LORD,

And let everyone stand in awe of him....

He made their hearts,

so he understands everything they do."

"That's in the Psalms?" I asked.

Joanne nodded. "Psalm 33, the New Living Translation, I

think. Not all the chapter. Just some of the verses. I love the part, 'He made their hearts, so he understands everything they do.'"

"*¡Gloria a Dios!*" Rosa Lupe exclaimed.

"Yes," Joanne said. "Glory to God."

"Is that what she said?"

"I think so, Mel. After listening to Spanish for a while, enough words sound similar to figure out what she's saying."

Rosa Lupe followed Joanne's comment with a long string of sentences that didn't contain a single similar-sounding word to our untrained ears.

Joanne laughed. "Well, so much for that theory!"

I went over to the ceramic water pitcher to wash up and found the pitcher was empty. "May I get some more water for you?" I asked Rosa Lupe, holding up the pitcher.

"Ah, sí, sí." She bustled over to where I stood. "*Necesitamos mas agua.*"

I tried to explain again that I could get the water, but she seemed to prefer that I keep the breakfast preparations going while she went for the water. Handing over the pitcher, I joined Joanne by the smoky stove and tried to nimbly flip one of the frying tortillas without burning my fingers.

"How does she do this? I need tongs or something. I can't believe she lives here with so little and is so giving and content."

"I know." Joanne stood beside me and tried her fingers at flipping the tortilla. She did it with more ease and speed than I could. "There's a lot about this place that reminds me of India."

"The poverty?"

"Yes, but also the peace and the generosity."

"I've never seen hospitality like this." I reached for another flattened tortilla and eased it onto the grill.

"*You* amaze me." Joanne looped her arm around my shoulder.

"Me? Why? Because I can cook tortillas?"

"No. I thought you would come undone when we pulled in last night. I didn't think you would be able to cope with all this."

"So I surprised you, huh?"

"Yes, you definitely surprised me."

Rosa Lupe returned with a full pitcher of water and a trail of hungry men behind her.

Hambre hombres, I thought to myself. None of them appeared too worse for wear after their night without a bed. I wondered who ended up on the table and who spent the night on the bench or floor. Since we hadn't needed our coats, I felt bad that I hadn't offered them when Joanne turned over our blankets.

"Buenas dias," Señor Valdepariso greeted us. He continued to talk, and our delightful interpreter, Matthew, jumped right in to let us know what our host was saying. It was refreshing to know what was being said.

"Miguel is not doing very well this morning," Matthew said. "By any chance did you find those aspirin?"

"Oh, I forgot. Let me get them." I rifled through my purse and found the bottle of generic ibuprofen. "It's not much, but you're welcome to keep it." I handed over the pills to Matthew.

I noticed that Rosa Lupe and her husband eyed the bottle as if it were a generous gift. I couldn't imagine what life would be like without the freedom to grab a couple of painkillers whenever a headache started up. What did these people do if they had an infection or a sore tooth? I never had visualized life without antibiotics or dentists. Clearly Matthew's arrival was a huge blessing. I also understood more why Joanne decided to stay so many years in India.

Matthew left with the ibuprofen and two tortillas for the recovering patient.

The three of us remaining "honored guests" were directed toward the rickety chairs around the wooden table where Rosa Lupe delivered warm tortillas to a platter in front of us as quickly as she could prepare them.

Cal updated Joanne and me on how poor Miguel had woken up moaning in the middle of the night and begging for more tequila.

"I wish I'd given you the bottle of painkillers last night," I said.

"I don't think they would have stayed down." Cal made a graphic facial expression for us.

Thankfully he didn't go into detail. Joanne quickly changed the topic and asked if Cal and Matthew were going back to San Felipe that morning.

"I don't know." Cal shrugged. The boy apparently had no need of plans to jump into this new day wholeheartedly. Had I ever felt that way, even as a child?

When Matthew returned with news that Miguel was much improved, Rosa Lupe offered him more tortillas, but he only took one. I wondered why this compassionate medic wasn't grabbing at the offers for food the way the rest of us were. I suspected he held back not because he was afraid the food wasn't sanitary, but rather because he was reluctant to take from the Valdeparisos' scant supply. He seemed the sort of man who would quietly go without rather than demand his fair share.

As he sat across the table from Joanne, I noticed the intensity of his warm brown eyes. He had to be at least our age or a little older, with the telltale feathery touches of gray hair showing above his ears. I liked the way he was leaning forward slightly, listening to my sister answer his question about where she served in India.

For someone who hadn't washed up or even brushed her hair this morning, Joanne looked lovely. She really did. I concluded that her glow had something to do with the filtered sunlight leaking through the scattered cracks in the cool adobe brick walls. She looked good in early winter light.

"Are you two eager to be on your way to San Felipe?" Matthew asked, automatically repeating his question in Spanish for the benefit of Rosa Lupe and her husband.

"Yes," I answered for both of us, although I wasn't in as great a hurry as I'd been the day before.

"Do you need a ride back to San Felipe?" Joanne asked.

"No, we'll stay a little longer." Matthew went on to explain in both languages that Señor Valdepariso had a truck and was experienced at repairing broken engines. He would drive them back to the stalled Baja bug to see if anything could be done on the spot to fix the car.

Señor Valdepariso nodded and continued to talk, looking at Joanne and me.

Matthew interpreted for us. "He says he has a brother who lives in San Felipe, and if you need anything, he would be honored for you to contact his brother, Juan Valdepariso."

"That's very kind, but we won't be in San Felipe long," Joanne said without providing any details. I was glad because, in the midst of such simplicity and hospitality, it would have sounded arrogant to announce we were the owners of beach-front property.

"Remember his name just in case. Juan Valdepariso. There's a reason for everything, you know," Matthew said.

"I agree." Joanne slipped me a see-someone-agrees-with-me look.

I would have gone along with their shared philosophy, but how does one explain what we had been through in the past twenty-four hours as having some special meaning? A delayed departure from the ship, the return to Ensenada for gas, the stop to watch the sun go down, and then this detour with Matthew and Cal. The course of events seemed far too complicated and random to be part of a divine design.

However, my sister was convinced God was in the midst of dreaming up something special for her. I was merely the "almost twin" who happened to be occupying the same sombrero-of-grace space with her at the moment.

"By the way," Matthew said, turning to me. "I understand you were admiring the beautiful guts last night."

"The what?" I had barely glanced at poor Miguel's broken leg last night. I didn't see any of his guts.

"Apparently you were admiring the night sky and said it was full of 'beautiful entrails.'"

"Oh no!" I covered my face with my hands. "I meant stars. Beautiful stars."

Matthew grinned, and his smile seemed to ignite Joanne's smile. "I think they knew what you meant."

"Good. Now how do I tell her good-bye and make a gracious exit?"

Matthew laughed. "I'm sure you'll figure that out when the time comes."

The time for good-byes came within twenty minutes of my asking. Joanne and I hugged Rosa Lupe as we stood in the full sunlight outside her home. The humble hacienda seemed even more dilapidated in the daylight. I paused to take a firm mental picture of this place and these people. Without a camera, my memory would be my only reminder of this extraordinary moment.

"The señora says that, if you're ever here again, you are welcome to come to her home," Matthew told us. "Her house is your house."

"*Mi casa es su casa,*" Rosa Lupe repeated to us with tears glistening in the corners of her eyes.

"Gracias," Joanne said. "Muchas gracias."

"Sí," I echoed. "Muchas gracias."

I shook Matthew's hand and gave Cal and Señor Valdepariso a wave before slipping into the driver's seat. Joanne was too busy shaking hands to notice that she ended up in shotgun position.

The Jeep's engine started right up, and I rebuked myself for being so critical of our slipshod car rental dealer in Ensenada. At least the lemon yellow beast ran. We could have been stuck in a wheezing Baja bug like Matthew and Cal.

I turned to offer a final wave to our send-off party. With Tom Sawyer charm, Cal placed his dirty hand over his mouth and threw a mock kiss at the two of us in our revved-up Jeep.

Blowing a kiss back at him, I called out, "I hope the rest of your vacation goes great for you and your dad."

Cal's forehead wrinkled. "My dad? He's not my dad; he's my uncle. He doesn't have any family, so he likes to borrow me."

On a crazy whim, I did something that to this day I don't think Joanne believes happened on purpose, but it did. I made the engine stall. All went quiet.

"You're not married?" I asked Matthew without batting an eyelash.

"No."

"Aunt Caroline died when I was a baby," Cal volunteered. "She was my mom's sister, just like you two are sisters."

"Is that right," I said without moving from my position. I

knew I was blocking Joanne's view of Matthew. The only thing I regretted at that moment was that I couldn't see my sister's face.

Señora Valdepariso said something to Matthew and pointed to a thin silver band on her finger. Then she pointed to me.

"The señora wants to know if both of you are married," Matthew interpreted.

"I am," I said quickly, feeling like Rosa Lupe was right there with me in this spontaneous matchmaking scheme. "But Joanne is available."

My sister pinched the underside of my upper arm with such a vengeance I knew I'd have a bruise for a month.

"Start the car," she growled, reaching for the key in the ignition.

The second thing I later regretted was that Joanne was so embarrassed and so determined to get out of there that she didn't see what I saw. The look on Matthew's face was priceless. The man was delightfully intrigued, and I knew it.

Unfortunately, Joanne didn't. She turned the key in the ignition, and the Jeep roared back to business, ready to hit the road. Everyone waved as I turned the Jeep around and headed down the bumpy dirt trail.

Everyone but Matthew.

He stood there, his startled expression frozen. I watched him in the rearview mirror.

"Why did you do that?" Joanne squawked.

"Turn around," I told her.

"Why?"

"Just do it. Turn around. Wave one more time."

This was the wrong moment for my usually pliable sister to adopt my stubborn characteristics.

"No," she said. "Keep driving."

"But, Joanne, you have to see his face."

"I've seen his face."

"Not looking like this, you haven't."

"Keep driving, Melanie. I'm too angry to talk to you right now."

"Please, Jo. Before it's too late. Turn and look at him."

She would not.

We endured the horrible ruts in dismal silence, feeling every jolt with already sore muscles. The route back to the highway seemed twice as long in the daylight as it had in the night. I used the rumbling ride to review what had just happened and to evaluate whether I had done the right thing in promoting Joanne the way I had.

A memory from summer camp came back to me with the bumps. The last night of camp all the girls in our cabin had "dates" to the final banquet except Joanne. A "date" simply meant that one of the boys from the camp had worked up the nerve to ask if he could sit by you at dinner. All the girls took showers and wore their one nice, clean outfit instead of grubby jeans to the "banquet."

I had secured a date by Thursday afternoon at archery

practice and had focused all my efforts after that on finding someone—anyone—to ask Joanne so that we could all sit at the same table together.

From the previous year at camp, I knew that all the girls who didn't have dates ended up at the table in the back of the dining hall across from the table with all the boys who hadn't showered all week and still thought girls had cooties.

In my desire to spare my sister the humiliation of being relegated to the back of the banquet hall, I went all out to solicit a date for her. All the really cool guys were already spoken for, but in my campaign, I'd inadvertently made it clear to all those cool guys that my sister was desperate. Or at least that's how she framed it for years afterward.

By Friday afternoon I'd managed to fix her up with the shyest guy at the camp. Two of his friends had to do the asking on his behalf. My mission was accomplished, so I was happy.

My sister, however, was not.

Joanne sat with us at the popular table beside a tall, slender, shy boy who didn't say one word to her the entire time. The cute and popular guys teased Joanne's date as their evening entertainment, and to my sister's way of thinking, all of this was much more humiliating than being relegated to the all-girl table. At least at the "leftover" table, someone would have spoken to her, and she wouldn't have felt the pity of all the cute guys, who now knew she wasn't capable of stirring up any admirers on her own.

Just about the time the Jeep connected with the main road,

my clueless brain connected with the fact that I had embarrassed my sister all over again.

"Joanne," I spoke above the sound of the wind coming at us. "I'm sorry. I shouldn't have done that. I didn't mean to embarrass you. I apologize. Really. I'm sorry."

For a moment Joanne didn't move. She was looking straight ahead at the two-lane road. She reached over and rubbed the back of my upper arm. "Sorry about the welt you're going to get there."

"That's okay. All my welts from the allergic reaction have gone away, so I guess I needed one more." I intended my comment to be funny, but instead of smiling at my joke, Joanne cried.

"You okay?" I glanced at her and then back at the road.

"I will be." Turning away from me, my sister went into a quiet place inside herself and didn't invite me to come along.

Twelve

The first thing I noticed when we were less than a kilometer outside of San Felipe was all the motor homes that seemed to have appeared out of nowhere. Joanne was driving now. We hadn't talked much during the past hour or so while traversing the desert on the winding road that lowered us into view of the spectacular coastal waters of the Sea of Cortez. The bright blue of the water and crisp white of the beach contrasted sharply with the muted grays and browns we had been viewing since we left Ensenada.

"Where should we go first?" Joanne asked.

"A gas station," I suggested.

"Good idea. We're almost out of gas."

I hadn't been concerned about filling up our tank as much as I was eager to use the facilities. If this sleepy town had any running water at the gas station—even from a spigot—I was going to wash my face and hands thoroughly and cool off the back of my neck.

By my watch it was nearly ten o'clock. The dust from the road and the sun in our faces, along with a mouthful of unbrushed teeth, made me feel grungier than I remembered ever feeling in my life.

Joanne pulled into the first Pemex station we saw. While she communicated with the attendant in English, I made use of the less-than-premium facilities. At least the black-encrusted sink had running water. I was learning to be thankful for little things. But I was careful not to drink any of the water, even the drops that lingered on my lips.

Our next stop was at an organized and fairly modern grocery store. We stocked up on food for our stay at Uncle Harlan's and on bottled water that was outrageously expensive but obviously a tourist favorite because of the label "Bottled in California." The water could have come from a garden hose on the other side of Tijuana, but Joanne and I fell for the marketing ploy and bought two cases.

Loading our abundance in the back of the Jeep, I noticed something significant as I lifted our straw sombreros and handed one to my sister.

"Joanne, where is our luggage?" I pictured us spending the rest of the week in our already sweaty T-shirts, dirt-streaked jeans, and the outlandishly floppy sombreros.

"I thought I told you." Joanne contentedly plopped her sombrero on her head. "I paid the guy at the gas station to keep our suitcases safe for us inside his office. I knew we'd be driving around town, and I didn't want to tote our luggage inside the bank."

"We didn't think this through." I let out a sigh and tightened my sombrero's string under my chin. "Since we can't lock up this vehicle, what are we going to do? We shouldn't have bought all this food yet."

"There's nothing perishable."

"I know, but we can't park the car and leave it all, can we?"

"Let's find Uncle Harlan's house and leave everything there, and then go to the bank," Joanne said. I noticed she was beginning to look "normal" in her sombrero, now that I'd seen her in it for nearly an entire day.

"We can't go to Uncle Harlan's first," I said. "The bank has the key to let us in."

"So we ask our guardian angels to keep an eye on the food while we're in the bank, then we pick up our luggage, and take all of it to Harlan's." Joanne twisted the top off a bottle of water and held it out to me.

"What? You want to see if I die when I drink it?"

"No, you paranoid petunia! I was trying to be polite."

"Oh. Thanks."

Joanne twisted off the lid on another bottle and took a long swig just to prove she was fearless or something. She came up coughing, and I paused before placing my lips to the bottle in my hand.

Her hand flew to her throat, and her eyes widened as she

gasped for air. Then, just as quickly, she straightened up and said, "Just kidding!"

A wild smile returned to Joanne's face for the first time since we had left the Valdeparisos' casa that morning. "I'm just giving you a hard time," she said with a ripple of giggles. The air around us filled with Joanne's huge laugh.

"You brat." I squeezed my water bottle so that a straight stream of the precious commodity zipped through the two feet of warm air that separated us. My aim was perfect. The water doused my sister's dust-caked cheek.

"Hey, don't start anything you can't finish." She squirted me back.

The shot of water from her bottle felt heavenly as it ran down my chin and neck.

"Oh, I can finish this all right. I have plenty of ammo." I squirted my laughing sibling with a stream that landed in her mouth.

Now she really was choking. That didn't stop her from squirting me again. This time she stuck the neck of the bottle down the back of my shirt and emptied the contents.

I did the same to her, laughing and threatening to reload with another bottle.

Joanne paused, looking over my shoulder. I turned my head to follow her line of sight. We had a small audience watching our water ballet. Two weathered-looking fishermen stood in the shade along with a distinguished gentleman wearing a dark business suit. They were grinning and speaking

Spanish; one of them pointed to Joanne.

"Come on." I reached for another bottle of water—this time to drink it. "We can finish this later. Without an audience."

Joanne pulled the car keys from her pocket and swung into the driver's seat with a gleam in her eye. "I'll hold you to that."

Backing up the Jeep, Joanne nearly collided with an off-road motorcycle that was going far too fast. The helmeted driver halted and motioned for us to go first. "I had no idea this was such a recreational destination, did you?" Joanne asked.

"No, San Felipe is a lot bigger than I thought it was going to be."

"And more spread out. I'm sure it wasn't much when Uncle Harlan first built his place in the sixties."

"I've been thinking about that. Joanne, what do you think his house looks like?"

"I don't think it's going to be very large. But you know how he and Aunt Winnie always have lived with the finest of everything. I'm thinking it's simple but elegant."

"That's what I thought at first, but now I'm not so sure. What if it's a little nothing place?" I asked. "Then what do we do?"

Joanne turned to look at me and then focused back on the traffic at the upcoming intersection. Clearly she never had considered that bleak possibility.

"We'll figure that out when we get there. I think it's going to be run-down and old, but it seemed to me the lawyer made it sound like something of value."

"I don't doubt the land is of value, especially since the area obviously is a growing tourist attraction. But don't we only lease the land from the Mexican government? It's not as if we can sell the land."

"Like I said, Mel, we'll figure that out when we get there. First, let's retrieve our luggage, go to the bank, pick up the key and directions, and see what we see. We'll know soon enough what we've inherited."

"I thought we were going to go to the bank first and *then* pick up our luggage." I felt perturbed that Joanne was messing up a perfectly good plan by switching the order of things—without conferring with me.

"I just realized we have no idea where the bank is, and the guy at the gas station spoke English. We might as well pick up the luggage now. Then one of us can stay in the car while the other goes into the bank."

It took everything within me not to open our suitcases inside the gas station office and do a careful inventory to make sure nothing had been touched. Joanne was much more trusting as usual and handed over several dollars to the attendant. He seemed grateful.

"Can you tell us how to get to this bank?" Joanne held up her copy of the official letter Aunt Winnie received last week and pointed to the letterhead.

The attendant seemed to study the paper a little too long in my estimation. Reaching over and snatching the paper, I read the name of the bank for him. "El Banco del Sol."

He spoke a few words of English and pointed the direction we had just come.

"Thanks." I nudged Joanne to move toward the car.

"Stop being so pushy," she said, when she pulled out of the gas station.

"He was reading the letter. I don't think we should let strangers know what we're doing here."

"Okay, fine. But you can be polite about it." Joanne drove past the grocery store, and a block later we spotted the bank. "How do you want to do this?" she asked.

"I'll go in with the letter and see if I can speak with the bank president. You don't mind being the one who waits in the car, do you?"

"No. Make sure you get a good map to the property and the key."

"I know." I started toward the front door of the bank and then stopped and turned around, realizing I might be taken a little more seriously if I weren't wearing a sombrero. Combing back my disarrayed hair with my dirty fingers, I said, "I wish I wasn't such a mess. The bank president isn't going to take me seriously."

"You can change if you think you need to, but—"

"Good idea." I got back in the Jeep and forced my sister to drive to the Pemex station, where I went into the despicable restroom and changed into my nice pants and a crumpled but clean blouse. I flipped my eyelashes a few times with a mascara wand and applied some lipstick. The whole process seemed ludicrous, but if Joanne and I were to be taken seriously as landowners, at least one of us should look the part.

"Ready?" Joanne asked when I climbed back into the Jeep.

"Yep. Drive slow so my hair won't flip out."

"Mel, your hair is—"

I shot her an evil eye, and she hushed up. She knew better than to make any comments about my hair or ears or any other of our "almost twin" features on sixth-grade-picture day or on going-to-meet-the-Mexican-bank-president day.

With renewed confidence I entered the bank holding the all-important letter. I walked up to a young woman who sat at what looked like a receptionist's desk.

"Pardon me. Do you speak English?"

"Yes."

"I need to speak with the bank president."

She nodded and walked to a large desk in the back corner. A gentleman rose and followed her to where I stood waiting.

With my best posture and my rehearsed lines ready, I greeted him with a cordial nod and offered my hand to shake. "My name is Melanie Holmquist. Your bank sent a letter to my aunt Winifred Clayton regarding some property owned by my deceased uncle Harlan Clayton. I'm here to process the necessary paperwork."

The man in the dark suit tilted his head and looked at me more closely. He then looked over my shoulder and seemed to be studying Joanne in the Jeep parked in front of the bank window.

A smile brightened his face. "The women with the water fight. I was going to place a bet on your friend."

Caught off guard, I stammered, "She's not my friend; she's my sister." All my efforts to appear professional were pointless.

"Won't you and your sister please come sit at my desk?"

"We have all our things in the car," I stammered once more.

He waited for a further explanation.

"We're not able to lock the car. Our clothes and food would be left out in the open if Joanne came in."

His expression changed. Apparently I had offended him by assuming that we might be robbed. With crisp words he said, "I will ask my guard to keep careful watch on your belongings."

I felt reprimanded. We still had business to transact, but my ability to impress him with my tidy appearance or my organized speech was nil at this point. He was no longer charmed to be talking to the woman who fearlessly participated in a water fight in front of the grocery store.

We walked together toward the front door, which he held open for me. As he spoke with the uniformed, armed employee seated by the front door, I called to Joanne to come inside.

My sister left her sombrero on the front seat and managed, despite all her scruffiness, to pick up the conversation where I had exploded a land mine with my distrust. I felt humbled. It was a different sort of humbling than I'd felt at the adobe house last night. This humility was the kind that reveals the truth about one's deepest and most unpleasant qualities, yet doesn't make the effort to cover those foibles with an excuse. I felt as if I'd slipped out from under that sombrero of grace and found the elements were merciless.

"I'm Joanne Clayton," she said, shaking his hand. I don't think she realized that across her cheek, where I'd first squirted the water, she now had a streak of clean skin while the rest of her cheek still was covered with dirt.

"Please come sit at my desk."

For the next twenty-five minutes, Joanne pretty much single-handedly managed the transaction. We were given the key inside a manila envelope, a hand-drawn map, and a stack of papers to sign, which we did in the presence of the notary who sat at the receptionist's desk. It was all surprisingly simple. We walked out of the bank the legal owners of Uncle Harlan's beach house. Or at least we were the legal beneficiaries because the bank was the holder of the title on all coastal properties held in trust by a Mexican bank.

"Would you like us to mail to you the final documents?" Señor Campaña, the bank president, asked.

"Do you mean this isn't everything?" I held up a small stack of signed forms.

"Now you must have the official release form from the government."

"How long will that take to get?" Joanne asked.

"Sometimes weeks. Sometimes a few days."

"We'll be here through Friday," I said.

"Come back Friday," he advised. "I will see what I can do."

"Piece of cake," Joanne said, as we exited the bank.

"It was pretty easy," I agreed. "If nothing else, we now have all the papers with us. I'm sure we can have them translated into English through Aunt Winnie's lawyer, and he can tell us if anything is missing."

"No, I'm saying I'm ready to celebrate with a piece of cake."

"We don't have any more chocolate cake. We left it with Rosa Lupe."

"Then let's find some."

"Now?"

"Sure. I saw a bakery back there. Let's buy something to take with us to the house."

We took our newly established positions in the car. Joanne was the driver, and I was the one with the map who gave directions. Joanne's side of our power-balance teeter-totter was up at the moment.

"Why were you so uptight when I first came into the bank?" Joanne asked.

I told her my foible of assuming our things would be stolen.

"I thought Señor Campaña was a nice man."

"Yes, well, he told me he was going to bet on you in our water fight."

"Did he really? Smart man. Now I know why I trusted him."

"He would have lost his bet," I said. "Turn left on Puerto Lobos."

"You wish," Joanne teased. "What do I do after I turn on Lobos?"

"Puerto Lobos," I corrected her. "And I would have taken you in a snap. Follow Puerto Lobos to the ocean and then left again on Ave Mar de Cortez."

"You would have taken me in a snap. Ha! That's something I'd like to see." Joanne grinned at the thought as she drove slowly past a mix of old and new in this curious town.

Small cantinas lined one part of the street where old men sat outside on chairs in the shade. It looked as if they were doing the same thing their grandfathers had done and were sitting in the same chairs their grandfathers had sat in. Yet, two blocks farther down the street, a bright, modern video rental store sported posters of the latest releases direct from Hollywood. Next to the video store was a newly landscaped park area complete with a fountain and bright tiles. It was a surprising combination of the past and present.

"Is that the bakery you saw earlier?" I asked.

"No, but it's definitely a bakery. Let's stop there."

We parked in front of a small shop that advertised *pasteles* in the window.

"I wonder what that means?" I said. "Do you suppose you can order your treats in pastel colors or something?"

"It's probably the Spanish word for 'pastries.'"

"Good thinking. Are you ready?"

"You go ahead," Joanne said. "I'll wait with the Jeep."

"But you're the one who wanted the cake. Shouldn't you be the one to pick out what you want?"

Joanne laughed.

"What's so funny?"

"Are you nervous about going in by yourself?"

"What if I am?"

"Listen, Mel, just because the bank meeting got off to a lumpy start, doesn't mean you'll have problems grabbing a cake for us."

"You're the one figuring out what the Spanish words mean. Like pasteles. I thought it had to do with color, but you figured out it was pastries. You'll figure out what to order in there. All the signs are going to be in Spanish, you know."

Joanne tapped her finger on the steering wheel. "Should we toss a coin to see who goes in?"

"No, I think you should go. You're the oldest."

Joanne really laughed at that one. "Oh, right, as if that has ever made any difference!"

"Come on." I used my best little-sister whine. "You got to wait in the car last time. It's my turn to sit this one out."

"You are such a baby." Joanne pushed open the Jeep door. "I can't believe you always get your way."

"Me!? Always get my way? You were the one who said you wanted cake!"

Joanne paused, blinked, and seemed to have no comeback. "Well, so I did. And here we are. In front of a bakery. Imagine that. I guess I'll go buy a cake."

I shook my head as she pranced into the store, chin held high.

A few yards away I spotted what looked like a rubbish bin and decided to throw away our empty water bottles. Getting out of the Jeep, I noticed a half-filled beer bottle sitting upright only inches from the back tire.

That probably explains why Joanne pulled into this spot at such a crazy angle. I might as well throw it away before we back over it. The last thing we need is a flat tire!

With all the bottles in hand, I headed toward the bin. A uniformed police officer stepped out of what looked like a barbershop, and with his hands resting on his wide belt, he spoke to me in Spanish.

I offered a congenial smile and nodded.

He's probably thanking me for cleaning up the streets a little.

"Just tidying up." I held up the bottles as he stepped closer.

He asked me something, and I returned a blank look. Reaching for the beer bottle, he shook it as if to verify it wasn't empty.

"It's not mine. It was over there on the street by our Jeep. I didn't want to back over it."

Does he think I was drinking the beer?

I vaguely remembered a warning the cruise personnel had issued when we took the shuttle into Ensenada. Joanne and I were still in a state of stunned silence because of the trauma with the toddler, but something was said about it being illegal to possess an open beer bottle on Ensenada's sidewalks. Did that law apply in San Felipe as well?

"It's not mine," I stated emphatically, pointing again to the Jeep. "I found it in the street."

With all the compassion of a stone, the officer reached for his handcuffs as he spoke to me in Spanish.

"No, no! You don't understand! I didn't do anything. I was just cleaning up. That's what I do best."

He held the handcuffs to the side and kept talking to me, his chin motioning toward the Jeep.

"Do you want to inspect the Jeep? Is that it? Are you asking if I have any more beer? Because I don't. It's just water. Do you want to see? You can come look. Let me just throw these bottles away over here and—"

As I took two steps away from him, he yelled something.

"Okay. I won't go anywhere. I'll just stand here. My sister is right over there, in the bakery, getting cake." I tried the only Spanish word I could think of. "Pastels. She's buying pastels."

"¿Pasteles?" he asked.

"Sí, pasteles."

Just then Joanne stepped out of the bakery, and from my throat came a terrified sounding, "Jo-anne! Over here! Come quick!"

Thirteen

My startled sister hurried over, carrying a thin cardboard box.

"Everything okay?" She looked at me and then at the officer.

"He thinks I was drinking. But that's not my bottle of beer. I was trying to clean up the street."

"She does that," Joanne said to the officer with a smile. "She likes things to be organized."

He wasn't impressed. The handcuffs made an irritating clinking as he slowly moved them from side to side. His eyes were fixed on the pastry box Joanne was holding.

"¿Pasteles?" He put down the beer bottle.

"Yes," Joanne said proudly. "I bought two dancing ladies and some sort of coconut cream cake, I think. It looked good, but the woman at the bakery couldn't tell me what it was."

Joanne turned to me. "The woman in the bakery spoke English. You should have gone in."

I couldn't believe Joanne was being so flippant and friendly with this guy. Opening the lid to the cake box, she nodded for the officer to look inside.

"Does that look like white cake to you? Or is it coconut?"

"He doesn't speak English," I whispered to Joanne. "I think he's threatening to arrest me."

"For throwing away rubbish?"

"No, I think because the beer bottle wasn't empty. Remember what they told us on the shuttle in Ensenada?"

Joanne looked confused. I doubted she remembered much of those announcements.

"Hey," Joanne said, as the officer reached into the box and lifted out the coconut covered piece of cake. "I meant for you to identify it for me, not take it."

An ancient system had gone into play between the officer and the two of us.

"No, that's okay." I quickly nodded at the Federale. "You can have that."

He returned his handcuffs to his belt loop, and with a satisfied expression took a big bite of the cake.

"I see how it is." Joanne closed the lid on the box. "Come on, let's leave while we still have our dancing ladies."

I had no idea what Joanne was talking about, but I remembered Aunt Winnie saying something on the phone the morning I left about eating a dancing lady for her. Apparently dancing ladies were a Mexican pastry.

To be on the safe side, I didn't throw away my empty water

bottles in case a law existed about not recycling plastic. I made Joanne cross at the corner so we wouldn't be jaywalking. We had just climbed into the Jeep, with me driving this time, when the officer called out to us. He was slowly coming across the street.

"Do you have any more money on you?" I asked Joanne.

"Yes, but I am not going to give that man cash for a bribe or a payoff or whatever you're suggesting. You're the one who always is standing up for justice and saying the world isn't fair. I can't believe you want to pay off this guy."

"I don't. I was asking if you had more money to buy a couple of pastries in case he wants to eat ours."

Joanne shook her head as we watched him approach. "It's still not fair."

The officer walked around the vehicle and seemed to be pointing out that we weren't lined up in the assigned parking space.

"I was trying not to run over the bottle of beer," Joanne said plainly.

Moving to the back of our Jeep, he patted the Mexican blanket that covered our groceries and gave a chin-up gesture asking, I assumed, something along the lines of, "What are you hiding under here?"

"Bottles of water," Joanne said with a slice to her words. "Are you thirsty now?"

He pulled back the blanket and helped himself to one of the bottles, holding it up as if to make sure we weren't smuggling vodka into the country.

"You're welcome to have that." I reached over and gave Joanne a nudge.

"That's right. Help yourself." Lowering her voice she added, "We know you will anyway."

He was satisfied with two bottles of water—apparently the going rate for parking crooked on this side of town.

"Adios," he said to us and waved us clear.

I backed up slowly as Joanne firmly held the pastry box in her lap. "Men like that...," she muttered under her breath.

"Hey, relax. It's okay. He didn't haul me off to jail. We have plenty of water. And you bought an extra piece of cake anyhow, right?"

Joanne's expression didn't uncloud. She was acting like me. I tried to remember all the wise things she had said to me in moments like this.

"There were so many like him in India." Joanne spoke through still-clenched teeth. "Those young girls would come to us and..." She couldn't finish her sentence.

I knew the medical team Joanne worked with specialized in restoring young women who were victims of slavery, specifically girls who had been sold into prostitution. Her prayer support letters had contained sanitized versions of the horrible injustices done to girls as young as nine years old, when they were sold by their parents into a life of abuse.

The intensity of what Joanne must have experienced over there never had connected to anything I could relate to. My daughters were safe. I was safe. Joanne was a saint. That's how I saw it. I preferred to stay sheltered and not to hear any specifics of her experiences, even after she came home, and we started our routine phone calls.

"You've seen a lot of injustice, haven't you?"

Joanne nodded. "Come on, let's get out of here."

I drove back the way we had come and turned on the street I remembered seeing listed on the map. "Now what?" I asked Joanne. "Can you pull out that paper and tell me where we turn next?"

"It looks like you keep heading toward the beach. We're looking for a short road called Mar Vista. When you reach Mar Vista, turn right, and it should be right there. On the beach, I guess."

"I'm getting excited," I said. "Are you?"

"I guess I am. It's like going after treasure in some ways. We're closer, but we still don't know what we're going to find."

"Didn't Señor Campaña at the bank say it would be easy to sell the house, if we didn't want to keep it?"

"Yes, I noticed that little comment, too. The key, I think, would be to find someone other than the bank to buy it."

"Of course, we might want to keep it," I commented, thinking of a lovely, tile-roofed house sitting on the sand next to the ocean like a fat hen settled into her nest.

I turned right on Mar Vista and stopped the Jeep. Before us stretched hundreds of yards of perfect, white sand broken only by an occasional palm tree that clung to a stretch of land close to the undeveloped road. Behind us were two spacious homes that looked as if they had been built only recently. In front of one house sat a shiny new pickup truck with a dune buggy attached to a trailer. The other house looked as if it was still under construction. Neither of those could have been Uncle Harlan's. But they looked like the beautiful start of an upscale neighborhood.

"So where's the house?" I looked at the map.

"I guess we have to go down this road a little farther," Joanne said.

The road wasn't paved, but that didn't surprise us. Clumps of some sort of overgrown beach grass sprouted to our left. Shooting up from the center was a single, rather spectacular palm tree.

I smiled. "It's over there. That's Uncle Harlan's palm tree. Do you remember? From the photo?"

"I see jungle-style weeds and a palm tree, but where's the house?"

"Let's find out." I drove a quarter of a mile to the left, parallel with the beach.

Then the dwelling came into plain view. I stopped the Jeep so we could take in the full ambience of our newly inherited beachfront property.

"It's...a...trailer," Joanne said slowly. "A sci-fi-style silver trailer."

"I think they called them Airstreams." I turned off the engine and got out. "You coming?"

Joanne, the normally buoyant one, sat with her two dancing ladies balanced in the box on her lap and chewed on her lower lip.

"I've never seen wrought iron bars on trailer windows before," she said. "Have you?"

"Uncle Harlan was clever. We'll give him that. Come on. I have the key here. Let's see what's inside."

"Why? Can't we sell it as is?"

"Without looking inside? It could be wonderful. Airstreams are retro, and retro is in. Where's your sense of adventure, Joanne? This is too bizarre. I'm turning into you, and you're turning into me. How did that happen?"

"Let me hold the key." Joanne got out of the Jeep but still held the pastry box under her arm.

"Why do you want the key?"

"I just do. Let me open the door."

"Why?"

"Okay, you know what? Never mind. You open the door. Go ahead. You do it."

I stood there staring at my discombobulated sister, trying to figure out what was going on in that head of hers.

"Here." I held out the key. "You open the door."

She looked at the key, blinked, put the dancing ladies on the hood of the Jeep, and took the key from me.

Neither of us spoke as we stepped onto the large cement slab that formed the front patio area as well as the solid foundation for the silver trailer. The meshed lattice covering over the patio was in need of repair, but it was easy to imagine that at one time it had provided lovely shade.

A large lock ingeniously blocked the front door's keyhole.

"Oh, great," Joanne said. "We only have one key."

"Try it on the padlock."

It worked. We exchanged thrilled glances. It felt as if we were unbolting a weathered lock on a forgotten treasure chest.

"Here." Joanne handed over the key. "You try the door's lock."

I tried to insert the same key into the front door, but it was too large. Our hopes sank.

"We don't have another key." I tried again. "This one is too big."

Joanne took the key from me and tried it upside down. No good. "Why would Uncle Harlan do this?"

"Who knows? We can go back to town and find a locksmith or check back at the bank to see if we missed any additional envelopes."

"Did you look through all the paperwork?" Joanne asked. "Maybe a second key was taped to one of the papers."

"I don't think so, but I'll look." I went back to the Jeep and pulled out a bottle of water. "You want one, Joanne?"

"Yes, please."

I brought the water, the pastries, and the official papers.

"We can't celebrate with our pastries, yet," Joanne said. "We're locked out."

"So? We're here. We made it all the way to Ensenada and all the way from Ensenada to San Felipe. We got to the bank, we signed all the papers, narrowly escaped imprisonment, and now we're here. We made it, Joanne. That fact, in and of itself, is worth celebrating, don't you think?"

"You're right."

Joanne and I sat together on the dirty cement slab in front of the door. First we looked through all the papers and the manila envelope. No extra key popped out. With resignation we opened the pastry box and lifted out the two slightly drooping dancing ladies.

"Why do you suppose these are called dancing ladies?" I held up the cream-puff type of dessert.

"Don't you see it? This puffy part on the bottom is like the twirling skirt, the creamy stuff is the lady, and this smaller top slice of pastry is her head."

"Or maybe it's her hat," I suggested.

"Her sombrero," Joanne said with a faint chuckle. "These are little Sisterchicks in sombreros."

"That's better than being a couple of Sisterchicks in the slammer, like we almost were!"

"Here's to being a couple of free birds." Joanne held up her pastry as a toast so we could "clink" the dough skirts and say "cheers."

"You're sure calm about all this," Joanne said.

"We accomplished something; we made it here. That feels like a huge step."

"We aren't inside yet."

"So? We'll figure it out." I wiped my cream-tinged fingers

on the side of the pastry box in lieu of a napkin. "Why do you suppose Uncle Harlan would put that massive lock on the door so it covered the normal lock?"

Joanne thought a moment, her tongue reaching for a dot of pastry flake that had stuck to her top lip like a snowflake. "I have no idea. Should we call Aunt Winnie?"

"She only came here one time. I doubt she would know."

"Only one time?"

I nodded. "Yup, only one time."

Like a watchdog waking at the slightest sound of a snapped twig, Joanne sat up straight and looked at me. "One time," she repeated. "That's it! Uncle Harlan put that big lock on there so it would be secure, but he'd only have to unlock the door one time."

She hopped up and tried the door handle. Her theory worked; the door opened.

"You're a genius, Jo!"

We stood back as the stale air escaped the hollowed-out silver bullet.

"All I needed was a little brain food." She laughed. "Are you sure we're ready to venture into the unknown?"

"Last one in is a crybaby." I took the single step up into the trailer. The first sight that caught my eye made me scream and jump back. I bumped into Joanne, who was on her way in.

"What is it?"

"I thought it was a person, but now I'm not so sure." My hand flew to my chest. "Look!"

Joanne stood behind me with her hands on my shoulders, gazing at the long figure "sitting" on the sofa, "wearing" a fishing hat, and "reading" the newspaper.

"What in the world is that?" Joanne asked. "It almost looks like a fish."

I burst out laughing and tilted my head to get a better view of the long-nosed, four-foot-long, shimmering blue-scaled fish.

"I can't believe it! Uncle Harlan's marlin!"

"Uncle Harlan's what?"

"His fish! Aunt Winnie told me about this creature. They argued about this fish for years. I thought it was mounted on a piece of wood. I didn't know it hung around like a stuffed member of the family."

"Uncle Harlan's marlin." Joanne slowly walked over and touched the well-preserved dummy. "We have very strange relatives, Melanie. Does that concern you the way it concerns me?"

"All the time."

I slid past the mannequin fish and opened the screened windows to allow some air to flow through the wrought iron burglar protection bars. "Open those windows in the front, will you?"

"Did you see this furniture?" Joanne leaned over to pull back the curtains and open the slatted windows. "This is leather. I don't think this was standard issue for these trailers."

"It isn't as dirty in here as I thought it would be." I opened the final window. The fresh air and light gave the space a surprising sense of livability for such confined quarters. "This is really nice."

"For a trailer," Joanne reminded me.

"I know. I thought it would be worse."

"So did I." Joanne stood in front of the great marlin, as if examining a work of art in a museum. "Uncle Harlan poked this guy's swordfish nose through the top of the hat. Did you see that?"

"How did he attach the newspaper?"

"You have to see this. I think it's a coat hanger. Look at how it's looped around here. Is that ingenious or what?"

"There might be other words for such manifestations of creativity." I looked for the date on the newspaper. "Like you said, we have very strange relatives. Look at this date, 1992. I'm surprised the paper didn't disintegrate."

"It feels as if we stepped inside a time capsule." Joanne reached for a framed color photograph on one of the built-in shelves. "Look, it's Aunt Winnie. She was so young! Check out those sunglasses. If the points stuck out the sides any farther, she'd have birds landing on them as a perch!"

I laughed. "Pink, even. Aunt Winnie, you were all class in your day. I want to know where she found the hot pink lipstick to match the glasses. We're definitely taking that picture back with us."

Joanne looked at me. "Is that what you're thinking? We should dismantle the place, take home whatever we can salvage, and sell the trailer?"

"I hadn't gone that far in my thinking, but you tell me. What would we do with this place?"

Joanne looked around. "I don't know. Let's bring the groceries in out of the sun and think about it. We have a couple of days to mull it over."

As she headed down the steps, she called over her shoulder, "Did you catch this view? I mean, really? This is incredible. It's like the cover of a travel magazine."

I joined Joanne at the door and gazed at the rolled-out white sand that stretched like an elegant rug between the turquoise waters and us. The radiant blue sky that met the sea was a different hue, but they blended perfectly at the horizon where a seamless line separated heaven from earth. A single fishing boat bobbed in the calm bay.

"I could live here," Joanne said.

"It's December," I reminded her. "How much heat do you like?"

"I've lived through my share of sweltering heat waves and drenching monsoons. I like it here. This is a nice place."

"Yes, it is." I followed Joanne to the Jeep where we began to unload our goods. The design of Uncle Harlan's little alcove began to make sense. He had built a wall around the sides and back of the trailer with some sort of large cement blocks that formed an embankment. On top of the embankment, he'd planted the hearty grasses that rose high enough to partially conceal the back side of the trailer from the nearest main road. The design undoubtedly had deterred many potential intruders from knowing the trailer was there. I felt fairly isolated and safer than if we were sitting out in plain view.

The ingenuity of his plan was that once you were in the trailer or on the front patio, the entire bay seemed to belong to you. I paused under the towering palm tree and looked up, smiling. Joanne stopped beside me with a bag of groceries in each hand and said, "Now all we need is a hammock."

"That's what Aunt Winnie said about this palm tree. Uncle Harlan planted it so he could string up his hammock. But we need two palm trees."

"No we don't. Do you see the hook?" Joanne nodded at a huge eyebolt that protruded from the trailer's end. The distance from the bolt to the palm tree seemed just far enough to comfortably hang a hammock. Or at least a clothesline. The beauty of the potential hammock location was that for part of the day the trailer provided shade and part of the day the palm tree provided shade.

"Clever Harlan," I said. "His recurring theme seems to be, 'why use two when one will do?'"

"Yes, clever Harlan and his dancing marlin. Why have two stuffed fish when one is all you need to frighten away bandidos? He could have taken his show on the road. Although the marlin's wardrobe would have taken up at least several steamer trunks, and that would have been hard on Harlan's back, since I would guess that the marlin was reluctant to help carry any of the luggage."

I laughed and gave my head a shake. Joanne didn't need

much encouragement for her imagination to ignite its quirky fuse. "Now I know where you get it," I said, carrying the rest of our supplies into the trailer.

"Get what?"

"Your wit."

"Get what wit?"

Joanne said it so fast, and the 'get-what-wit' line came out so funny, that we both paused the same exact three seconds and then burst into laughter. I had to put down the groceries and place a supportive arm across my stomach while the tears rolled down my face. The insanity of all this was catching up with us.

"We have to move Mr. Marlin," Joanne said between her chortles. "Look at him, Mel. He's giving me the evil eye."

"He only has one eye," I spurted.

"Well, it's an evil one. I don't trust him. He's gotta go."

"Where?"

Joanne looked around the confined quarters. "How about back to sea? It'll be the sequel to *Free Willy*. You and I will free marlin, and they'll make a movie about us. Or," Joanne continued, wiping away her laughter tears with the back of her hand. "We could put up a sign at the road that says, 'Free Marlin,' and someone can come and take him away for us."

I held up my hand to stop her so I could catch my breath. "We can't set the old guy free."

"Why not?"

"Aunt Winnie wants him back. She wants the fish."

"Why? I thought you said the fish made them fight."

"It did."

"Well, I can't imagine *why!*" Joanne said with fresh sarcasm that started us on another laughing jag.

"All I know is that the last thing Aunt Winnie said to me right before I left was, 'Melanie, I want that fish. I want you to get my Harlan's fish and bring it back to me.'"

Joanne opened her mouth and her eyes wide. "Melanie, you sounded exactly like her! Don't do that again! That was frightening!"

We sniffed together and caught our breath. I leaned against the counter. "Ahh, the wonders of heredity."

"No joke," Joanne said. "So, what do we do with the fish?"

"Ignore him. At least for now."

"I don't think that if we ignore him his feelings will be hurt sufficiently for him to go away."

"We can cover him with a blanket," I suggested.

Joanne reached for one of our Mexican blankets. Instead of draping it over him, she treated the fish like a big doll, laying him on his side on the couch and tucking him in with the blanket.

I probably would have laughed again, but something about Joanne's actions was endearing. They were tender, motherly, and nurselike.

In typical sisterly fashion, we set to work side by side, unpacking our groceries and examining the contents of each of the cupboards and drawers. I thought I scored when I found a broom to sweep off the patio. But Joanne trumped me when she found the deluxe-size hammock made from thick, unbreakable nylon cords.

She was quite proud of herself and went right outside to set up Uncle Harlan's hammock. It worked like a honeybee, and Joanne called for me to come see her once she had managed to clamber into the swinging contraption.

"Now, *that* looks like it was worth the drive from Ensenada," I said.

"You know it." Joanne stretched out her arms behind her head and swayed back and forth with her legs crossed at the ankles. "I think I'll sleep out here tonight."

"I wish I had a camera," I said. "Aunt Winnie has to see how Harlan's palm tree sprouted and how relaxed you look in his little paradise."

"If you had a camera, I'd take a picture of you right now, too. You know this is your childhood dream come true."

"Why do you say that?" I leaned on the broom's handle.

"Your favorite books, remember? The Boxcar Children. You are now the owner of a shiny silver boxcar, and you can set up house to your heart's content. All you need is a little dump where you can dig up a chipped cup, and some berry bushes so you can harvest our dinner."

For a moment I considered using the broom to swat my sassy sis on her sagging backside or at least using it to rock her boat. But she was right.

When we were children, I always wanted to be Jessie from

the Boxcar Children books. One time I tried to convince Joanne to play dress up with me. I told her she could play the role of Henry, the older brother who left the boxcar to "mow the doctor's lawn" and then came back and fixed things. Joanne said she would rather be Violet and lie on the couch coughing and fanning herself, as if she had a fever.

Here we were, grown-up Boxcar Children, and she was playing Violet by lounging in the hammock and fanning herself. We were living out a silly sort of childhood dream. I was, indeed, sweeping the porch of my own shiny silver boxcar.

You didn't really have anything to do with this silly little dream, did you, God? This is more like one of Your personal little jokes, right?

Squinting, I looked up into the flawless, sapphire sky and wondered if God had heard me.

Fourteen

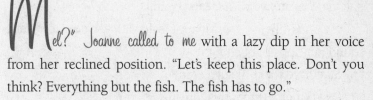

"Mel?" Joanne called to me with a lazy dip in her voice from her reclined position. "Let's keep this place. Don't you think? Everything but the fish. The fish has to go."

"Scoot over." I muscled my way onto the hammock.

"It's not going to hold both of us."

"Yes it will. Uncle Harlan made it, right? It's designed to stand the test of time."

"He should have made two," Joanne protested, inching to the side so I could position myself with my head at the opposite end from her head.

"Why make two when one will do?" I adjusted my hips slightly and—voilà!—we both fit.

"This isn't so bad," Joanne said. "No sudden moves, and we should be okay. Although you better keep your feet away from my face, or I'll topple you."

"Same goes for your feet."

We lilted from side to side with comfortable ease and remarked about the peacefulness and simple beauty of the place.

"The colors are true," Joanne said. "The blue is really blue, not fogged-over gray-blue like the sky I've been living under. And there isn't any gray here, did you notice that? Silver, of course, in the trailer, but not gray. The clinic where I work is all gray. It's not white. It's gray. I'm tired of gray."

"The dentist's office where I work is creamy vanilla and pale blue. I can live with creamy vanilla."

"Sounds like a latte," Joanne said. "Doesn't an iced latte sound delicious right about now?"

"We have water," I suggested.

"No, I'm not thirsty. Just dreamy."

We rocked together in silence a few more minutes before I lifted my head a couple of inches to see Joanne's face. I wanted to see her expression when I asked the question that still plagued me from that morning.

"Jo?"

"Hmm?" Her eyes were closed.

"What were you feeling when Matthew said he wasn't married?"

Her eyes flew open. Her gaze pierced mine. I didn't flinch. A single tear came out of her heart and took a shy stroll in the sunlight across Joanne's cheek. "I don't know."

"Yes you do. What did you think of him?"

"I thought he was marvelous. Skilled and compassionate. He was wonderful. I assumed he was married, so of course I didn't allow myself even an inch of hope."

"And how did you feel when you found out he wasn't married?"

"Too much."

"Too much what?"

"Too much of everything. I felt ripped off, like why didn't I know he was single when we picked him up? He didn't wear a ring, but a lot of doctors and nurses don't because they have to wash their hands all the time. I felt embarrassed, too."

"I know. I already apologized, but I am sorry that I embarrassed you by saying you were available."

"I was more embarrassed by the flood of feelings that came over me." Joanne's first shy tear now was joined by a whole club of droplets that had congregated in a corner of her heart. Their meeting was adjourned, and all the teary colleagues came out together, scrambling down my sister's face, as if no one had told them the location for their next meeting.

"It's crazy, I know." Joanne sniffed. "Or maybe I should say I know that if I think about him, it will drive me crazy. Been there. Done that. Gained ten pounds."

I suddenly understood her need to head to the bakery and stock up on "dainties," as Aunt Winnie called them.

"I'm hopeless." Joanne used her T-shirt's sleeve to wipe her dripping nose. "I should have turned around and waved like you told me to. Now I'll never see him again."

"Oh, come on!" I snapped with all the finesse of a bull-dozer driver who's a little inebriated on hormones. "What happened to all your great spiritual insights from a couple of nights ago? Remember when you were saying you were in love with God?"

"I still am."

"I don't doubt that. But you said that didn't mean you were going to take a vow of solitude, that you still wanted to get married, right? You said you had surrendered to God's will and to His kingdom coming, and now you were waiting for His dreams to come true."

"Yes, I believe that."

"Well, what if Matthew is God's dream come true for you?"

Joanne looked at me, as if I were the one making up the fairy-tale endings. I chuckled at her incredulous expression. "I'm not the one coming up with this stuff. You told me that everything happens for a reason and that we were on God's time schedule, right?"

"Yes."

"So, doesn't it seem to you that our schedule was altered all day long yesterday so we would end up at the right spot in the road to stop and watch the sunset when Matthew's car died? Wouldn't you call that a divine appointment?"

"I hadn't thought of it that way."

"Joanne! You were the one who offered him a ride, not me. You have been the one all along saying that God has unfulfilled dreams for you."

"You're right. I missed it entirely. It can't be a coincidence that we met when we did. Oh, wow, God might really be doing something here."

Returning the same expression my sister gave me on the ship when I confessed that I had control issues, I grinned at her. "Oh, really?"

"Hey, be nice," Joanne said.

"I am being nice. I'm giving you some free emotional advice to balance out the free medical advice you give me. My advice is to release whatever bungled-up disappointments you have from the past and turn your heart toward this new relationship. Trust me, Jo, when we were driving away, if you would have turned around and seen him the way I saw him, you would know right now how much he wanted you to come back."

Joanne let out a long sigh. It was a mind-cleansing sort of sigh. "You're right."

"I *love* it when you say that," I teased.

We rocked silently for a few moments while Joanne seemed to be sinking into deep contemplation. I broke her concentration by asking, "What are you going to do next?"

"What do you mean what am I going to do next?"

"Well, Matthew probably is staying in San Felipe tonight, if he got his car fixed. We could check all the hotels to see if he's staying in town."

"Or not," Joanne said.

"Do you have a better idea?"

"Yes. I'm going to wait."

"For what?"

"For God to have our paths cross again."

"Why? Your paths already crossed. We both agree. He is Dreamboat of the Year. You have to find him. Come on! God helps those who help themselves."

"Where did you hear that?" Joanne glared at me with one eye squinted open.

"Isn't it in the Bible?"

"No. Definitely not."

"I think I read it on one of the laminated prayer cards at Aunt Winnie's. Where I heard it doesn't matter. The point is, you should plan your attack and attack your plan."

Joanne chuckled. "I wish you could hear yourself, Mel. Relax. If this is God's doing, He'll complete it. What He starts, He finishes."

"With no help from you. Is that it?"

"That's what the grace part is all about. It's His will that's accomplished, not mine."

Now my sister was bugging me. First, she didn't recognize the obvious signs about Matthew, and then she put all the responsibility back on God to make something miraculous happen.

"I'm going to finish cleaning up," I said, eager to get back to a task that would work out my exasperation. "Hold on to your side of the hammock while I climb out."

We successfully completed my departure from the hammock without either of us ending up on the ground. I swept while Joanne slept. The afternoon turned the pages to the day's story with languid, long-armed motions. It was siesta time in this quiet cove. Even the insects seemed to be napping.

I was the only one who needed to be busy.

As the afternoon heat rose, I cheerfully changed into a pair of shorts, pulled my hair up in a clip, and continued to set up house inside the trailer. To my delight, Mr. Marlin fit inside the broom closet just fine, as long as I kept him at an angle so that his long, swordfishlike nose could stick out at the top.

No skeletons in Uncle Harlan's closet. Just a nosey fish!

Within an hour or so I had everything tidy and organized. The trailer was roomier than it looked from the outside, and with a few more items from the grocery store, I thought that Joanne and I could live here several weeks if we needed to.

Popping outside to check on my lounging sis, I noticed a string of motorized vehicles with wide tires that looked like souped-up tricycles roaring across the sand. The noise was annoying, but they looked fun as the drivers spun around in wide circles.

"What do you think?" Joanne asked. "Should we rent a couple of those and have a race or two?"

"Sure. Why not? How was your nap?"

"Heavenly. I was serious when I said I'm going to sleep out here tonight."

"I made up both beds, just in case you change your mind."

"Thanks." Joanne pulled herself up and looked around. "I like it here. I like it here a lot."

"I made a list of a few things we still need at the store."

"Of course you did."

"What did you say?"

"Nothing. Go on, Mel. You were saying we need a few things at the store."

"Do you want to go with me, or should I just go?"

"Oh, now look who's the brave one, eh? You sure got your second wind once we arrived."

"I like to attain goals," I said plainly.

"Yes, you do." Joanne stretched. "I'll go with you. Be sure to bring the key. I'll put the big padlock back in place."

We headed the opposite direction of how we had come when we reached the main road because Joanne insisted we see if another grocery store was nearby so we wouldn't have to return to the older part of town. Her instincts proved to be right. A large, newly built grocery store was located not more than half a mile away. Not far down the road from the grocery store was a gated area with a guard station and a fancy sign that read, "Rio del Mar Resort."

"Can you believe this?" I said. "It's a new development. A new city being built outside the old city."

As soon as we entered the grocery store, we realized the new grocery store catered to North American tourists. For starters, the store was air-conditioned. Many of the signs were in English. The freezer section by the front door was stocked with familiar ice cream treats like the brands we bought at home.

I made quick work of our shopping needs, but at the checkout counter I couldn't help but ask a few questions since the employee spoke perfect English.

"Yes, it's a resort," the cashier explained. "But you buy the house and rent it out if you want. It's not going to be a hotel. The main resort hotel in San Felipe is Costa del Sur, in case that's the one you're trying to find. It's south of here."

"No, I was curious about this resort."

"The construction started a few weeks ago. You can still buy property. Not many of the lots have been bought yet. The clubhouse already is built with the pool. They have an office, if you want to ask questions."

"Thank you. We may have a look."

She handed me the receipt. "Have a nice day."

It seemed sad, in a way. I preferred the sound of the many voices speaking Spanish in the grocery store we had gone to earlier in the old part of town. This air-conditioned, shiny store felt commercial, and as if this local girl had sold out to the corporate North American mogul who was transforming her sleepy fishing town into a money-making venture.

Joanne reached for the grocery bags along with one of the gallon-sized jugs of water. "I wonder how Uncle Harlan would have viewed this news."

I turned to the checkout clerk and said, "By any chance do you know a man named Matthew who is visiting San Felipe with his nephew, Cal? Cal is about eight. This high."

She shook her head.

"Melanie." Joanne's bristly words swept me out of the store. "You don't have to play junior detective, you know. I don't intend to search for Matthew all over town."

"Okay," I said reluctantly. "Sorry. I just thought it wouldn't hurt to ask."

"Don't ask anymore," she said firmly.

"Okay, relax. I won't."

"Good. Now, do you want to check out this resort?"

"We might as well."

The guard at the small booth let us in without asking any questions. We drove down smoothly paved streets to a clubhouse and office that looked out at the ocean. The measured-off lots looked like a setup for a cookie-cutter suburban development.

"How depressing," Joanne said. "In six months this place will turn into a little dollhouse world. Let's go in the office and find out how much the lots are going for."

We stepped into an air-conditioned office and immediately felt chilled. A gentleman wearing expensive resort clothing greeted us in English and Spanish. He seemed to be eyeing our tousled appearance, as if to evaluate the potential of our actually purchasing one of his many soon-to-be-snatched-up lots.

"We're interested in one of your brochures." I wanted to cut off his presentation the moment he started it. "We have to go because we have groceries in the car."

"I see." He reached for a slick pamphlet. "Are you staying at the Costa del Sur?"

"No."

"Camping on the beach?" he ventured.

"No."

"Do you mind if I ask where you're staying?"

Joanne stepped in and took over. "We're staying at our uncle's old place." It was the truth, even though the trailer was now legally ours. At least the salesman stopped probing.

"If you have time to come back, I'd be happy to take you on a tour of our facilities and point out the lots that are still available. After the tour you're entitled to a coupon good for a margarita at our clubhouse bar and free use of our swimming pool."

"Thanks." We turned to go.

"De nada," he answered us then added, "Mi casa es su casa."

Joanne and I looked at each other and shook our heads all the way back to the Jeep. That California boy had no idea what it meant to say that his house was our house.

"How much?" Joanne asked as we pulled out of the parking spot. She was driving, and I was flipping through the brochure.

"I don't believe it," I said.

"How much for a lot?"

"They start at two hundred thousand dollars and go up to four hundred thousand, depending on the size and how much of an ocean view it has."

"That's U.S. dollars, not pesos, right?"

"Right."

"Are you saying they're charging two hundred thousand dollars just for the lot?"

"No, that includes the house. They give four different floor plans to choose from. And get this. There are more than three hundred lots still available."

"The big question is how will this development affect Uncle Harlan's place."

"Good question."

After we put away the groceries, Joanne and I made sandwiches from the packaged turkey breast we had bought and munched on a bag of baby carrots. Our trailer didn't have working electricity or water, but since we would be there such a short time, we thought it was best to make do without. I don't think either of us would have been happy with that decision if we hadn't stayed with Rosa Lupe and seen how cleverly she coped with neither of those modern conveniences.

Our late afternoon meal was a combination of lunch and dinner, so it seemed fitting to leisurely stroll barefoot along the beach at sunset. I had bought a flashlight and extra batteries and carried it with us on our walk just in case it became too dark on the way back.

The evening breeze skittered across the water on kitten's paws, quietly stretching and taking its precious time to join us as we walked. Facing east meant the sun was actually going to set behind us and not into the water, the way it did whenever we had viewed the close of the day in British Columbia. The eastern sky was slow to dim as Joanne and I leaned low, looking for seashells. I loved the sensation of the warm, sugar white sand between my toes.

"What are you thinking?" I asked Joanne as a fleet of amber- and scarlet-shaded clouds scuttled out to sea.

"I'm thinking lots of things. What are you thinking?"

"That I can't remember my other life."

"What does that mean?"

"That means I feel as if I've been gone from home for years, not just a few days. I feel as if I have new spaces opening up in my brain, and I have time to think. I feel renewed."

"So do I," Joanne said. "Getting out of our comfort drones is a good thing."

"Don't you mean comfort zones?"

"They might be zones for you, but for me, when I get comfortable, I turn into a drone."

"Joanne, you don't have to answer this if you don't want to, but I have to ask. Why did you jump in the water after that child?"

"I thought he was going to drown."

"But you didn't even think about it. You just ran and jumped in. I could never do that."

"Yes you could. If you had seen all the suffering and loss of life I saw in India and you were presented with a situation where it seemed possible you could save a life if you acted immediately, you would have jumped in, too."

We had turned and were now headed back up the beach toward our hideaway.

"Do you think you'll ever go back to India?"

"Possibly. One day. What I'd rather do is raise an army of support for the work that's going on there."

"What do you mean?"

"I want to find a way to let people know what's going on in India and how young girls are being freed from forced prostitution. If I go back to India, I'm one person. That's helpful, of course. Very helpful. But if I can find ten people or a hundred people who will pray and contribute to the ministry, that's even more helpful. "

"Are you doing that now? I don't remember seeing any letters from you that asked for financial support for them."

"I haven't sent out any letters. I don't know where to begin. I'm terrible at organizing and communicating and all the other stuff necessary to build a support base. That's a bigger challenge to me than getting back on a plane and working at the center for the rest of my life."

Writing a simple letter sounded elementary to me. I had organized a fund-raiser for Joy's school choir while I had the flu two years ago, and when it turned out to be the biggest draw they'd ever had, they asked me to do it every year. I did it this year practically in my sleep.

"I know a thing or two about organizing," I said. "Why don't you keep me in mind, if you need help sometime?"

By the look on Joanne's face in the dimming light, I saw

she never had thought of me as a resource for such a project. "You're right, Mel."

"You know, I think that's the third time today you've told me I was right. I love it when you say those three little words: 'You're right, Mel. You're right, Mel.'"

"You know what they say about pride," Joanne warned.

"Wear it with honor?"

"No, I was thinking of the verse in Proverbs that says pride goes before a fall." She caught my ankle with her foot and tried to bring me down to the sand. I hopped quickly and avoided the tumble.

"How many times do I have to warn you not to start something you can't finish, Joanna Banana?"

She took off down the beach before I could trip her. I ran after her in the firm, moist sand, but she was in much better shape than I. I'd never catch her.

Zigzagging into the shallow water, Joanne tried to get me wet as her bare feet kicked up a spray of salt water. I retaliated with a splash in her direction, and Joanne let out a loud yelp.

"I didn't even get you wet," I called.

She screamed, and I knew something was really wrong.

"Are you okay? What happened?"

Joanne hopped on one foot and wailed, "I stepped on something. Owww! I can't see. Where's your flashlight?"

I quickly turned the light on her foot. We saw nothing. No gash or blood. Only a slight puncture on the fleshy upper pad.

"Ow, ow, ow, ow!" Joanne cried.

Turning the flashlight on the sand where she had been standing, I searched for the culprit, expecting to find the top of a ballpoint pen or something. No evidence lay in the wet sand.

"It hurts! It hurts! It hurts!"

"Okay, Joanne, let's get you back to the trailer. Can you lean on my shoulder and hobble along?"

We did a crazy hop-shuffle dance step. I'd never seen Joanne fall apart like she was now.

"It hurts," she whimpered, breathing hard.

"You don't have any idea what it was?"

"No!" she screamed. "It hurts!"

"Listen, Jo, I'll drive you to the clinic I saw in town. Do you remember seeing it by the gas station? No matter. Just stay calm, and I'll drive as fast as I can."

With my sister whimpering in the seat beside me, I drove like a crazy woman through town, barely stopping at the "Alto" signs.

"Here's a bottle of water." I reached behind me when we rolled to a stop at an intersection, and I heard the bottle rattle. "Pour some water over your foot. Maybe a little piece of shell is stuck in there. Hold on. I'm going to make a turn up here."

With fierce determination, I clutched the steering wheel and drove my sister to the closest thing to a hospital this town had to offer. She didn't have two broken legs, but I had jumped into the emergency as fully as if she did.

Fifteen

The good thing about taking a nurse-practitioner to a clinic is that she understands her diagnosis long before you do. And that's an especially good thing when the diagnosis is mostly in Spanish.

Our helpful doctor was certain that a sea creature, possibly a stingray, had stung Joanne. He made her plunge her foot into a pan of steaming hot water. As soon as the water cooled, more scalding hot water was delivered. When I informed the doctor that our accommodations didn't include electricity or running water, he insisted we stay at the twenty-four-hour clinic with the ready supply of boiling water until he felt confident a sufficient amount of the poison had been extracted from her foot.

While Joanne soaked, she quietly whimpered. I felt so bad for her. She barely had moaned after she was hoisted up from

Ensenada's water with the rope. For her to react like this, it must really hurt.

After the first two hours of rotating buckets of hot water, she said she could tell a difference. The sharp, burning pain was decreasing. She could partially wiggle her toes again. The panic was lifting from her eyes.

I bought bottles of Coke from a machine in the lobby, and we sat in metal chairs flipping through Mexican tabloids. Some popular Mexican television star was marrying some other popular Mexican television star, but some other blond woman wasn't happy about it. We figured out that critical bit of news from the pictures. What we didn't know was if it was happening in real life or on a soap opera.

Sometime close to midnight the doctor indicated he was going home and another doctor was coming on duty. I have to say that I had been very good the whole time we were at the clinic. My suspicion was that this was the clinic Matthew was associated with, and therefore the same clinic that received the dispatch about Miguel's broken leg. The thought of asking about Matthew had plagued me for several hours, but I wanted to honor Joanne's resolute request that I keep my fingers out of the matchmaking bowl.

Still, every twinkling Christmas light inside my brain lit up when the doctor said he was leaving. If God was dreaming up a charming surprise for my sister, how great would it be for Matthew to walk in and to see Joanne sitting there, helpless, with her hair going every which way, unbathed except for her swollen foot that was stuck in a bucket?

Well, maybe that scene wouldn't be exceptionally romantic, but it would still work. Instead of the Cinderella slipper, Matthew could slip Joanne's bare foot into another pan of scalding water, and they could live happily ever after.

That's how I would have written the story.

Apparently God had a different plot in mind and wasn't looking for someone with control issues to step in and help Him out. God is deliberate.

To my credit, I didn't say a word when the new doctor came on duty and turned out to be all of twenty-something, wearing too much aftershave and a red bowling shirt. When we left at two-thirty in the morning, I didn't sidle up to the doctor and ask if he knew Matthew. I didn't leave a trail of clues for Matthew to follow if he wanted to find the "Joanne Clayton" who was logged in at 6:55 p.m. on Wednesday, December 3. I was hands-off out of respect for Joanne's wishes.

And it was killing me.

The beds I'd made up earlier that day inside the trailer were a welcome sight by flashlight. Joanne said she had a screaming headache, and I realized I hadn't replaced the bottle of aspirin I had given away. I prepared a cold, wet paper towel and stood by Joanne's side, placing the soothing friend on her forehead.

"Just like when we had chicken pox," she said.

"It's not as effective as the aspirin would have been."

"Ibuprofen," she corrected me.

241

"Fine, ibuprofen." With a smirk I added, "If I had tequila, I'd give it to you."

"If you had tequila, the way I feel right now, I'd drink it."

"You must be delirious," I teased.

"I'm actually doing lots better. You can leave the paper towel. It's helping."

"And your foot?"

"It's better. I would never have known to soak it in hot water. Especially such scalding hot water. It seems to have worked, though. Thanks, Mel, for driving me to the clinic and for taking such good care of me."

"De nada," I said, crawling into my little bed. The sheets weren't exactly freshly cleaned, but they were better than what we had slept on the night before.

"Sleep deep, Joanne."

"Dream deeper," she answered me.

I don't know if I dreamed deeper, but I certainly slept deeper than I had the first few nights of this trip. The trailer stayed cool and dark, which allowed Joanne and me to sleep until after ten-thirty that morning. Usually neither of us slept that long, but after what we had demanded of our minds, emotions, and bodies the previous few days, it was a wonder we didn't hibernate for the entire day in an effort to rejuvenate.

Joanne's foot was much better, she said, but I noticed she hobbled around as she tidied up her side of the trailer. I had purchased some boxed oatmeal bars for our breakfast and pulled them out along with a glass bottle of what I took to be

Mexican orange juice that didn't need refrigeration.

"This is orange pop." Joanne placed her paper cup on the top of the collapsible kitchen table.

"Sorry about that."

"I don't mind. The sweetness surprised me."

"I think that's because it's so warm. Would you like a banana, Joanna Banana?"

"Sure, Melly Jelly Belly. What's on our schedule for today?"

It took me a moment to think before I answered, "Nothing." I couldn't remember a day in my adult life when the complete schedule could be listed with that singular word.

"We don't need to go back to the bank until tomorrow, right?" Joanne asked.

"Right."

"And we don't have to talk to a Realtor about selling the place because we're in agreement that we both want to keep it. At least for now."

"Right," I said again.

As if she needed to convince me further she added, "For the investment possibilities alone it seems too soon to sell."

"I know. I agree. And I'm sure Ethan will agree, too."

"I'm definitely coming back. We both will have to come back sometime when we can stay longer."

"And we'll bring a flyswatter." I flapped my hand in the air at a pesky fly that was determined to land on my banana peel.

"Flyswatter and what else? I know you're dying to make a list of some sort." Joanne didn't say it in a rude way. She said it like she knew me well enough to understand what was enjoyable for me, and she was willing to invest part of her free day in doing something I considered fun. Her gesture warmed me because it had been a long time since anyone, especially another woman, had volunteered to do something simply because she knew it would be a treat for me.

"Why don't we do that now?" she asked. "Where's your little notepad?"

"Here." I pulled out my pad and pen and started slowly, making sure I hadn't misread her invitation to join me in a little organizing fest. "We could use new silverware."

"At least we have silverware here," Joanne said. "I don't think Rosa Lupe had much silverware. You know, I was thinking about how we need to leave pretty early Saturday to get back to the cruise ship by five o'clock."

"Right."

"What if we leave nice and early? We could stop by the Valdeparisos' to see how Miguel is doing. We could even take a little gift to Rosa Lupe."

My task-motivated mind began to compose a list of all the things the dear woman could use like silverware and a few cooking items. "Great idea. What if we pulled all the extra items out of here? We could give them to Rosa Lupe, and if and when you or I ever come back, we'll keep the list so we know what items we need to replace."

"¡Excellente! Let's get at it and make your day."

Joanne was right. It made me happy to inventory and set

aside all the items we felt good about taking to Rosa Lupe. The day before I'd been fairly thorough in throwing out old newspapers and some of Uncle Harlan's rusted fishing lures. Anything else of his, including a battered pair of fishing boots, I loaded into some of the collapsed cardboard boxes I'd found in the broom closet. Aunt Winnie wanted the big fish, but she might also appreciate these other odd reminders of her husband.

By noon Joanne and I had accomplished the task and had a stack of useful items for Rosa Lupe.

"I hope she won't take any of this the wrong way," I said.

"No gift is misunderstood when the heart of the giver comes with the gift," Joanne said. "I know she'll see our heart in this. Now, if you don't mind, I have a hammock waiting with my name on it."

"It is getting stuffy in here," I said. "How's your foot doing?"

"Better. You don't mind if I take a nap, do you?"

"Not at all, Sleeping Beauty."

"What are you going to do?"

"I thought I might use some of our water to do a better job cleaning up the silverware and the frying pan."

"It is siesta time, you know."

"I'll try not to disturb you."

While Joanne turned the shaded hammock into a perfect little nest, I filled a basin with water and went to work on the old flatware. Remembering a trick Jessie used in the Boxcar Children, I padded out to the sand and scooped up a handful, which I carried back and used to rub off some of the ancient fish gut stains.

What do you know! It worked!

Alone in my private bliss, I kept staring out at the serenely beautiful ocean and wishing I had a camera. It struck me that I had seen disposable cameras at the grocery store by the resort. While Joanne slept, I hiked the half mile or so down to the grocery store, bought a camera, a small bottle of ibuprofen, and a cold bottle of iced tea. Life seemed so simple, and it seemed so good.

I only saw one person on my walk and guessed that Joanne was right about this being siesta hour. I also wondered if I was safer because I was in the greater orbit of the new resort. Yesterday I'd barely been able to cross the street in the older part of San Felipe without having a run-in with the law. Here I felt as if I were in "Little America."

Joanne was still snoozing when I returned to our hideaway. I snapped her picture and then stood back to take a lengthwise picture of the palm tree. The quiet snap of the disposable camera apparently was loud enough to wake Joanne.

"What are you doing?"

"I bought a camera. Smile!"

"No! Not until I wake up."

"Here." I handed her the camera. "Take a picture of me by Uncle Harlan's tree." I started to pose with my palm resting on the trunk of the grand palm when I had an idea. "Wait!"

"Good grief! I was just about to take it. What are you doing?"

"You'll see." I went into the trailer, fished out the black-

and-white photo of Uncle Harlan watering the fledgling palm tree, and my hunch was right. He had used the same basin I'd just used to clean the flatware.

"Let me get in the same position," I said, studying the old photo. Holding the basin just so, I looked up at Joanne and offered a big grin as I poured out the water the same way Uncle Harlan had.

"Now?" Joanne asked.

"Yes! Now!" I tried to bark through my fixed smile. "Take-the-ficture-efore-all-the-water's-gone."

"Got it," Joanne said. "Did you take one of our little cottage by the sea?"

"Not yet."

Joanne handed the camera to me, and I backed up so I could capture the whole trailer, complete with Joanne in the attached hammock.

"You know, this place isn't so bad," I called out to Joanne, pressing the button. "It's not at all what I imagined, but it has potential. Some patio chairs would help, and a couple of big clay pots with some hearty flowers."

"Excuse me." A man appeared in front of the camera. I hadn't seen him come around the side of our sequestered fortress, and the sight of another tourist made me jump. He was wearing white shorts and a polo shirt with an expensive-looking pair of sunglasses.

"I'm sorry to startle you. I heard you speaking English, and I came over to see if I might ask a few questions."

I realized he was the one tourist I'd spotted while walking to the store. Apparently he didn't need a siesta, either.

He pulled a business card from his pocket and said he was looking for a small place to buy for a weekend retirement getaway. He wondered if I knew who owned the "pristine location" on which our trailer was parked.

"Yes, I know the owner," I said, unwilling to let down my guard with this guy.

"Would you be so kind as to pass on my card, and if they are interested in selling, I'd be interested in talking with them."

"I'll pass on the information."

He gave a courteous nod and went on his way.

"We could be sitting on a little gold mine," Joanne said, after I joined her in the hammock and we were certain our intruder was off our property. "Let me see his card. California address. That guy is an investor for sure. He's not looking for a weekend getaway. We're keeping this place, Mel."

"Hey, we already agreed on that this morning. You don't have to convince me."

"There is one thing I might have to convince you about," Joanne said.

"What's that?"

"I think we should rent one of those sand buggies and go for a ride."

"What about your foot?"

"Much improved. See?" She held up her wrinkled hoof for my inspection a few inches from my face.

"I don't want that thing in my face. It is better, though. The swelling is gone."

"I know. Let's go have a last romp in the sea."

"Okay," I said. "Maybe we can find whatever it was that bit you and run over it."

"Now there's a lovely, aggressive thought."

Joanne and I drove down the road to the rental shack where we were given a condensed course on everything we needed to know about all-terrain vehicles, also called ATVs. We rented the two-seater instead of two separate ATVs. It only seemed appropriate after all the togetherness we had been experiencing.

The real decision came when we had to agree on who was going to drive first. Since Joanne had been so nice about helping me clean and make lists in the trailer that morning, and since renting one of these noisemakers was her idea, I acquiesced and let her drive.

With my arms around her middle and her hands in place on the throttle, we puttered off down the sand, appearing, I'm sure, like a couple of wacky women stuck in a midlife identity bubble.

Who cared? Hardly anyone was on the beach to see us as Joanne picked up speed, and we zipped through the shallow water, letting out a string of wild "yahoooies!"

We laughed and spun donuts in the sand and splashed through the water like a couple of teenagers.

"This is great!" I yelled. "Don't you love this?"

"Love it!" she called back over her shoulder.

We motored for a long stretch along the gorgeous beach before I convinced Joanne to stop and let me have a turn. I took the reins and sent our flying machine over a series of small sand dunes. On the last one, Joanne yelled in my ear to stop showing off. I didn't mind the accusation. The fun part was, she was the only one I was showing off for.

We cruised our way back to the rental shack, feeling the sun on our shoulders. Returning our wide-tire magic carpet a minute before our one-hour rental time was up, we thanked the owner in Spanish.

"De nada." He handed Joanne our copy of the rental agreement while she and I debated what we should do for dinner.

I had bread and peanut butter back at the trailer along with more carrot sticks. Joanne wasn't impressed. She thought we should go out to dinner. I was apprehensive.

"You like *camarones*?" the gentleman at the ATV rental shack asked us.

"¿Camarones?" I asked.

"Fresh today." He pointed to a cart across the street where a man was cooking up something that smelled wonderful.

"Let's look," Joanne said. "We don't have to buy anything."

As we approached the cart, the man opened an ice chest to show us his catch for the day. The chest was packed with large prawns.

"¿Camarones?" Joanne pointed to the tiger shrimp.

"Sí, camarones."

"Let's buy a pound," Joanne said. "Or a kilo, or however he sells them. We can cook them ourselves. I saw a round grill in the closet."

Joanne was speaking my language. A Boxcar Children banquet on the beach. I was game.

"One pound, please." I held up one finger.

"Let's get two," Joanne suggested. "Dos. Dos kilos, *por favor*."

"Impressive Spanish there, Jo!"

"I'm catching on." She pulled some money from her pocket and settled with the cart vendor. He handed me the smelly fellows in a sticky plastic bag.

"How do you say, *butter?*" she asked the vendor.

He shook his head.

"Butter." She pointed to a half-used stick of what looked like margarine that he was using to grease his grill.

"*Mantequilla,*" he said.

"Okay. That one may take a little longer for me to learn. Let's get some butter at the grocery store and see if they have any garlic powder. It wouldn't hurt to see if they have charcoal as well."

Mission accomplished at the extremely convenient grocery store, we returned to our beachfront property a little stiff from our dune buggy jaunt. Making fun of each other for hobbling around like old ladies, Joanne and I went to work hollowing out a pit in the sand, setting fire to the charcoal, and placing the grill just so.

Working together, we peeled the plump prawns and rinsed each one before dipping them in the melted garlic butter and cooking them over the red-hot coals.

Our Mexican blankets came in handy once again as we spread them on the sand and settled into the warm pockets of unspoiled beach. When the sun began to lower, so did our voices. The colors that spread across the night sky were fainter and paler than they had been the previous night. The air was still, and we were in no hurry to go anywhere or do anything. Each succulent shrimp was enjoyed as if it were the first time we had ever tasted such a delicacy and the last time we would ever be together.

As the soft blush of the day took her leave, the obscurity of deep night took her place as our dinner companion. She came to our fire wearing a velvet cloak studded with diamonds, and we welcomed her without fear.

"So many stars." Joanne drew the blanket tighter around her shoulders. "Did you ever know so many stars were up there?"

"They seem closer here, don't they? If we had a long enough net we could catch some. Like fish."

"Would that make them starfish?" Joanne asked with a giggle.

"At least that's more poetic than whatever it was I said in Spanish the other night."

"Beautiful entrails," Joanne remembered.

"Oh, yeah."

We chuckled.

"I love being with you," Joanne said.

"Me, too. I wish we could have gotten along this well when we were growing up."

"I know."

"I've been thinking about your moving to Vancouver." I'd actually been thinking about how Matthew said he lived in Vancouver, but I didn't bring that up. Instead I said, "I think when you get there, we should plan a time to meet every week or at least every two weeks."

"Organizing us already," Joanne said with a tease in her voice.

"I'm just saying that if we don't have a set time, life gets hectic, and then all of a sudden it's been two months and we haven't seen each other, even if we live only a few miles apart."

"I agree. It's a good idea. We'll schedule sister time as soon as I relocate. Assuming, that is, that I can make this change. If I can, I'd like to transition by the end of the year, but that might be too ambitious."

"I don't think so. It's good to have specific goals. Besides, you know you're welcome to stay with us as long as you want."

"Thanks, Mel."

"De nada." I scooted closer in the sand to my big sister and rested my head on her shoulder.

She rested her head on top of mine, and together we watched a shooting star streak across the sky. Then, as if I weren't there or as if she didn't mind that I was, Joanne talked aloud to God, telling Him how great He was and how amazing

His creation was. She unabashedly poured out her heart to Jesus Christ, and that's when I knew she really, truly was in love with Him.

Sixteen

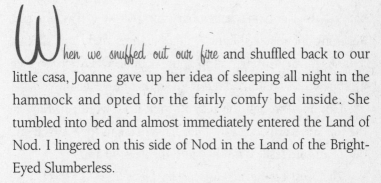

When we snuffed out our fire and shuffled back to our little casa, Joanne gave up her idea of sleeping all night in the hammock and opted for the fairly comfy bed inside. She tumbled into bed and almost immediately entered the Land of Nod. I lingered on this side of Nod in the Land of the Bright-Eyed Slumberless.

It wasn't as if I was lying in the dark listening for bandidos. I just couldn't fall asleep. Life seemed to be closing in on me.

Not life as I knew it in Langley. There, life was all about schedules and timetables. I felt secure when I was operating with the unbendable reality of numbers. Columns and lists and dependable routines were the equation that equaled life in my understanding. All the beauty I knew came from paint by numbers, following the rules. I could do it. All of it, and some-how make it pretty.

But tonight on the beach by the fire listening to Joanne talk to Christ the way a woman confides in her best friend, I saw no numbers or columns or rules. Only broad strokes of vibrant colors nearly visible in the darkness. Her passionate dialogue with Christ made me desire oh so much more than what my life of formulas had produced for me. The elusive remedy seemed so close I could almost feel it breathing on me.

I turned to face the small window above my bed that I'd left open. A line from Joanne's Augustine quote kept chasing around in my wide-awake brain. It was the part about God bathing us. I couldn't remember exactly how it was phrased. Reaching for my flashlight, I flipped the switch and spotted Joanne's journal sitting on top of the counter where she had left it. I knew she wouldn't mind if I read that quote again.

Flipping through the pages I found the word *Augustine* at the top and started to read. "You have made us for Yourself and our hearts are restless till they find their rest in You."

That wasn't the quote I was looking for.

Further down I found the part I remembered—the haunting portion she had read to me on the ship. "You were with me, but I was not with You. You called me, You shouted to me, You broke past my deafness. You bathed me in Your light, You wrapped me in Your splendor..."

That was it. "You bathed me in Your light." That's what I was trying to remember.

Joanne had written sideways down the edge of the page:

My heart has heard you say, "Come and talk with me."
And my heart responds, "LORD, I am coming." Psalm
27:8, NLT.

Closing Joanne's journal, I turned off the flashlight and
reclined in the darkness.

In the deepest part of my spirit I heard an echo of the
words I'd just read: *"Come and talk with me."*

The thought was so distinct that I responded with one of
my usual defenses: *Why? What did I do wrong?*

No further thought came to me. Could that truly have
been God shouting at me? Breaking through my deafness? If
that thought was from God, had I responded the right way?

With the flashlight turned back on, I read the verse from
Psalm 27 one more time.

*The right response should have been, "Lord, I'm coming." Is that
it? Is that what I should have said to You? I'm not accustomed to
turning to You. I'm always trying to make sure I stay off Your radar.
I don't want to do anything wrong. I think I'd feel too embarrassed if
I turned toward You.*

In the cool closeness of the trailer, I remembered the scene at
the Valdeparisos' as we drove away from Matthew. I kept telling
Joanne to turn around and look at him, but she wouldn't. She
didn't see him the way I was saw him in the rearview mirror—
openhearted, willing, hopeful. She was embarrassed and angry.
That combination equaled an unbecoming stubbornness. She

wouldn't turn, no matter how sincerely I had urged her.

Is that me? Am I too embarrassed and angry and stubborn to turn and see You the way Joanne sees You?

I held my breath and strained my ears. I wasn't used to speaking so plainly with God in my thoughts. I was as trusting as a child that He would answer.

Come and talk with me.

My heart pounded faster. This time in the stillness I didn't question the invitation that resonated in my thoughts, but rather I whispered, "Lord, I am coming."

Silence followed. Sweet, calming silence. No words were needed. I had turned and faced Christ instead of driving away from Him or ducking from His gaze. I didn't know what would happen next, but I knew I was on a new road and a journey was beginning.

What did happen next was sleep. Deep, restorative, life-giving sleep. Sweet slumber followed by a washing of light.

I felt the warmth on my forehead before I opened my eyes. It was barely morning. Just first light. But that first light had slipped past the wrought iron bars, through the screen, and down the open slats of the window above my bed. The light touched me and my spirit responded with, "Lord, I am coming."

Bathed in light, I was feeling so alive. More alive than I'd ever felt. How long had God been softly calling to me, but I'd been too stubborn or self-absorbed to stop, turn around, and listen?

With quiet movements, I slipped into my shorts and tennis shoes and prepared to tiptoe outside.

"Melanie, are you okay?" Joanne turned over and squinted at me.

"I'm going for a walk," I whispered. "Everything is good. Very good."

"Do you mind if I come with you?"

"You don't have to."

"I want to."

A few moments later we stepped out into the fresh, new day and stood with our faces to the rising sun, bathed in light—spectacular, translucent, tropical light.

The tide was out at least fifteen feet from where the waves had touched the shore the day before. In that wide expanse of moist sand stretched out a harvest of shells waiting for treasure seekers like my eager sister and me to come collect.

We strolled through the white sand close together, but each keeping company with her own thoughts. I found myself confessing. I told Christ I was bossy.

I imagined His response to be identical to Joanne's: "Oh, really?"

I couldn't tell Him anything He didn't already know. So, since that truth didn't scare Him away, I went on to tell my unseen companion that I wanted to be washed clean. Washed in His light. I told Him I wanted to be close like this every moment of every day, and somehow I knew that was all He had ever wanted from our relationship, too.

I remembered the prayer I'd whispered our night on the cruise ship. Instead of a confession or an honest dialogue with God, I had told him what I would do. I would improve. I would fix my anger problem. I would take control.

This morning I knew I didn't possess the power within myself to initiate or complete lasting changes in my life. Only God could do that. I'd been too busy trying to do it myself. I hadn't stopped and turned to Him.

Now that everything was out in the open, in full light, I saw clearly that in the past I might have had the honorable quality of obedience to God, but I hadn't had the closeness Joanne experienced with Him.

I tried to explain all this to my sister as we strolled along the beach.

Joanne listened to every word before she said, "God came after you, didn't He?"

I paused before I understood, and then I answered, "Yes. That's exactly what happened. God pursued me, just like you said the other night. It was as if He called out, 'Come,' and I responded."

"Told you," Joanne said with a grin as mischievous as the one she wore on the way to my sixteenth birthday party. "I think this was what He had in mind all along when He created us, this closeness."

I nodded, and we made our way back along the shore with our arms linked and our wet tennis shoes filling with sand. The rest of the way back was spent in the sweetest discussion of things we had never talked about before. I loved feeling this close to my sister. Closeness is a good thing.

After a simple breakfast, Joanne and I drove to the bank where we hoped all the final papers would be ready and waiting for us.

I was the one who was to speak with Señor Campaña. I also was the one to squawk when we were told he was out and wouldn't be back until Monday.

"Did he leave any papers for us?" Joanne asked.

"Uno momento." The receptionist walked back to his desk and shuffled around some of the stacks of papers.

"No, no papers for you," she said, returning to her front desk. "Please come back on Monday."

"We won't be able to come back on Monday," Joanne said patiently. "Would you write down our names and addresses and please have Señor Campaña mail the papers to us as soon as they arrive?"

She nodded, but I was less than confident that our message would ever reach the bank president. I made sure we had her full name as well as the bank phone number before we left. We might not be able to come in on Monday, but if nothing else, we could turn in all this information to Aunt Winnie's lawyer so he could follow up for us.

We found a restaurant that looked like a popular spot for many Americans, judging by the number of vehicles with U.S. license plates parked out front.

A song from a British group popular in the eighties was

playing in English on the speakers overhead as we entered and found an open booth by the window. I ordered number three on the menu: a tamale and a shredded beef burrito. Joanne ordered the special of the day: fish tacos.

As we waited for our food, I told Joanne I didn't think I could be as calm as she was about the bank situation.

"I wanted to have everything finalized," I told her.

"I know."

"We could have driven back to Ensenada a day earlier."

"I know," she said again. "But we stayed, and I'm glad we did. It'll work out. You'll see."

"Joanne, I'm worried about something."

"What's that?"

"I don't think I'm very good at trusting God the way you do. You're so confident."

"Not all the time."

"I think I was better at being an uptight, rigid sort of Christian. I'm much better at helping God out than sitting back and relying on Him to dream up the ending to our situation here."

Joanne laughed. "I think He's already dreamed up the ending. And you know what else? Relinquishment is—"

"I know, I know. Relinquishment is a beautiful thing."

I brought that line up again later that afternoon when we took a final stroll on the beach. With shoes on our feet to protect us from any burrowing stingrays, Joanne and I waded into the warm water and gazed out at the spectacular turquoise horizon.

"What is your line about surrender?" I asked.

"You mean relinquishing?"

"Yes." I bent to scoop a handful of salt water and fling it through the air. "We never exactly finished our water fight from the other day so I wondered if you were relinquishing or ready to watch me finish what I started a couple of days ago."

Before she could answer, I scooped up two handfuls of water and tossed it at her. "Where's that bank *presidente* now? I'll show him where to place his bets."

Joanne and I entered into an all-out water fight with our only spectators being a few ATV drivers spinning donuts in the sand and whatever evil stingrays popped their heads up to hear where all the laughter was coming from.

The water fight was a grand tie, we decided, and we were a grand, sopping mess. The playfulness, the freedom to act like girls again, and the release of energy all had seemed like such a great idea when we started the water war.

But after sunset, when we had organized our things for an early departure the next morning, Joanne and I complained about how our hair and skin had been crusted by the salty brine. We lovingly blamed the other for starting something we both wished we hadn't finished.

The next morning we rose with the sun and packed the Jeep. Joanne kept shaking her head, and I finally said, "Are you okay?"

"It's the salt water and the way it dried in my hair. It's driving me crazy."

"We have enough bottled water," I said. "You can wash your hair, if you want."

"You would like an excuse to douse me with another bucket of water, wouldn't you?"

"It's up to you, but I was thinking about asking you to pour a bottle or two over me. This crusted feeling is awful."

"Why didn't you say so?" Joanne said. "You don't have to ask me twice. Where's the water?"

We took turns, sudsing up with a small bottle of shampoo Joanne pulled from her suitcase and pouring plastic bottles of water over each other's head. Standing on the patio in our shorts and T-shirts, shaking our heads like dogs, we coaxed the early morning air to dry us.

"I don't think I rinsed out all the shampoo," I moaned.

"It doesn't matter, really," Joanne said. "As soon as we get in the Jeep, we'll air dry. And if our hair is still really bad, we can hide under our sombreros."

"I guess. Let's finish loading up and get on the road."

"We're leaving the fish, right?" Joanne asked after we put our suitcases and other boxes of essentials for Aunt Winnie and Rosa Lupe into the Jeep.

"No, of course not. We need to take him," I said.

"You can't be serious."

"Aunt Winnie was serious. She wants that fish."

"Do you always give Aunt Winnie what she wants?"

"When it's within my power, yes. Wait until you move to Vancouver. You'll do the same."

Joanne shook her head. "I doubt it. You are a much kinder woman than I am, sweet Melanie."

 Since Joanne was always the sweet and kind one growing up, I didn't mind being accused of exhibiting those qualities.

"Come on," I said. "Mr. Marlin is the last thing we have to load. Let's stick him in the backseat."

"I can't believe we're doing this."

Joanne helped me maneuver the silent, one-eyed former watchdog out of the closet and through the front door. We positioned him horizontally across the backseat, but his long, sharp nose protruded too far out the side.

"He'll have to sit up," Joanne said. "We could tie a little flag to his nose. It would look like one of those long antennas on top of the Baja bugs."

We repositioned him, and I made a face. "I don't like the way he looks."

"Oh, really?" Joanne said with a scoffing choke in her throat. "So now do you want to leave him?"

"No, I mean I don't like the way he looks sitting up. He's too stiff. Maybe we should put his tail on the floor and lean him against the backseat instead of having the tail on the seat."

Joanne's mouth twitched, and I knew she was growing impatient as I adjusted Mr. Marlin without her assistance.

"That's better." I buckled the seat belt around his middle. "Let's wrap him in a blanket so he won't look so stiff."

"You wrap your fish," Joanne said. "I'm taking down the hammock and locking up everything."

I used both of our Mexican blankets to cover Mr. Marlin and realized, when I stepped back, that it looked like he was wearing a serape. All that could be seen was that menacing eye and his protruding snout.

"What do you think?" I asked Joanne. "All we need is an extra sombrero to cover up his face."

"Here, he can use yours." Joanne picked up my shabby sombrero from the front seat and tossed it over his pointy beak.

"You don't mind if his nose pokes a hole through the top, do you?" Joanne added as an afterthought. The hat already was harpooned.

"I guess not."

We stood back and looked at him, turning our heads right and then left.

"He looks like a short passenger taking a long siesta," Joanne said.

"It's kind of creepy."

"You said it. Now we can both go in the bakery. We have Mr. Marlin to guard our luggage."

"Let's take a picture," I said.

"A picture of what?"

"Of us. With Mr. Marlin. I want a picture, even if you don't."

I dug in my purse for the camera, and Joanne finally loosened up when she took a shot of me in the backseat with my arm around Mr. Marlin.

Not to be outdone, Joanne handed me the camera and

clambered into the Jeep. She positioned herself so it looked as if she were sitting on Santa Marlin's lap and posed as if she were telling him what she wanted for Christmas. We made up crazy poses with our under-serape fish and finally got on the road when the sun was well up and busy illuminating the new day.

With our untalkative hitchhiker seat-belted in the backseat, we made our one-hour-and-twenty-minute bumpy ride to Rosa Lupe's. She came outside as soon as she heard our vehicle and greeted us with more loving excitement than I think our mother ever had.

Language wasn't a barrier. It didn't matter that we didn't have an interpreter this time, nor did it matter that we looked like a couple of sea urchins with stiff hair and dirty clothes. She hugged us with teary eyes.

Then she looked at Mr. Marlin and at the two of us as if waiting for an introduction.

"That's Uncle Harlan's fish." Joanne pulled up the sombrero so Rosa Lupe could glimpse the singular eye that followed you no matter where you stood.

She appeared confused and slightly frightened at first, but then she smiled and nodded and said something that I suspected was along the lines of, "You two burrito-brains are completely loco."

"Don't worry," Joanne said. "We're not leaving him here with you. My sister wouldn't hear of it. But we brought you a few other goodies."

Our presentation of the frying pan, can opener, and plastic mixing bowl met with expressions of appreciation. The real treat that she laughed and clapped her hands over was the cake. Joanne and I had made a final stop at the grocery store by the resort and bought a few treats for Rosa Lupe.

With eager hand motions Rosa Lupe invited us to come inside to eat.

"No, we need to get going," Joanne said. "We just wanted to leave these few things for you and to say hello."

"We have to get to Ensenada before our ship sails at five o'clock," I added.

"¿Ensenada?" Rosa Lupe repeated.

"Sí, Ensenada," Joanne repeated. "We have to get on a ship and head back home today. Back to our casas."

"Sus casas, ah, sí," she said and then picked up her side of the conversation. We listened attentively for several minutes as she visited with us enthusiastically. Only one word stood out in Rosa Lupe's long paragraph that both Joanne and I understood. *Mateo*.

We had both heard that name used several times when we were here before. *Mateo* was Spanish for "Matthew."

"What about Mateo?" I asked, since I doubted Joanne would pipe up.

The señora had plenty to tell us about Mateo. It was terrible not to be able to understand any of it.

"And how is Miguel and his leg?" Joanne asked, pointing to her leg.

The señora led us out to where Joanne and Matthew had first treated Miguel, talking all the way. We found the patient seated on a bench outside his humble home with his leg elevated. He looked much better than he had when we first found him.

Rosa Lupe made the introductions, and Miguel shook our hands, saying *gracias* a lot.

"You're looking much better," Joanne said compassionately. "I have more painkillers for you that I'll leave with Rosa Lupe. They're in my purse. I'm sure she'll give them to you when you need them. One or two every four hours for pain."

"Joanne." I stopped her from confusing the guy further as she held up first one finger, then two, and then four. "He has no idea what you're saying. Just leave the aspirin with Rosa Lupe."

"Ibuprofen," Joanne corrected me.

I kept my mouth shut after that and followed Joanne and Rosa Lupe back to our Jeep. I figured that sometimes big sisters just need to know they're right about something. Joanne always was right about medications.

"We need to go." Joanne gave Rosa Lupe a tight hug. I wondered if the hug had been offensive to Rosa Lupe since we were so dirty and smelly. Rosa Lupe, on the other hand, smelled like fresh soap and a smoky blend of melted lard and warm flour tortillas.

I hugged her, too, drawing in the friendly fragrance of this sweet woman who had shared all she had with us, including her bed.

"I wish I spoke Spanish." I felt my eyes filling with tears. "I wish I could tell you what you've meant to me, Rosa Lupe."

She patted my cheek, catching the first tear and placing it on her cheek as if she was holding it there for me for safekeeping.

Joanne and I couldn't leave. We couldn't make ourselves let go of this dear woman's hand and get in the Jeep and drive off. The fellowship, without words, was so sweet. We lingered, smiling, speaking a bit, hugging again.

At last we climbed into the Jeep and left. Both of us kept looking over our shoulders and waving until we were so far down the rutted trail that the dust we were kicking up blocked our view of her.

"What a woman," I said.

"Yes," Joanne agreed. "What a woman."

Seventeen

Do you want anything?" Joanne asked as we approached Ensenada, having made the journey without incident. "Souvenirs? Water? Another dancing lady?"

"All I want is a bath. A long, hot bath. What about you?"

"I might grab a souvenir if I see one, but I'm with you. A warm shower would be heavenly."

It's funny how relative things are based on your life experience. When we first docked in Ensenada and I looked down on the city from the balcony of our cabin, I thought the dirt soccer field and floating scent of burning rubbish was the most uncivilized sight I'd ever seen. Driving through town and watching cars run the yellow lights and make up their own private lanes to drive in, I thought we were in the midst of barbarians.

Reentering Ensenada now after the experiences we'd been

through, I felt happy to see the sight of such a big town and so many urban developments, such as the Pemex stations and the huge Mexican flag that waved from a tremendously high pole at the harbor's entrance. I felt a friendly familiarity with Ensenada and the sound of honking horns.

We had gone through several stoplights in town when I realized that people were looking at us. Yes, the mud-splattered, canary yellow Jeep was a sight to behold along with the driver (Joanne, this time) and the front-seat passenger (me, this time) both decked out in frayed straw sombreros.

But I think the evil eye of our serape-draped hitchhiker was what caught people's attention. Either that or the dirty gym sock that Joanne had peeled off her sweaty foot halfway here and tied around Mr. Marlin's extended beak so that we could look like a souped-up desert vehicle.

"I think we've aired our dirty laundry long enough," I told Joanne.

"We're almost to the car rental place. Let people stare. They won't see us again for a while. If they don't like it, let them eat cake!"

"We gave the pastries to Rosa Lupe, remember? We don't have any cake to offer."

"Yes, but I've been thinking about the dessert cart that will be coming past our table tonight at dinner. If they have coconut cake, I'm having two pieces."

I thought of our charming dinner guests from the first part of our cruise and regretted that they wouldn't be on the return portion with us. We would have a tale or two to tell at the dinner table tonight.

When we pulled into the car rental shop, the gold-toothed fellow was nowhere to be seen. A different man was working, and he seemed delighted to try out his English on us as well as arrange a ride for us back to the ship. Fish included for no extra charge.

Joanne kept apologizing for how dirty we got the Jeep, but he wisely said, with his palms open to the front of the vehicle, "Here is a picture of your beautiful trip."

We knew what he meant, and he was right. Nothing had been dainty or sanitary about our journey, and yet the results had been beautiful and life changing. No "car wash" would take that away from us.

Pulling up to the front of the dock where the cruise ship was calmly moored, our friendly car rental employee was grateful for the large tip we handed him. He carried our luggage and boxes as far as the ship's crew would let him, which was about ten feet from the gangway. He went back to the car and carried Mr. Marlin for us under one arm. Without his blanket covering, Mr. Marlin wasn't nearly as intriguing.

The ship's personnel considered Mr. Marlin to be an unregistered guest and suggested we leave him in his country of birth.

"We can't do that." Joanne stood as firm as I would have if I had been the first to speak up. Clearly, we'd had an effect on each other's personalities during the past week.

"Would you be so kind as to call Sven for us?" Joanne said. "He knows us."

When Sven appeared, I wished I'd had the camera ready. I could have used one of the last photos to capture his flabbergasted look. All the suave, smooth-sailing lingo seemed to have abandoned him when he saw the three of us. He began to speak to us as if we were a pack of hooligans trying to stow away.

That is, until Joanne and I removed our battered sombreros, and Sven realized it was us, his favorite Platinum Crown cruisers.

With the assistance of Sven and two other stewards, we were quickly taken to our suite along with our dusty luggage. Mr. Marlin was delivered at the same time, wrapped in our now-filthy Mexican blankets.

"I'm sure you must be eager for a shower," Sven suggested. "I'll see to it that more towels are brought for you." He gave a low bow and exited, I suspect, holding his breath.

The instant the door closed, Joanne and I laughed.

"Look at us!" I turned my sister around so she could see her reflection in the mirror above the built-in dresser. We were in the same stateroom, peering into the same mirror we had looked in only five days earlier and complained that our noses were too funny and our mouths too imbalanced.

All those imperfections didn't matter in the face of what greeted us in the reflection now. No attention was drawn to our noses or mouths. Those two features were about the only things on us that hadn't radically been altered. Our hair had suffered the most. It stuck out in frightening, wind-blown dreadlocks.

"Who was that mythical woman whose hair turned into snakes?" Joanne asked. "Wasn't it Methuselah?"

"No, Medusa."

"Well, we could give Medusa a little competition."

"Look how dirty we are!" I turned my head and ran a finger down the side of my neck the same way I would run a finger across the top of the refrigerator and make a fuss over how long it had been since I'd cleaned up there.

"My teeth feel so gritty." Joanne smiled big. "I think I caught half the bugs in Baja in my teeth."

"That's what you get for smiling so much," I teased. Turning halfway around, I noticed a long dark streak down the back of my T-shirt. "How long has that been there?"

"Since the ATV yesterday."

"We went out in the ATV two days ago."

"Okay, so since the ATV ride two days ago."

"I didn't wear this shirt, did I?"

"Yes."

"And you didn't tell me I had a big splotch on it?"

"It seemed pointless. Who cared? I didn't care. I usually was looking at the front of you, anyhow. You didn't know it was there."

"I'm going to throw away these clothes," I said. "I'm serious. I don't think I'll ever get them clean. Do you want the shower first?"

"You don't mind?"

"No, I want to take a long bath. You said you wanted a shower. I'm guessing a shower will take less time than a bath."

"Don't count on it." Joanne stepped into the bathroom. "Would you be a honey and hand me that luxurious bathrobe hanging in the closet?"

"Here you go." I couldn't wait to soak in the tub and wrap up in the other plush robe. These items were a much greater luxury on the return trip than they had been on the way to Mexico. I kept thinking how much of the world lived like Rosa Lupe did. Only a minuscule percentage of the earth's population has ever gone on a luxury cruise or been afforded the use of plush bathrobes or even soaked in a hot tub, for that matter.

My understanding of life and of the world in general had expanded so far that I knew it would be difficult to return to my complacent world of suburbia without doing something to organize assistance to those in need.

As I arranged our luggage and found a place for Mr. Marlin behind the drawn-open curtain that covered our sliding glass window, I thought of Joanne's comments earlier about the need in India and how she didn't know how to organize support. With a nod and a smile at my frightening reflection as I passed the mirror, I knew I could pitch a couple of ideas at her that we could work on once she relocated to Vancouver.

A knock sounded at the door. Sven stood there with extra towels and an envelope with Joanne's name on it. "Would you see to it that your sister receives these?"

"I will. Thank you." I closed the door, wondering if I should be tipping all these helpful staff personnel.

"You know, we might have enough time," Joanne said about ten minutes later as she stepped out of the bathroom in her robe, rosy cheeked and smelling divine.

"Enough time for what?"

"We might have enough time for a massage before dinner."

"We're still at the six-thirty seating, aren't we?" I asked.

"I think so. I guess that doesn't give us enough time."

"Why don't you call and order up some pampering specialties for us for tomorrow?"

As soon as I got into the bathroom, I realized a shower was a better idea than a bath. With a shower all the dirt at least had a place to go instead of floating around me in the tub and potentially soaking further into my skin. I stood under the showerhead long enough to soothe my shoulder muscles and to thoroughly rinse off all the lather I'd worked up with the lovely cleansing products provided in our stateroom.

"That was short," Joanne said when I came out.

"I know. I thought I'd be in there for an hour, but once I was clean, I was done."

"Same with me. Did you think about Rosa Lupe?"

"I did. I thought about what a luxury all this is."

"Does it make you feel guilty to be going home in such style?"

"Actually, it makes me feel grateful. I don't think I appreciated any of this as much on the cruise down here."

Joanne nodded. "You're going to appreciate it even more tomorrow. We have deep-conditioning hair treatments scheduled at eleven. I tried to get facials or massages, but they were all booked up."

"Good thinking on the hair treatments."

"That's what I thought."

"Did you see that envelope Sven brought for you?"

"No, where is it?"

"It's with the extra towels."

"Oh, I saw it."

"What was it?"

"I don't know. I didn't open it. It's on ship stationery, so it's probably our bill for the extra assistance we had with our rental car. I'm too content to look at any bills. What are you wearing to dinner?"

"Black pants, white blouse; same as I wore the other night. What about you?"

"I overdressed last time. I'll go for casual this time, too."

We fluffed up our hair, slipped into our cleanest casual clothes, and didn't bother with makeup. It felt so good to be clean; we were happy to have freshly scrubbed faces to show off.

As soon as we entered the dining room, we realized it was formal night, and we were way underdressed. Nevertheless, the hostess took us to our table.

"I can't believe it," I muttered to Joanne. "We have managed to wear the wrong thing to every single meal so far on this ship, coming and going."

"Who cares?" Joanne smiled as we paraded past the captain's table where one woman in a strapless gown with diamonds dripping from her earlobes and circling her neck watched us as we walked to our table and sat down.

"Good evening," Joanne said cordially to the others already seated at our table. "I'm Joanne. This is my sister, Melanie."

The three couples at our table were all in their early twenties. All three women were dressed in dazzling, revealing gowns. All of them were drinking heavily, and clearly they hadn't expected us to break into their private party. When one of the men made an off-color joke, he turned to me and apologized, as if I were his mother.

Joanne tried unsuccessfully to start a conversation. I found out from the woman next to me that none of the three couples were married. They were on a business trip. Two of the young women kept fussing with their gowns as if this were prom night and they hadn't bought the right size. The third woman had an especially high-pitched laugh, and she kept swatting her "date" on the arm and saying, "Get outta here."

He didn't, but we did.

Joanne and I lasted through our waiter's explanation of our dinner selections before reaching over and tapping each other on the leg under the table. I knew Joanne was thinking what I was thinking. Excusing ourselves, we exited the posh company and took the elevator down to the main lobby.

"What a depressing setup," I said.

"You were thinking the same thing I was. What is that

verse in Proverbs? Something about how it's better to eat crumbs served with love than a slab of prime rib in the presence of hatred."

"Exactly. I was comparing that bunch to what it was like eating dinner at Rosa Lupe's."

"No comparison. Let's see if we can come up with some other place to eat." Joanne headed for the front desk.

The desk clerk informed us that a full buffet dinner was offered to guests on the top deck behind the sushi bar. And, if we didn't get enough at the open buffet, the midnight buffet would be in full swing at eleven-thirty after the last show.

Taking the stairs instead of the elevator, Joanne and I prepared to eat heartily this evening. We knew we would be dining where love was served because we were dining with our new best friends.

I started out slowly at the salad bar, intending to leave lots of room for the fish and beef. But what filled my plate wasn't the salads but the potatoes. The selection included scalloped, garlic mashed, and twice-baked potatoes. I think I could have eaten only potatoes for dinner and been content.

Joanne was thrilled with the three different selections of fish and the chicken Kiev as well as the end cut of prime rib. We selected a table by the window. Even though the sun had set and all was darkness on the ocean, we could spot an occasional star flickering in the distance that made us both nostalgic for our simple fireside dinner of camarones on the beach.

"I need a walk on deck before I visit the dessert counter," Joanne said. "Are you with me?"

"All the way."

We strolled in the brisk night air and breathed in deeply.

"I have to confess something to you," Joanne said, as we rounded the back of the ship and headed down the less windy side.

"What's that?"

"I've been thinking about Matthew."

I smiled, but I don't think she could see my face.

"I've been thinking about him a lot, and I know that's crazy because I barely know him. The thing is, I've had so many disappointments with men over the years that I don't dare to dream anymore. I wish I'd turned toward him when you told me to, Mel. He has no way of knowing that my heart is toward him, and that makes me sad. Everything you said was true. God's timing was precise. I just didn't respond the way I should have when I had the chance. So that's my confession. You were right. I was too proud to even wave good-bye, and it's breaking my heart."

She cried softly. I wrapped my arms around her, and in true Joanne fashion, she sniveled for about a minute and a half and was done. Bucking up, she straightened her posture. "I'm okay. I had to tell you, though. Next time you tell me to turn around, I promise I'll do it."

I paused a moment and then said, "Joanne, turn around."

She did. No one was behind us. She turned to me with a quizzical look.

"I was testing you." I grinned widely.

"You brat!"

"What? Did you think Matthew would be standing there or something?"

"No."

"Joanne, listen, at the risk of sounding a lot like you sounded to me on our first night on the cruise, I now happen to believe that God is a big dreamer, like you said. He doesn't give up. I have no idea what's going to happen, but I know you're in good hands."

"I know," Joanne said. "I really am content. More content than I've ever been before. I thought it would be a good idea if I confessed to you what I was feeling about Matthew instead of holding it in."

"I'm glad you told me."

We continued our stroll, and I bravely did something I had never done. I prayed aloud as we walked. It was short and simple, but it seemed like a good idea. Something Joanne would do. I asked God that, if He had any dreams for Joanne and Matthew, He would make them come true.

I considered adding a P.S. along the lines of, "And please make my sister smart enough to respond the right way next time, if you do set up a next time with Matthew." I didn't add it, though. Joanne probably had prayed a few of those P.S.'s for me along the way. She had been eager for me to respond wholeheartedly to Christ, and yet she patiently had kept her private prayers for me to herself.

Having completed one loop of the deck, Joanne and I returned to the dessert counter of the upper-deck buffet and treated ourselves to three desserts each. Mine were all chocolate. Small pieces. Joanne found a coconut macaroon, and that satisfied her urge for coconut cake at least for the time being.

All the food in our bellies put us in a strange sort of stupor we hadn't experienced during the past few days in Mexico. We meandered through some of the onboard shops, trying on jewelry we knew we'd never buy and admiring the craftsmanship of the Mexican silver. The shopping wasn't particularly special, but it did make up for our not having strolled through the shops in Ensenada.

At ten o'clock we wandered into the theater and landed terrific balcony seats for the second performance of "Broadway's Best." A waiter came by asking if we wanted to order something to drink before the show began. We both ordered ginger ale to settle our full stomachs. He looked a little disappointed, as if he knew he could make a larger tip on the more exotic drinks.

I noticed when he delivered the ginger ales they came with a bendable straw and a whole maraschino cherry. In other words, a child's nonalcoholic beverage.

For the next hour we sipped our Shirley Temples and tapped our feet while a cast of energetic quick-change artists performed portions of more than twenty Broadway shows. We decided we would have been even more impressed with their abilities if we'd ever seen one of the twenty Broadway shows.

But the music was familiar and the presentation entertaining.

"Almost eleven-thirty," Joanne said, as we followed the crowd out of the theater. "Ready for the midnight buffet?"

I said yes, but the truth was I was more ready for bed. It was strange how we had so quickly conformed to the opportunities offered us. After-dinner shows and then dinner again after the shows.

The midnight buffet was really something. We had been told the ice sculptures were worth the viewing, and they were. I counted four different ice sculptures. My favorite was the palm tree that dripped small droplets from the end of each frond and refreshed the plate of grapes and strawberries. It reminded me of Uncle Harlan's great palm tree.

All the food at the buffet was Mexican. We tried the carne asada, taquitos, fish tacos, tamales, and chicken enchiladas. Every bite was better than the last. We both declared we never had tasted such excellent Mexican food in Vancouver.

"Although we haven't tried looking," Joanne pointed out. "What if we make that one of the goals of our weekly get-togethers? We can try every Mexican restaurant in the phone book and decide which ones come closest to this."

"You'd really do that with me?"

Joanne nodded, sincere in her expression and her words.

"I'll hold you to it," I said. "Things like that drive Ethan up a wall. He has his tried-and-true favorite places to eat out and doesn't see any reason to experience new places."

"He'll never know what he's missing," Joanne said with a

grin. "Now, do you suppose we could ask Sven to come with a cart and roll us back to our rooms?"

"No kidding. That was delicious and decadent, but I'm definitely not going to eat breakfast in the morning."

"We'll see," Joanne said. "Come on. I've been dying to get back to our room and see what kind of animal they shaped our towels into."

It was a bunny rabbit. I took a picture of Joanne holding it in her lap.

Settling in with the gentle sway of the ship's motion as we headed north, I thought of how crisp and clean the bleached sheets felt.

Last night we were using our fingers to brush our teeth because we didn't want to dig in our suitcases in the dark to find our toothbrushes. Tonight we were returning to folded towel animals on our beds, and if we so required, we might have been able to order an assistant to brush our teeth for us.

But we didn't.

The deep-conditioning hair treatment the next morning at eleven was as much pampering as either of us wanted that day. When we realized how much we were paying for these amenities, even with the discount I received for the body wrap gone bad, it seemed best to forego any other elaborate treatments.

"Perhaps another time—on another cruise," I said when the spa receptionist informed me she had an opening for a facial, if I was interested.

"Do you suppose we're learning to be content?" Joanne asked.

"Maybe so. What would make you feel content with the rest of this day?"

Joanne looked at me as if no one had ever asked her that before.

The two of us spent the remainder of the day doing what we both decided would make us most content. We wrapped up in our robes, sat out on our deck, and read aloud to each other while sipping hot tea that room service delivered in sturdy blue pottery teapots with matching mugs. Joanne went for the coconut cream tea while I couldn't turn down the offer of chocolate mint tea. We asked about coconut cake and ended up with a plate of coconut macaroons that were delivered with the tea.

Neither of us had any complaints.

Well, maybe we had one. In the morning we were docking in San Pedro at eight o'clock. Real life would soon be upon us, complete with winter's chill and Christmas preparations. A certain hammock and a certain palm tree lingered in both our minds.

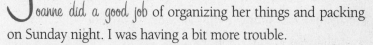

Eighteen

Joanne did a good job of organizing her things and packing on Sunday night. I was having a bit more trouble.

A notice had been delivered under our door giving specifications for disembarking the ship. We found out several key pieces of information. First, we were to place in the envelope provided our tip for all the services we had been given on the cruise, and we were informed of the expected amount. It added up to more than either of us would have spent, but we didn't want to put a black mark against Aunt Winnie's perfect sailing record, so we paid the suggested tip and sealed the envelope.

Next, we were informed that our luggage needed to be packed and tagged and set out in the hall before midnight. That's where Joanne excelled, and I was running into difficulties. The Harlan mementos I had packed up for Aunt

Winnie were bursting out of the flimsy box, and I was reluctant to leave the box in the hall for the steward to cart off the ship for me.

"The box is the least of your challenges," Joanne said. "All you need is some packing tape or twine. It's the fish you should worry about. You can't leave Mr. Marlin in the hall all night."

"I don't plan to. I'm going to carry him off the ship."

"You can't carry him."

"Yes I can. He's not that heavy."

"It's his nose," Joanne said.

"What about his nose?"

"It's a deadly weapon. How do you plan to get that ridiculous fish off this ship without harpooning someone?"

"They got it on the ship for us."

"I know, but the halls weren't crowded with travelers all trying to disembark at the same time."

"I can wrap him in the blanket and—"

"It's not going to work."

What followed was an argument that must have ranked right up there with the sort of arguments Harlan and Winnie had over this preposterous fish. Joanne said I would never get Mr. Marlin all the way home and I should give up now and throw him overboard.

"Can't do that," I said. "Clean ocean policy, remember? Didn't you read the notice on the back of the door? No throwing anything overboard."

"It's organic. It's going back to its original habitat."

"It's a thirty-year-old pickled, varnished marlin. There's nothing organic about this guy any longer. The point is, I told Aunt Winnie I would bring Harlan's fish back to her, and I'm going to try my best to keep my word."

"Melanie, Aunt Winnie doesn't even know where the fish is. She didn't know Mr. Marlin was in the trailer, did she? She won't know that you tried to stuff him in your suitcase to get him home."

"No, but I know. We got him this far; I can't give up now."

Joanne stood with her hands on her hips, glaring at me.

"I like your idea," I said.

"My idea?"

"What if I did try to stuff him in my suitcase? In pieces. I could saw him in half or maybe into three pieces, what with the nose being so long and all."

"And then what? Glue him back together at Aunt Winnie's? I don't think so, Mel."

"Okay, what if I just cut off the nose?"

"What if you leave Mr. Marlin under your bed for the maid to find once we're off the ship?"

"Joanne!"

"You could buy a different fish at home and give it to Aunt Winnie, and it would have the same sentiment for her."

"Look at this face." I pulled Mr. Marlin out from behind the curtain and laid him out on my bed. "Where am I ever going to find another fish with a face like that? Aunt Winnie would remember this face."

Joanne sighed. "I have a feeling I'm going to spend the rest of my life trying to forget that face."

"I'll cut off the nose. That should do it. Then I can wrap the body in trash bags and duct tape and check it through as luggage."

"Melanie, are you hearing yourself? Even if you get the stiff through baggage claim, you can't keep the beak in your carry-on luggage. On the way here airport security searched my purse and confiscated my nail file. You think they're going to let you go traipsing through X-ray with a swordfish nose in your wallet?"

"Maybe if I wrap it really well."

"That does it." Joanne went to the phone, picked it up, and dialed.

"Who are you calling? It's almost midnight."

"Hello." Joanne ignored my question. "Sven? This is Joanne Clayton. Oh. He is? You are? Yes. And by any chance could you bring a saw, some duct tape, and some trash bags. That's right. Oh, and some twine. Yes, please. Thank you."

She hung up and announced to me that Sven was unavailable but his assistant, Georgio, was on his way.

"What are you going to do when you get home and you can't dial up Sven every time you have a little problem?" I said with a sassy air.

Joanne stared me down. "I guess I'll have to call you."

I knew no other person on this earth whom I could talk to the way Joanne and I were talking to each other now. It had been years since we had fallen into this feisty back-talk way of communicating, but it felt good. We could express our mutual frustration, yet both of us knew it was in love.

Georgio appeared with the requested items and an expression of curiosity. His Italian accent was in full swing when he entered the room and spotted Mr. Marlin stretched out across my bed with the bath towel bunny to keep him company.

"I'm thinking of sawing off the nose," I said. "Just so I can wrap him up and get him loaded on the plane."

"No, no, no, no, no!" Georgio said.

"That's what I told her," Joanne said.

"This is a black marlin. Not very common. Difficult to catch. I know a lot about these fish."

"Is it valuable?" Joanne asked.

"Not so much, now, I think, but certainly to the fisherman who caught it. Was that one of you?"

"No, our Uncle Harlan caught it. A long time ago."

"So this is your Uncle Harlan's marlin." Georgio grinned, as if he were the first one to notice the play on words.

"Yes," Joanne said. "This grumpy-looking beast with the evil eye is Uncle Harlan's marlin. And now my sister thinks she can get it back to Canada. I've been trying to tell her it can't be done."

"No, it's not a problem."

"It's a huge problem," Joanne said.

"No, I can ship this fish anywhere in the world. Where do you want him to go?"

I jumped in quickly before Joanne had a chance to voice, in her current brazen tone, exactly where she wanted this fish to go. "Vancouver, BC. I have the address right here."

Reaching for some paper to copy Aunt Winnie's address, I found the envelope that had been delivered for Joanne earlier on top of the extra towels. I tossed it to her and said, "You better look at this in case there's anything we haven't covered yet."

Georgio pulled out one of his cards for me, and I copied Aunt Winnie's address on the back of the card with strict instructions that the shipping cost didn't matter. The important thing was for the fish to get there.

"Not a problem. I have shipped worse than this before."

"Worse?" I questioned.

"Larger items and more fragile such as big clay pots and one time a rocking chair the guest bought in Ensenada. Your fish is not a problem. It's a beautiful fish. Do you know the females are the largest? The males are never more than 140 kilos—about 300 pounds to you. This is a small one. But the small ones are fast. They can run on the surface for a long time, and you think you have them, but then they dive very deep and for a long time. When they leap from the water, you can see a faint blue line, right here."

He traced his finger along the side before ceasing his lecture on black marlins. With both arms, Georgio lifted his new friend. "Do not worry. I will take good care to see that he gets to your home in one piece."

"That's better than what I was about to do." I scooted

ahead of him to open the door. "Thanks, Georgio. I really appreciate it."

"Ciao!" He called over his shoulder.

I stood by the open door, watching as he maneuvered his way down the narrow hallway lined with our neighbors' luggage.

"Joanne," I called softly, "you should see this. It looks like Georgio is doing the samba with Mr. Marlin. Isn't that the dance where you take a few steps, stop, step some more and stop again? That's what he's doing. It's hilarious."

Joanne didn't answer. Ever since I'd handed her the envelope with her name on it, she hadn't said a word. I closed the door and looked at her. She was sitting on the edge of our small love seat with the open envelope in her lap and some paper in her hand. Her eyes were fixed on the paper, and her mouth was open.

"Uh-oh, give me the bad news. How much more do we owe in tips and service fees?"

"Ten thousand dollars," Joanne stated without breathing.

"What? Pesos, not dollars, right? Did you say ten thousand? What for?"

I snatched the paper out of Joanne's hand and read a handwritten note in beautiful cursive loops.

Ms. Clayton,

I have inquired as to how I might present to you my thanks and have been informed that you disembarked the ship. My most humble apologies for not giving this to you in person. You saved my son's life, and I will forever be your servant. Please accept this small check offered from my heart for a debt I can never repay.

"Joanne."

"I know."

"Ten thousand dollars?"

"U.S. ten thousand dollars."

"Did you see her return address? She's from Morocco."

"I know."

"This is..."

"I know."

We sat together in silence, staring at the letter and the cashier's check.

"I guess you can move to Vancouver now without hesitation," I said after a few moments.

"I didn't need money to make my move possible. I don't need this." She waved the check at me. "This isn't for me. It's for those girls in India. This will buy freedom for so many young girls. It will make them safe."

Aside from the low-sounding hum of the ship's mighty engines, all was quiet. My sister had risked everything to save one life, and now she would be instrumental in saving many. This had to be a God-dream.

"What if," I said slowly, "what if you offered this money to the ministry you worked with in India, and they used it as a matching donation?"

"What are you talking about?"

My organizational way of thinking was kicking into full gear. "Have you ever seen a matching grant? The organization sends out letters requesting donations, and your seed money is used to match their donations up to ten thousand dollars. It's done all the time. Donors are asked to give by a certain date. That way you end up with twenty thousand, hopefully."

"I think you and I have some planning to do."

"Planning is a sweet word in my vocabulary," I said with a smile.

Someone knocked on our door. It was one of the stewards checking to see if we had any luggage to put out since it was past midnight. Joanne had hers ready, and I scrambled to close my suitcase.

After we handed over the bags, instead of crawling into bed, Joanne and I sat up talking. We formulated a plan for her move to Vancouver by the end of the year and how we would all spend Christmas together, even if she hadn't packed up everything and moved from Toronto.

The night slipped by as we snatched a few early morning hours of sleep. By eight o'clock Monday morning we were so tired yet so satisfied, we were barely able to get ourselves off the ship with our carry-on bags and make our way through customs.

"Mr. Marlin would never have made it this far," Joanne kept telling me.

"So you've told me."

"I hope Aunt Winnie doesn't get so sentimental when the fish arrives that she puts him in a place of prominence in her apartment," Joanne said. "I cringe at the thought of that beady eye following me around every time I go to visit her."

"All I care about is that he's on his way and I don't have to think about him anymore."

We picked up our checked luggage and chatted on the shuttle to LAX. The first thing I did when we were inside the airport terminal was to call Ethan. Our conversation was completely different from the one we'd had a week earlier when I apologized for the brick-face kiss and being so uptight. I told him I couldn't wait to see him and that I loved him with all my heart.

Everything seemed wonderful until Joanne and I got past check-in and realized we were going through security at separate gates. She was flying back to Toronto, and I was flying to Vancouver.

"This isn't really good-bye." I gave my dear sister a tight hug. "It's just 'see you later.'"

"Just a few weeks, and we can start checking out Mexican restaurants in Vancouver."

I nodded, keeping my teeth clenched so I wouldn't cry.

"I love you, Melly Jelly Belly." Joanne hugged me one more time and planted a kiss just above my ear in my freshly conditioned, clean hair.

"I love you, too, Joanna Banana." I kissed her cheek, and one of her salty tears touched my lips.

"Adios." She pulled away and gave me a smile.

"Adios," I echoed. We started in our opposite directions through the crowded terminal. I stopped before turning down the wing where my gate was located, intending to wave at Joanne one last time.

Turn around, Joanne. Look over your shoulder.

She kept walking and would soon be out of range.

Impulsively, I called out her name.

Joanne turned to glance over her shoulder, and with my free hand I waved and blew her a lopsided kiss.

She attempted to do the same, but she was still moving away from me. Before the kiss left her fingers, Joanne ran right into the chest of another traveler, causing her shoulder bag to tip and spill half its contents in the pathway of the oncoming travelers.

Oh, Joanne! I chuckled and wove my way back through the crowd to help her out. *You and I can make it all the way to San Felipe and back without an accident, but we can't make it through the airport!*

I was almost to where she stood with her back to me when I stopped. My mouth dropped open, and my eyes stretched wide. Her wallet, brush, and a pack of gum remained on the ground as the man she had run into wrapped his arms around her in a hug.

"Joanne!" I scrambled to pick up the dropped items and held them out as she pulled away from the stranger's embrace.

That's when I saw his face.

Matthew!

I couldn't move. I couldn't cry. I couldn't laugh. It was like a dream. A sweet, gigantic, larger-than-life dream. I was watching one of God's dreams come true.

"I looked everywhere for you in San Felipe." Matthew smiled at my sister. "I checked the hotels and rental houses, but no one had a record of you. Then I saw your name on the log at the clinic Thursday morning, and I knew you were still in town. Are you okay?"

Joanne nodded, all smiles. "I was stung by a stingray. But my foot is fine now. It's good to see you."

"It's good to see you, too."

"So, how did you know we'd be here?" I asked. "Or is this a coincidence?" I gave Joanne a subtle wink.

Fixing his gaze on Joanne he said, "Do you remember telling me you missed the opportunity to be hands-on at work?"

Joanne shook her head.

"It was when you were holding Miguel down while I reset the tibia. I know you were joking about the hands-on part because Miguel was such a challenge to restrain, but I asked how long you were going to be on vacation, and you said you were flying home Monday. I hoped your flight was through LAX."

With a shy grin he added, "I've been here since five o'clock this morning checking every flight headed for Canada."

Joanne laughed that great, big, effervescent laugh of hers,

and I thought, *He came after you, Joanne. He pursued you. He found you, and you found him.*

"And here you are," Matthew said, still grinning.

"Here I am," Joanne said.

"So, may I buy you ladies a cup of coffee?"

Joanne turned to look at me. Her face was bathed in light.

I handed Joanne the items that had fallen from her shoulder bag. "I have a plane to catch. But, ah...I'll see you later."

"Hasta la vista," Matthew said. Then, I'm sure for my benefit, he translated his farewell by adding, "That means 'I'll see you later.'"

"Yes," I said with a big smile. "I'm sure I will hasta la vista you."

Part of me was dying to stay there and just watch. My sister was a lit-up ball of glimmers. I could almost imagine that if I pinched her just right, she would burst and millions of minute particles of brilliance, like ecstatic stars, would fill the terminal.

Turning and making my way back to the gate where a flight to Vancouver, BC was waiting for me, all I could think of were Augustine's words,

"I came to love you late, O Beauty so ancient and new; I came to love you late."

Epilogue

Everything in me changed after that trip to Mexico two years ago. I went from knowing God by the numbers to growing into a close relationship with Christ. That affected how I loved Ethan and our girls and everyone else, including my new brother-in-law, Matthew.

Yes, he fell for my sister in a big way, and she fell right along with him. It was the most adorable thing to watch the two of them together. Joanne brought Matthew home for Christmas right after our cruise, and Aunt Winnie kept saying, "Is this Russell?"

My ever-clever sister said, "No, Aunt Winnie. You keep forgetting. Russell is my dog."

Matthew and Joanne now live about twenty minutes from us, but they're hardly ever home. In the five months since they've been married, they have been to India once to carry out the work I've been helping Joanne to organize. They've been to San Felipe twice. The first time was for their honeymoon. I know. I would have selected a location other than the silver time capsule for my honeymoon. But then, I'm not Joanne, and she's not me. We're almost twins, but not completely twins.

Part of the reason they returned to San Felipe the second time was to finalize the paperwork on the property. Nearly a year after Joanne and I signed the papers at El Banco del Sol, we still hadn't received our approved copies. On their last trip, Matthew negotiated with Señor Campaña with far more success than Joanne and I had. As of two months ago, Joanne and I officially became joint owners of Uncle Harlan's beachfront property.

To date, over 250 of the 300 lots at the resort down the road from us have been purchased, and construction has been nonstop. Joanne and I continue to collect business cards and phone calls from soft-spoken folks who nonchalantly tell us they wouldn't mind taking the property off of our hands, seeing as the trailer is so run-down and all.

What those investors managed to discover, but Joanne and I failed to figure out, was that Uncle's Harlan's property isn't just the cement slab and bunkered area where the trailer is located. Uncle Harlan owned the equivalent of nearly ten acres, and it's all beachfront. His property, or now I should get used to saying, our property, ends at the edge of the Rio del Mar Resort. It seems the resort won't be able to set up the kinds of beachfront concessions they would like unless they can purchase some of our property.

It's a problem my husband has loved working on. He and Matthew have approached it like a big game of chess and have made one trip to San Felipe together and have another one planned for early spring. The two of them are determined to go fishing on this upcoming trip. Both men have promised, or should I say threatened, to bring home a marlin for Joanne and me.

I should mention that Uncle Harlan's marlin arrived at Aunt Winnie's safe and unharmed, nose intact. Georgio used so much bubble wrap that you would have thought the shipping box contained a small whale instead of that grumpy black marlin with the creepy evil eye.

I will always be glad that I was at Aunt Winnie's apartment the afternoon Mr. Marlin was delivered. I will always regret that my sister was also there, freshly moved from Toronto. Aunt Winnie circled the beast in her Scoot-About and barked out directions for Joanne and me as we set the poor thing free. We unwrapped and unwrapped until the shimmering blue line could almost be seen striped across his leaping body.

"Here he is!" I announced, as the last layer of padding was pulled away. "Mr. Marlin!"

Aunt Winnie leaned close, eyes squinting. "That's him all right," she declared with an unbridled disdain as poignant as any line ever delivered by Captain Ahab. "Hideous, isn't he?"

Joanne and I kept our lips sealed.

"Throw him back in the sea!" Aunt Winnie shouted with a wave of her hand. "I don't ever want to see that ugly creature again. Who's ready for tea? Is it hot in here to you?"

"Told you." Joanne leaned close so that only I heard her.

Sometimes it's good for a younger sister to affirm her older sister, so I smiled sweetly and said, "You were right, Joanne."

Then I reached over and pinched her good on the underside of her arm. Just because.

Log on to www.sisterchicks.com for updates on Robin's next Sisterchick novel—*Sisterchicks Down Under*—coming April 2005!

Discussion Questions

1. Why do you think Melanie felt a wave of panic when she arrived in San Pedro and saw the huge cruise ship? Have you ever had a similar feeling?

2. Do you think you would have tried eating something exotic like escargot the way Melanie and Joanne did their first night on the cruise? Share a time when you've done something outside of your comfort zone. How did you feel afterward?

3. The first evening on the cruise, Joanne and Melanie's dinner companion Robert tells them about how God is always dreaming up adventures we could never imagine. What are some of the God-adventures you've experienced, and how were you changed by them?

4. If you've been blessed with a biological sister, what do you most enjoy about her? How has she impacted your life?

5. Joanne reads the following Augustine quote to Melanie.
    What part of this quote did you relate to? Why?

    > "I came to love you late, O Beauty so ancient
    > and new; I came to love you late. You were
    > within me and I was outside where I rushed
    > about wildly searching for you like some
    > monster loose in your beautiful world. You
    > were with me, but I was not with you. You
    > called me, you shouted to me. You broke
    > past my deafness. You bathed me in your
    > light, you wrapped me in your splendor, you
    > sent my blindness reeling. You gave out such
    > a delightful fragrance, and I drew it in and
    > came breathing hard after you. I tasted, and
    > it made me hunger and thirst; you touched
    > me, and I burned to know your peace."

6. Have you ever been in a situation like Melanie was with
    Rosa Lupe, where you were a stranger and yet you were
    treated to extravagant hospitality? How did that make
    you feel?

7. What was it that made Melanie, Joanne, and Rosa Lupe
    connect as true Sisterchicks despite the language barrier?
    Have you ever bonded instantly with a fellow
    Sisterchick? Details, please!

8. When was the last time you felt the freedom to do
   something spontaneous and fun like the water fight
   Melanie and Joanne started in the street in San Felipe?

9. Are you more like Melanie when it comes to having fun
   by cleaning up like the Boxcar Children? Or would you
   rather relax in a hammock like Joanne? What are the
   benefits and drawbacks of each?

10. Do Melanie and Joanne remind you of a couple of sisters
    in the town of Bethany who opened their home to Jesus
    and his friends in the New Testament? What are some of
    the similarities? (Refer to the book of Luke chapter 10
    and the book of John chapter 11.)

11. Why do you think it was difficult for Melanie to
    relinquish her life and enter into a more free, open, and
    grace-filled relationship with the Lord like her sister
    had?

12. Joanne tells Melanie she's "protected under a sombrero of
    God's grace." How has wearing that sombrero affected
    you?

13. Joanne is entering her next season of life with a new
    dream and a new love, and Melanie is experiencing an
    exciting, fresh relationship with Christ. What does the

next season of your life look like? Have you embraced it, or are you keeping the rocking chair of worry busy without going anywhere? What are some ways you can passionately pursue life?

Sisterchick *n.*: a friend who shares the deepest wonders of your heart, loves you like a sister, and provides a reality check when you're being a brat.

Helsinki or Bust!
Ohh, yeah...these gals are gone!

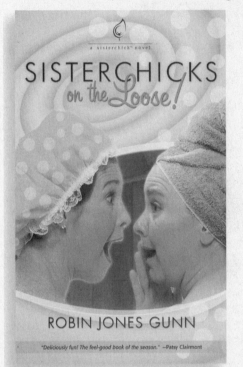

"Deliciously fun! *Sisterchicks on the Loose* is the feel-good book of the season!"

—PATSY CLAIRMONT,
Women of Faith speaker and author of *Stardust on My Pillow*

Meet two very real women who have become unlikely best friends. Sharon is the quiet mother of four; Penny is a former flower child. Their twenty-year friendship takes a surprising leap when Penny plans an impulsive trip to seek out her only living relatives in Finland. The land of reindeer and saunas holds infinite zaniness for these two sisterchicks. They find their hearts filling with a new zest for life and a fresh view of the almighty God who compressed the stars with His hands and flung them across the universe.

ISBN 1-59052-198-6

Sisterchick *n.*: a friend who shares the deepest wonders of your heart, loves you like a sister, and provides a reality check when you're being a brat.

Former College Roomies Make Waves on Waikiki

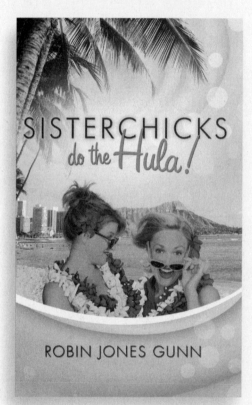

Some dreams take a while before they come true. Best friends Hope and Laurie never made it to Hawaii during their college years. But when they're about to turn forty, the islands still beckon, and off they go—with an unexpected stowaway on board. A little pineapple, a little sunshine, and a surprising little surfing lesson give these two sisterchicks all their crazy hearts could hope for—and more—as they enter the next season of their lives with a splash and with a beautiful vision of what God has dreamed up for them.

ISBN 1-59052-226-5

C'mon and say, "G'day!" and join two
Sisterchicks on their adventure to the
land of kangaroos and koalas in...

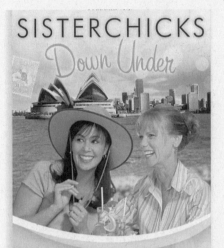

Coming in 2005!

Deb joins her husband for a three-month trip Down Under, when he's hired by a film studio in Wellington. Leaving behind all that's familiar in her comfortable corner in Southern California, Deb realizes that the past twenty years have been so tightly woven into the life of her only daughter that she's not sure of who she is on her own or with her husband.

In her isolation, Deb contemplates reinventing herself. But before her crazy schemes take flight, she meets Kelli at the Chocolate Fish Café. Even though the two women are very different at first glance, they share a common sisterchick heart and instantly forge a friendship that takes them on a journey to Australia and back to New Zealand for a road trip driving on the "wrong" side of the road. On the journey, both Deb and Kelli find that God has returned to them the truest part of themselves that was set aside so many years ago.

ISBN 1-59052-411-X

THE GLENBROOKE SERIES

by Robin Jones Gunn

COME TO GLENBROOKE...

A QUIET PLACE WHERE SOULS ARE REFRESHED

I magine a circle of friends who enter into each other's lives during that poignant season when love comes their way. Imagine the sweetness of having those friends to depend on as the journey into marriage and motherhood begins.

Meet the women of Glenbrooke: Jessica, Teri, Lauren, Alissa, Shelly, Meredith, Leah, and Genevieve. When their lives intersect in this small town, the door to friendship is opened and hearts come in to stay.

Perfectly crafted, heartwarming, and rich in truth, Robin's Glenbrooke novels have delighted half a million readers with their insights and charm. All souls looking to be refreshed are warmly invited to come to Glenbrooke.

SECRETS
Glenbrooke Series #1
Beginning her new life in a small Oregon town, high school English teacher Jessica Morgan tries desperately to hide the details of her past.

1-59052-240-0

WHISPERS
Glenbrooke Series #2
Teri went to Maui hoping to start a relationship with one special man. But romance becomes much more complicated when she finds herself pursued by three.

1-59052-192-7

ECHOES
Glenbrooke Series #3
Lauren Phillips "connects" on the Internet with a man known only as "K.C." Is she willing to risk everything...including another broken heart?

1-59052-193-5

SUNSETS
Glenbrooke Series #4
Alissa loves her new job as a Pasadena travel agent. Will an abrupt meeting with a stranger in an espresso shop leave her feeling that all men are like the one she's been hurt by recently?

1-59052-238-9

CLOUDS
Glenbrooke Series #5
After Shelly Graham and her old boyfriend cross paths in Germany, both must face the truth about their feelings.

1-59052-230-3

WATERFALLS
Glenbrooke Series #6
Meri thinks she's finally met the man of her dreams...until she finds out he's movie star Jacob Wilde, promptly puts her foot in her mouth, and ruins everything.

1-59052-231-1

WOODLANDS
Glenbrooke Series #7
Leah Hudson has the gift of giving, but questions her own motives, and God's purposes, when she meets a man she prays will love her just for herself.

1-59052-237-0

WILDFLOWERS
Glenbrooke Series #8
Genevieve Ahrens has invested lots of time and money in renovating the Wildflowers Café. Now her heart needs the same attention.

1-59052-239-7

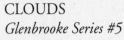

Visit

www.letstalkfiction.com

today!

Fiction Readers Unite!

Y ou've just found a new way to feed your fiction addiction. Letstalkfiction.com is a place where fiction readers can come together to learn about new fiction releases from Multnomah. You can read about the latest book releases, catch a behind-the-scenes look at the your favorite authors, sign up to receive the most current book information, and much more. Everything you need to make the most out of your fictional world can be found at www.letstalkfiction.com. Come and join the network!